Pentru A,
cu nuelt c

Catrina

MW00682973

# *About the author*

C. R. Preston is an only child. As such, he does not like to share food, be wrong, or lose at Monopoly. At the tender age of four he learned how to write and immediately began practicing his Nobel Prize acceptance speech. Before becoming a successful writer, C.R. spent two years sleeve-polishing the multiple degrees he earned from University of Toronto. Presently, he is living in sin with his life partner and their 13 plants. Due to his recent rise to fame, the writer would like to maintain his whereabouts secret, in order to keep his stalkers at bay.

# Acknowledgments:

*I would like to thank the following people for their help and support during the writing of* The Spanish Guru.

To my readers for their positive energy and feedback. Thank you for buying my book!

To my editor, Michelle Horn, for her patience and advice.

To Mike Petroianu for his dazzling cover design.

To the good folks at Empire State Publishing.

To Magda Mucha for her deadlines.

To Andreea Iorga for the energy and work she has put into promoting this book.

To my friends, who are bizarre enough to provide me with inspiration on a daily basis (particularly on Wednesdays).

And most of all, to Julian Avram, who believed in me and without whom this book would have been another icon on my desktop.

# THE SPANISH GURU

C.R. PRESTON

EMPIRE STATE PUBLISHING

This is a work of fiction. Names, characters, and incidents are products of author's imagination or are used fictitiously and are not to be construed as real. Any resemblance to actual events, organizations, or persons, living or dead, is entirely coincidental.

The Spanish Guru. Copyright © 2010 by Catrinel Ionescu. All rights reserved. No part of this book may be used or reproduced in any manner whatsoever without written permission except in the case of brief quotations embodied in critical articles and reviews.

Published by arrangement with Empire State Publishing.
ISBN-10: 0-9845457-0-0
ISBN-13: 978-0-9845457-0-4
http://www.empirestatebooks.com

*To my parents*

# CHAPTER 1

# SUPPLY AND DEMAND

Sometime in the early part of the twenty-first century, in the capital city of a certain ex-communist country, a pack of stray dogs crossed the main boulevard, making their way between car bumpers, huge huffing buses bursting at the seams with passengers, and impudent scooter wheels. The light turned green for a moment, shining like a small beacon of hope in a sea of feverish engines and dust. But nothing moved. From one end of the boulevard to the other, as far as the eye could see, traffic had been brought to a halt. Seen from above, the conglomerate of vehicles appeared to be a single creature—frustrated, unwashed, and colourful—struggling to break loose from the confining fences made of gray apartment buildings that contoured the length of the boulevard. Probing the sidewalks with wheels heating in the midday sun, the creature huffed and puffed, unable to swing its formidable tail. Small circles of exhaust smoke disappeared into the greyish skyline, and for an instant, the creature breathed in. Suddenly, a deafening symphony of honks broke out, shaking the balcony windows of the apartment buildings.

rage, as if to say, "That's not fair."

"Yeah, yeah," waved the driver of the black Mercedes. "If you want fairness, better move to another place. He-he-he," he chuckled. "So much for traffic jams being democratic, huh, Mr. Pector?"

* * *

Hotel Lido had been a landmark of the city through multiple political systems. It had been built as an elegant baroque establishment under the Habsburg monarchy, kept as a place to isolate foreign visitors from the realities of communism during the socialist republic decades, and turned into a place of leisure for the wealthy after the revolution. Now, only months away from having to function up to the standards of the European Union, the hotel was given a quick makeover in the form of a spa, complete with an entertainment team reminiscent of those they had at tropical resorts. Where to find good-looking men who could teach fitness classes and get the old gals hanging by the poolside excited enough to move? The hotel manager turned to the man in charge of placing beautiful people at the right spots and making a profit out of it.

Placido Pector stepped out of the black Mercedes. He looked at the facade of the building, noticing the high cornice carved with running leaf patterns. Massive gold letters spelled out the name of the hotel. The only visible signs of change were the dozen flags from around the world flanking the centerpiece above the front entrance, which was an indigo-coloured flag as big as a queen-sized bedsheet, with a golden wreath made of stars embroidered as its emblem.

"Nothing like a change of flags to authenticate new circumstances," he greeted the manager, who was waiting by the door.

"Yes," nodded the other man, shaking Placido's hand vigorously. "Do you like it?"

"That depends on the circumstances," he said, staring at the giant European Union flag.

"Well, this is what I wanted to show you," started the manager, holding the door open for Placido. "You know my business takes me around the world to see how other hotels operate. After all my travels, I have to say the Lido is as close as we'll ever get to a five-star establishment in this city. Especially now that I've opened up the spa," he added proudly.

Placido nodded absentmindedly as they crossed the lobby, heading for the outdoor pool at the back of the hotel.

"There's only one thing missing," the manager continued. "Customer loyalty."

"Come on," Placido gestured dismissively. "Where else do you expect a respectable foreigner to lodge? I bet they all come back to the Lido for lack of better options."

"True," agreed the manager. "Yet not many people travel to these parts of Europe. They used to when it was forbidden," he added, giving Placido a look that made him think of another time they both lived through. "Now that we're no longer a communist prison, they've lost interest. We are the newest member of the Union, the poor relative waiting for hand-me-downs. "

"That'll all change once we're no longer the newest member," remarked Placido.

The manager shook his head slowly and grabbing a hold of the metallic handle to the glass door, he rested his arm there for a moment. "But our habits will take much longer to change," he said. "We'll have to learn to respect, before others can respect us. Look at how we're treating our own. We hate our gypsies and we throw stones at our pride parade. Even our women," here he paused, and added, "we need them to be weak."

Prompted by this last observation, Placido raised a disproving eyebrow. Before he could say anything, the manager concluded, "The world no longer wants to know us, my friend. We get the odd investor and the rare businessman, but if I don't do something, I'm afraid our expenses will far exceed our earnings."

Placido returned the man's grave stare, as the manager showed him to the pool deck. A very high fence surrounded the deck, making the yellowish-gray sky the only possible scenery. Across the deck, a few palm trees grounded in large flowerpots marked the pool area with a precarious shade. Behind every tree, there was an incense can stuffed with burning cones meant to overpower the pungent smell of diesel coming from the boulevard. Slowly, the fragrant smoke curled up into the air, doing very little to cover the heavy odour of pollution.

The manager brought him to the bar, and after waving the bartender away, poured Placido a glass of his finest scotch whiskey. From four sets of speakers, the sharp sound of a trombone mixed with the playful rhythm of bongo drums. Over the salsa music, the men could still hear horns honking from the cars on the other side of the fence.

"So what did you have in mind?" asked Placido, knowing the manager was hoping he could help.

"Well," started the other man, pouring a glass for himself, "I figured if I can no longer rely on tourism, I must open up to the local clientele. The Lido must offer them something steady and attractive to come back to. As it happens, the demographics in this part of town are of a specific kind," he said, casting a glance across the pool deck, where a number of middle-aged women were lying back on beach chairs. "I have a market for a male . . . entertainer," he confided with a wink. Then, looking back to the women, he added, "Someone who can get them and their friends to spend their time and money at the Lido."

"Doesn't sound like much of a business plan," noted Placido, checking his wristwatch. "I mean I can get you a stud or two, if that's what you need, but I don't see how it'll help the Lido in the grand scheme of things."

The manager shook his head, "I'm afraid you're missing the big picture here," he said, spreading his arms widely. Placido looked away from the salt stains that had crystallized around the man's armpits.

"Land Retribution Act 143B," articulated the manager. "The land that once belonged to the nobility was stolen fifty years ago by the proletariat. But do you know what happened this week?" he asked. He was certain Placido, like most alert citizens of his country, knew. He said, "This stolen land was given back to the original owners. Well, to their legal heirs at any rate— most of the original owners died off years ago. Yet overnight, if you will, people from all walks of life inherited land. A villa in the country, a condominium downtown, even a cottage somewhere in ... Africa," he ended with aplomb.

Placido scratched his head. "Africa?" he repeated in disbelief.

"Yes," waved the manager. "Some people inherited land as far as Africa."

"Why Africa?"

The manager took another sip from his glass and lowered his voice as he leaned closer to Placido. "The socialist party tried to convert African countries to communism, and so large quantities of land were purchased in places like Libya, Gabon, and Angola. Courtesy of Land Retribution Act 143B, this land belongs to our people now."

Placido raised an incredulous eyebrow. "So what? Who needs land in Africa?"

"Why, the African people, of course," said the manager, clinking his glass against Placido's. "Land, irrespective of its geographical location, means money, my friend. And there is lots of money to be made from this particular land retribution act."

Placido took another swallow of fine import whiskey, this time swirling it in his mouth. The manager crossed his arms, hiding the sweat stains on his dark suit, and lowered his voice again. "So you see, my old friend, a *stud* or two is not what I need. *We* need a clever, athletic-looking chap who can bring in this new money. Someone who can provide us with the leverage we need so that I can get investors, and you can keep doing what it is that you're doing," he added with a meaningful stare. "These women are the wives of new money and old money together. They are the wives of ministers, judges, and executives. What do you think they would do to prevent their husbands from finding out about their . . . indiscretions?"

"Almost anything," replied Placido, holding his hand over his chin pensively.

Placido Pector thought about it for a few days. He could have sent dozens of beautiful women if asked to: redheads that made any man go wild with passion, brunettes with eyes of Caribbean blue, blonds with legs up to their necks who could recite Shakespearean sonnets while beating any man in tennis. But it was not men he was asked to cater to. It was the wealthiest wives of the city that needed to be pleased. This unforeseen demand made way for a supplier of beauty to set a new precedent. Placido needed a new type of product, an untapped resource in a post-communist country: the beautiful and useless male.

This male had to be easy on the eyes, not keen on feeling useful, and comfortable with taking what life offered him in exchange for not much other than looking pretty. He thought of the men he knew, most of them eager to cheat and steal as long as it followed a reasonably masculine code of conduct. They were the product of a society where the value of a man rested in his ability to provide for his family, for his woman. What self-respecting man would be willing to make a living off the good will of wealthy women? Thieves would not. Nor would other members of the underground world. It had to be a sort of man without clear qualifications, without consistent revenue, and with a love of self so great that he might consider letting others in on it. It also had to be a fellow who knew how to dress and undress, according to the occasion. Suddenly, while brainstorming these unlikely qualities, he heard himself describe his favourite betting horse.

Placido remembered that Leborio Borzelini, who until that day had been the undisputed arm-wrestling champion of every pub east of the Rhine River by virtue of his speed, was only good for two things: surprising big guys with a quick offense and stealing their women. If he wasn't so damn good at finding excuses for himself, Placido would have thrown him to the dogs a long time ago. But he thought the kid had something special. He could talk a nun into becoming a burlesque dancer and then convince her to cut him in on the profits.

Placido had plenty of beautiful women who specialized in getting powerful men to do his bidding. And until now, he did not think of finding a man to do the same for powerful women. As any bold inventor, Placido could not help but wonder which of his creations would be more effective. Would a beautiful female be the master of manipulation, or would a young Adonis surpass her charms? Hard to tell, he decided. Manipulation was difficult to measure. Leborio would certainly shed some light on this issue, as soon as he would undertake his new task teaching some sort of fitness class at the Lido Spa and Pool. At any rate, it would make for a most interesting social experiment, the old man thought.

"Get up, my champion." The gangster gently kicked Leborio out of his afternoon meditation. "You're getting a promotion."

* * *

If there was a man Leborio Borzelini feared and, implicitly, respected, that man was Placido Pector. Without being very tall, Placido commanded anxiety of anyone he came across. He made local warlords, politicians, and celebrities nervous. He was one of those local characters who never made the news because they chose to stay out of the spotlight but were rumoured to be behind all respectable heists and illicit operations. No longer a spring chicken, Placido had only one son, legitimate or otherwise, who could not have fallen farther from the tree that was his father. In fact, if the father had been an apple tree, as far as Leborio was concerned, the son had come out a tomato.

Thinking about it, Leborio found it pathetic that Armin Pector was still in junior high at the age of eighteen—what made it laughable were the junior's motives for choosing to stay there. Besides the advantage of being the only ninth-grade student who could vote, Leborio suspected that Armin's primary reason for repeating ninth grade so many times had to do with picking up girls. Sharing a learning space with considerably younger female colleagues improved his odds at getting to know them better. Girls seemed to like older guys. Even if a fellow was not particularly good-looking, a girl forced to see his face every day for a year might eventually change her mind about him. Of course, this theory only worked on rookies, and this was why Armin chose to stay in ninth grade, to his father's embarrassment and exasperation.

As far as Leborio could tell, Placido was a good father and would never have said anything unsupportive to his son. The only sign of disappointment he had ever witnessed was the day he heard Placido ask what he took to be a rhetorical question.

"Who am I going to leave my business to?"

Leborio did not answer and counted on the universe to point out the obvious. He could almost picture himself riding in Placido's inconspicuous black Mercedes. He saw no reason to upgrade to a more noticeable car and attract unwanted attention from the authorities. He also saw himself commanding Placido's people, living in Placido's house, sleeping with Placido's wife—or even better, with his mistress. There was only one thing standing between him and Placido's lifestyle: Armin Pector. Leborio knew too well that despite Placido's no-nonsense personality, he was reluctant to recognize his son's shortcomings. The father held on to the hope that one day his son would rise up to the Pector name and make him proud.

"He's still young," he told Leborio with a sigh. "One of these days, he'll snap out of it."

Out of what, stupidity or high school? thought the younger man. The way Leborio saw things, he owed it to his boss to sever the useless rudiment of familial ties, should the opportunity ever arise.

The opportunity presented itself with the "promotion," as Placido liked to refer to it. Leborio had been dozing off all morning on a black leather couch at the back of Neon Lounge, Placido Pector's trendiest nightclub. Luckily, he slept with one eye open and most people assumed he was in fact meditating. When Placido kicked him gently, Leborio pushed his shiny dark waves behind his ears and straightened the crisp white collar on his knock-off Dolce shirt. He had been waiting for this moment. At last, the head of local organized crime had seen the signs the universe was sending him and had decided to retire, leaving him, Leborio Borzelini, in charge of operations. His good-for-nothing son would stay out of the picture.

"You're going to work the ladies over at the Lido," announced Placido. "They're looking for a good-looking chap with athletic inclinations, who can, shall we say, *entertain* the old gals."

Seeing that Leborio stiffened at the edge of the couch into a figure shaped like a four, he pressed on, "Don't pout, dear boy. You haven't got the lips for it," he said, gently kicking his foot. "These gals are not that old you know. Some of them don't look half bad, either. You'll like it; you'll see. It's just your cup of tea: no work and lots of women to roam about you. You can teach them how to—what do you call that mumbo jumbo?"

Leborio's eyes widened in disbelief. The old man was serious. He was going to send him to strut his stuff at the Lido like one of his cheap dolls—granted, though, they really weren't that cheap. That was how Placido saw him, just another pawn in the corrupt booby trap he had spread about the changing city.

"What mumbo jumbo?" he brought himself to ask.

"The one where you look like you're sleeping."

"Meditating?"

"Yes, you can teach them how to meditate. While they're doing it, you can either find out something juicy about their husbands or unburden them of their jewels. But the jewels would have to be top-notch. None of that cubic zirconium or Swarovski crap. They'd have to be real diamonds, big diamonds, like the ones they use to make for queens and lock up in museums. We don't jeopardize our name for any old rock, you understand."

Before accepting this new assignment, the younger man could only bring himself to utter one thing. "Why me?"

Placido looked rather surprised. He took a few steps back to open his desk drawer, reached into a carved wooden box, and pulled out a thick cigar and a gold-plated lighter.

"Everyone has a talent," he said after a while, puffing on the cigar to light it up. "Yours, my dear boy, is to get yourself out of impossible situations."

Leborio suppressed a cough and turned his face away from the cloud of smoke. Paying no mind to his discomfort, Placido went on, "I'm sending you into a minefield because I am certain that you will map it out for others less intuitive than you, and help me turn this into a successful expansion of the business. Think of it as an internship. If you succeed, well, there might just be a place for you in upper management, ruling some part of the city." He puffed on his cigar with great gusto. "Think about it! It's an untapped industry. And you'll be the head of research, if you will."

"What if I refuse?"

Placido frowned. "That would be a shame. As I said, you are good at some things. What you are not good at is working for your money in the conventional sense of the word. And I wish you to never have to do so. You know what they say, if you do what you like and are good at, you'll never have to work a day in your life."

"And this is the best you think I can do for myself?" Leborio stood up from the couch.

"By no means. But this is as good a start as any, and it's better than most," he said, blowing a yellow cloud of smoke in the young man's face. "It's an unexploited market, and you could be its pioneer. The laws of supply and demand, my boy, the laws of supply and demand! This is a golden opportunity. Think about it."

Leborio thought about it during the next few meditations. Not long after, he became part of the Hotel Lido Spa and Swimming Pool entertainment team. Apparenlty settled in his new routine, Leborio Borzelini began planning to take charge of his destiny, against all odds—even against Placido. But Placido was a dangerous man, and Leborio knew to tread cautiously for now. Because he was a person who believed that when life gave one lemons one absolutely had to turn them into lemonade, he decided there were opportunities in becoming a yoga teacher at the Lido. This would give him ample time to figure out a way of eliminating the competition. Young Armin Pector's weakness had always been women. And women had always been Leborio's strong point.

· CHAPTER 2 ·

# DIAMONDS ARE A GIRL'S BEST FRIEND

In the shade of a colourful umbrella, Leborio Borzelini stretched out his magnificent arms and whispered, "*Inhalamos.* Inhale."

Half a dozen well-aged women sporting Versace sunglasses eagerly followed his lead. Holding their breath for a moment, the women awaited instructions. With a deliberate and hypnotic movement, his muscles rippling beneath his olive skin, he brought his arms down, letting them hang just a little lower than the leg line of his turquoise swimming trunks. He closed his eyes for a moment, like a conductor before his orchestra. Almost immediately, he heard them sigh and knew that behind the designer shades, the women's eyes rested on his body.

"*Exhalamos.* Exhale," he commanded, as all arms descended slowly to the ground.

A few more *inhalamos/exhalamos* stretches and he would move on to the lunges, which announced the beginning of the end for his afternoon yoga class. Leborio emptied his lungs and thought about the first yoga book he'd ever read. It was written by an illustrious

Tibetan monk whose name sounded like a French delicacy, and it professed the benefits of compassionate love for all God's creatures. According to this wise monk, the highest state of consciousness one could attain in this fleeting life was to become a guru, a channel between God and humanity. The guru's mere presence enlightened those around him. This was why his job was really fairly simple. All one had to do was be. Leborio thought it sounded like the sort of job he was cut out for. Soon after reading the monk's book, he began practicing yoga by meditating to the sounds of his favourite music. This process was rather challenging during his teenage years, as his musical inclinations were partial to the heavy metal movement. But by his early twenties, with practice and perseverance, Leborio found it increasingly less difficult to focus. Of course, his musical taste had changed by then to electronica. Without the distraction of lyrics, one could empty the mind and float on the wings of imagination to the sounds of an oscillating number of beats per minute.

One day, while meditating to the new release of a British music producer turned deejay, Leborio fell asleep and dreamed he was flying over his house, down to the main boulevard of the city, and into the Costa Rican embassy, where he sat down at the conference table and had tea with the ambassador. This had been a most pleasant vision, and when he awoke, he proceeded to download British music from Henry Purcell to Fat Boy Slim and Juno Reactor. Having figured out the secret to attaining a trance-like state of mind, Leborio felt confident he could help others toward a path of blissfulness.

"*Inhalamos. Exhalamos.* Good. Now let's go to lunges, ladies."

Perla Galanis nudged her friend, Rita, whose plump pout opened up like a purposeful fish mouth before a healthy wiggly worm.

"Oh, I do hope he turns his back for the lunges," she said, just as Leborio commanded the women to exhale.

"Keep your mind out of the gutter," Rita hissed back. "This one is mine!"

Perla shot her a look but said nothing. She was too much of a lady to dignify Rita with a response. Not that she couldn't think of one. After all, Rita deserved to be placed in front of an old-fashioned mirror, not like these new department store slimming lenses that made any old whale look as thin as a model so she would buy whatever she tried on. No. Rita ought to have been placed in front of a mirror that reflected her paunch and the ripples on the back of her thighs that either fierce hail or untreated cellulite had bestowed on her. To think the woman didn't even have the decency to cover up in public.

There she was, showing her pear-shaped booty in a two-piece Brazilian bikini on the deck of the Lido Hotel pool and obstructing the view of perfect, golden-skinned Leborio. A woman of her age! Why, the shamelessness of it all left Perla red-faced. Of course, her red face could have been from spending too much time in the sun earlier that morning. Her skin could only take so much tanning by the poolside with the aluminum collar around her neck. They called it a *tan optimizer*, and for the price she paid for one of those gizmos, she also received a transparent bottle of clear lotion that smelled like baby oil and was called *tan enhancer*. Armed with a complete tanning kit, Perla was napping by the poolside that morning until Leborio's soothing voice woke her up to join the yoga class.

"Will you be joining us this afternoon, Mrs. Galanis?"

"Oh, but of course, Leborio. I wouldn't miss your class for the world." And then blushing at her own eagerness, she added, "I find yoga is very good for the joints." But only old people complained about joint aches, and she was not that old. She felt the need to explain, just in case he might place her in the same age bracket as those other housewives. "A young woman can never be too careful about her joints if she plans to have an active old age—which I'm still quite far from reaching," she smiled. "Better to be safe than sorry."

"You look quite well, Mrs. Galanis," he said, smiling back. "Regular exercise and eating healthy will keep you in good shape well into your forties," he added with a wink.

"Perla," mumbled the flustered sexagenarian. "Just call me Perla."

She thought he smiled at her during yoga, and worked on her stretches with that much more dedication. Once the class was over, Perla sighed as she watched Leborio walk away. Dear Leborio had the keen eye of a trained professional, she thought. He was able to recognize the hard work she had put into her tight little body. Surely, there were thirty-year-olds who envied the firmness of her shoulders. Her skin had never looked as good as it did with the sunny glow she had acquired during the past few months. She wondered if the tanning kit had anything to do with it. Perhaps. Or perhaps it was the flutter in her stomach that made her light up the way she did before she'd married George. It was as if a beam of light from the sky pierced the clouds and spread over her platinum blond French twist, covering her with a warm and fuzzy halo.

I am in love with a real man, she thought.

There was no telling if this real man returned the passionate love she felt for him. But one could argue that there was passion in his occasional winks. Younger men felt intimidated by women of maturity and hardly ever acted on their passions. She would have to find a way to let her beloved know that the coast was clear despite the formality of titles married people adopted. She might have been Mrs. Galanis in name. In her heart, helped largely by George's obsessive love for reading politics in bed, Perla was a free woman—free to find her way to true love.

She waited until after she had showered to knock on the door to the spa. A pretty brunette dressed in a white lab coat opened the door with a toothy smile spread all across her flawless face. The girl looked young enough to be in high school, remarked Perla.

"Can I help you ma'am?"

Raising an eyebrow, Perla walked past the girl right up to the service counter. Ma'am! The nerve of this girl! You don't call someone ma'am unless they look like a ma'am. And Perla certainly did not. She put her elbows on top of the counter and interlocked her fingers.

"I'm interested in a massage."

"I can take you right now," offered the girl.

"No," protested Perla. "I mean, no, thank you. I am a loyal client of Mr. Borzelini."

"Umm, Leborio is booked for the rest of the day I'm afraid," said the girl, shifting her weight from one foot to the other. "I can take you if you'd like, or we can make an appointment for tomorrow."

Perla had not anticipated this. Faced with an obstacle as prosaic as an appointment, Perla Galanis turned away and started to leave, feeling as if a dark cloud had descended upon her. She grabbed a hold of the shiny knob on the tinted glass door. Reflected in the glass, a gentle light shone from behind her, contouring a male-shaped halo. The clouds parted once again as Leborio's unmistakable form appeared in the doorway.

"Snejana, hand me a bottle of eucalyptus oil, will you?" she heard him ask the girl. His eyes rested on her beaming face for a second. Then, taking notice of the older woman, he said, "Perla, how is your afternoon so far?"

Her face lit up as she turned to look at him.

"Wonderful, thank you. Of course, it would be even better if I could get a massage. But I understand you're busy for the rest of the day."

"Today, I'm afraid I am busy. But come back tomorrow, and I will be all yours."

*Mine*, she thought. He should be *mine*. He *will* be mine.

"All right. I will come back tomorrow," she nodded, inspired by a newfound confidence. "Don't work too hard, Leborio."

"I won't," he winked again, adjusting his turquoise Speedos with the hand that wasn't holding the eucalyptus oil. "Oh, Perla, before you go, I meant to compliment you on your earrings. They look most becoming on you."

She touched her ears instinctively, rubbing the heart-shaped diamonds with the tips of her fingers. George had bought them for her last summer at an auction in Monte Carlo.

"Thank you. They once belonged to Maria Callas. A gift from Aristotle Onassis, I would think."

Leborio took a closer look and marvelled at the workmanship. She heard him utter the word *exquisite*, and for a moment allowed herself to believe he meant her. Not entirely impossible, after all. Perla had once been the Queen of the Ball at the spring Danube River Festival, before the festival morphed into the spring socialist republic workers' parade. George's oldest friend swore he heard him call Perla exquisite as he watched her wave from her shell-shaped chariot. And if she had been exquisite once, she could be exquisite again.

"Will you close the door from the inside, dear boy? I'm getting cold in here."

Behind Leborio, the door to the massage room opened wide enough to allow Rita to stand in it. Leborio excused himself and followed her into the room, leaving Perla livid with rage in the middle of the spa antechamber. Why, that collagen-injected, old fish! How dare she make such a fool of herself at her age, going after a man who could be her son, a man she could never aspire to understand! And the way she spoke to him. This was not how one should speak to . . . an artist! Perla had some trouble finding the exact word to define Leborio's title and settled on artist. He wasn't really an artist in as much as he did not produce palpable art. There was no great Borzelini masterpiece out there to be sold post-mortem for an outrageous price; no moonlight sonata to listen to and think of gentle Leborio conducting the national orchestra with the kind of passion that makes the hair of a man jump out of its coif and into his face. No. There will be no great masterpiece bearing his name for posterity. But there was now, and he was special enough without producing anything of value. This was not how one should speak to a Leborio Borzelini.

Oblivious to Perla's noble inner conflict about defining the essence of Leborio Borzelini, the toothy girl wondered if the old lady was having a heart attack. At first, she stood still in the middle of the room, and then she trembled, turned red, and broke into a sweat that caused her mascara to melt. Snejana watched her quietly, afraid she might have to call the ambulance and spoil her afternoon. If the ambulance was called, the manager would have to step in, and that would be it for the rest of the day. She would have to pretend to do something useful, like clean the glass shelves, restock products, and make calls to confirm appointments. It had happened a few times before when an old gal passed out. What could be expected of them at their age? Of course, there was no telling how old they really were, with all the face-lifts and tummy tucks they invested in. A waste of money, really. Just because one couldn't tell their age didn't mean they didn't look old. Snejana examined the woman from the corner of her eye, wondering about her age. Her skin had the tangerine finish of animal hides, rigid and stretched like the face of a cat nailed to a tree.

"Should I put you down for tomorrow?" she asked gingerly, afraid to test Perla's regenerative capacity just yet.

The old lady stared her down in contempt and nodded.

Perla knew her type all too well. One look at the girl told her she was the impervious and callous sort, who looked fresh for the picking in her youth only to wilt into a big old mare like Rita. From a few feet away, the girl's most striking features were her unusually long neck and legs, somehow unbalanced against the rest of her willowy body and her thin but widely set hips. Poor girl, she told herself. She's made only for breeding. She wondered what Leborio thought of her and pictured laughing about it with him over an alcohol-free cocktail.

"How well put!" he would observe. "She does remind one of some sort of a large creature. An ostrich perhaps?"

"Doesn't she?" Perla would throw her head back, laughing. "I thought you'd see it too."

"Oh, Perla, few women have your wit and sense of style. Lucky is the man who has your heart," he would say, pressing his bow-shaped lips against her well-manicured hand. "You truly are exquisite. Just like those diamond earrings of yours."

One day, she thought, putting an end to her daydream. Until then, she would continue to surprise him with her wit and sense of style. Her wit she would have to work on. Not that she didn't have a sharp wit. But every time she saw Leborio, she was tongue-tied. Luckily, there was her unmatched sense of style, manifested mostly through her jewellery collection. Diamonds were a girl's best friend, Perla thought, idly playing with the earrings. And there were plenty more where they came from.

# CHAPTER 3

# THE SPANISH GURU

You could always tell a lady from a simple woman by looking at her nails, thought Snejana as she filed the tip of her pinkie nail. Young girls often think about the meaning behind words like "woman" and "lady" and find themselves puzzled over which one they would rather use when describing themselves. In her view, woman was too generic. It was like describing a dog by calling it a dog. Border Collie sounded fancier. It sounded like a title, and it represented a long line of careful breeding that clearly set Lassie apart from regular dogs. To be called a lady was the human equivalent of a female pedigree. These New Age feminist groups had it all wrong, she thought, carefully inspecting her other hand. They advocate the term *woman* as a tool of empowerment for females and criticize *ladies* for being too dainty and delicate. Not that I am delicate, she thought, beginning to work on her index finger.

Snejana's hair was not as polished as her nails. It was cut sharply, like an ancient Egyptian wig of an uncertain colour. Straight bangs barely brushed against her forehead, accentuating her angular, almost square shoulder frame. Her neck was unusually long and thin. It held her elongated head up, softly angled between a tilt and a turn, in the way of a Modigliani painting.

She was taller than most men she knew, a strong-boned girl with childbearing hips. At least, this was how Leborio had described them when they first met at her mother's healing institute. She took his observation to heart, and stopped eating altogether until her hips became less favourable to bearing children. And now, he teased her about it every chance he got.

"You're too thin. Why are you doing this to yourself? In less than three months, you went from a fine specimen to a coat hanger. Really, you have to start eating something instead of looming around my place like a big, gloomy bird."

Flattered by his notice of the drastic change, she continued chewing on carrots from breakfast to supper and spending her evenings under the guru's balcony, throwing pebbles at the window, hoping he'd let her in. Leborio was stingy with compliments, and she knew he really meant to tell her she looked fabulous. Just a few more pounds to go and Snejana could be the first woman in her family to fit into a size zero. The first lady, she corrected herself, checking her nails for confirmation.

"You're losing a dangerous amount of weight," noticed her mother. "I know you young girls all want to look like that actress—what's her name? Athena Jeudi. But I worry about your health."

"There's nothing to worry about. I want to reach my comfort zone," she said, quoting something she had read in a fitness magazine.

"Your comfort zone can't possibly be less than 110 pounds."

Snejana rolled her big gray eyes. On anyone else, those eyes would have looked almost profound. But there was something about the way she stared with an unquestioning and vacant expression, blinking contently at exact intervals, that made her look like a cross between

Marvin the Martian and the Road Runner

She put away the nail file and began to doodle. There were benefits to being the only child of a renowned healer, she thought, but arguing on matters of nutrition could not be one of them. She smiled, remembering the first time she saw Leborio. Clad in a plum silk shirt and an immaculate pair of white trousers, he walked right past the front desk of her mother's healing center, where Snejana was sketching something waiting for the switch-phone to ring. He walked past the dozen people waiting for their turn, and right into Simina's healing room.

At first, Snejana was rooted to her seat in shock. No one did that to mother. She dropped the pencil she had been using to shade in the outline of a Christ-like figure on a piece of tissue paper and tried to listen in. Curiosity eventually got the better of her, and she went to stand in the doorway.

"Nice drawings," she heard him say to her mother, as he took a closer look at the religious icons on the wall. His arms folded under the pits of his silk shirt, and the contorted but rather frightening heads of two intertwined snakes peeked out with jaws wide open. Had they been real, the snakes would have probably consumed Leborio's nipples long ago.

"They are pictures of saints and of the Virgin Mary," her mother said quietly. She glanced at the embroidered snakes on his shirt and looked away. "If you are here to see me, you must make an appointment at the front desk."

As if he hadn't heard any of this, Leborio strolled over to the window and checked to see if the ledge was clean before he leaned against it. Making himself comfortable, Leborio smiled at the bamboozled patient lying on the table in front of him.

"Oh, I am just going to watch today," he explained, at last, in a tone of voice one could only describe as somnolent. "I find it very relaxing when other people get healed. Does that make me more compassionate, do you suppose? I've always had a finely tuned sensibility for human energy. I can sense anyone's inner being just by being in the same room with them."

Snejana saw her mother's patient look up as if he expected her to remove the intruder. His face contorted from the pillow marks, the man clicked his tongue disapprovingly, and reached to pull a corner of the sheet already covering him. Her mother helped him tuck it under his belly and turned to Leborio. With her hands on her hips, Simina said, "Can you sense *my* inner being?"

The young healing aficionado must have indeed sensed her inner being, because without a word he stood up straight, tidied his white trousers, and headed for the door. Before walking out, he turned and left her with an afterthought.

"My name is Leborio. Leborio Borzelini," he added in the cool, detached tone of a British spy. "You will see me soon I hope."

Moving across the hallway with regal elegance, Leborio made Snejana think of Baron Harkonnen and his floating device. She sighed as she followed him back to the desk and sat down. Only he wasn't overweight, she noted. On the contrary, his weight seemed to be perfectly spread out.

He parked his floating device at her desk. "Tuesday evening works for me," he said, crossing his arms.

She stared at him with her mouth open. Did he not know people waited to see her mother for months and sometimes years? She rolled a colourful pencil between her knuckles, unsure of how to answer. With his luscious black waves and piercing dark gaze, he was unusually handsome. Snejana had the sensitive eye of a portrait artist and thought handsome people deserved preferential treatment.

"You may draw me if you want," he added magnanimously, just before she penciled him in.

Amazed at his mind-reading abilities, Snejana asked if he was a medium or a healer like her mother.

"Simina is your mother," he said, with the familiarity of one who had known her for years. "Yes. I can see the resemblance in your posture. You are both very . . . straight. Also, you both have childbearing hips. But, yes, you are very observant to notice my paranormal abilities. I too work with the powers of the universe." He paused for an instant and added solemnly, "I am a guru."

"A guru," she repeated. "Like for yoga?"

"That is only one of the teachings a guru must carry out."

"What type of yoga?"

The question seemed to take him by surprise as he reflected for a moment. "Spanish," he said with finality. "I am a Spanish guru."

It was so hard to keep track of yoga styles with all these celebrities endorsing it: from Ashtanga to Kripalu to yogalates and now to Spanish. Snejana wondered if Spanish yoga was the strenuous type. It had to be. The guru was very well built. She places her hands on her lap, covering the sides of her thighs. Did he mean her hips were too big? She had never thought of it until then.

The girl stared at him with her mouth slightly open, as if watching an illusionist produce a rabbit from an empty hat. He unclipped a gold-plated pen from his shirt pocket and clicked it a few times with his thumb.

"Nice pen," she muttered shyly.

"Thanks. I keep if for autographs."

Her eyes opened widely for a moment. "Are you famous?" she blurted.

With the graceful flourish of a musketeer, the guru waved his pen in the air and said, "Not yet, but that's just a technicality."

She watched him take a business card from her desk as he said, "Very well. Give me your number." He rested the tip of the pen expectantly over the blank side of the card. "I suppose I could take you out for lemonade sometime."

Snejana had never been asked out for lemonade by any boy before. Especially not by a clebrity-in-the-making. Other boys had asked her to the movies, the mall, and even dance parties. But never to drink lemonade. She willingly wrote her number on the card and underlined her name.

Later that week, he called her well after midnight and made a date for the next morning. They did not go for lemonade but strolled through a park for a few hours until he sat down on a bench and let her rub his back for him.

"Let's see if you're anything like your mother," he said. And after a while, he added, "You're actually quite good. I will get you a job where I teach."

Snejana blushed. Then she could rub his back all the time, the girl thought happily, unaware that she too could read minds.

Months later, things had not panned out exactly as she'd thought. She put the nail filer away in a drawer and checked the time. Another day of work where she didn't get to see him, she sighed. This was not what she had signed up for. Leborio spent his afternoons at the Hotel Lido pool teaching the old gals how to stretch, massaging them, and returning smiles, while Snejana answered the phone and filed her nails at the spa. They hardly saw each other in the day. At night, he was always busy with important matters he could not discuss over the phone. She tried to distract herself with paraffin treatments for her hands and baby-carrots for her figure, but, in the end, seeing Leborio was all she could think of.

One of these nights, I'm going to ambush him, she decided, grabbing her handbag on her way out.

# CHAPTER 4

# THE SOPHIE NECKLACE

The grandfather clock in the reading room had to be wound once a week, and George liked to do it himself on a Monday morning. He kept the key in the pocket of his housecoat and only took it out to coil the clock. Standing at a little over five feet, George climbed up a stout stepladder to reach the keyhole. As the silver key turned the tiny wheels of another week, George thought about his accomplishments and set new resolutions for the week ahead with the same excitement a woman determined to lose weight embraces New Year's Day.

A new Monday meant new business opportunities, possible acquisitions, and investments, bringing him closer to a seat in the senate. Senator Galanis, he thought, sounded very becoming. And who was to say he would not make a fine minister or even a memorable president? His father had once told him it was the moral duty of every man of a certain social standing to become involved in politics. If we who control the cargo do not steer the ship, then who will, reflected George, putting the silver key back in his pocket.

Simple men could not be expected to make wise decisions. After all, they had other, more pressing issues to think about, such as earning enough money to feed their families, putting their kids through college, and buying cemetery plots. George, who had been born into money, never worried about it too much. He had a cook to take care of feeding the family and a wife to worry about the kids. As for the cemetery plots, he had already commissioned a marble mausoleum to be built in his posthumous honour. Of course, Perla would be buried by his side, in her own Taj Mahal-shaped sarcophagus. Gently stroking his thick moustache, he pictured his wife lying there peacefully, clad in her best pastel dress suit, wearing a string of large pearls around her neck. Alive or dead, Perla looked the part of the politician's wife. A veritable Jackie Kennedy, that one. Except she would have to lay low on the tanning, he thought. Lately, she was beginning to look a little orange.

"Good morning, dear."

Prompted by her buoyant voice, George Galanis turned to face his own Jackie O. and nearly fell off the ladder. Framed by a low-cut blouse, a necklace as thick as a dog collar hung over her décolleté. The necklace consisted of thirty mine-cut diamonds set into a single thread, with a fringe of alternating round and pear-shaped stones. Small diamond clusters were mounted on top of each other across the necklace to make it look more brilliant.

"Are you wearing the Sophie necklace, darling?" he asked, holding on to the clock as he came down the ladder.

"Why, yes. Thank you for noticing it."

Perla stood in front of the hallway mirror, backcombing the crown of her head with her fingers. "Do you think my hair has enough volume, Georgie?"

Her husband descended on firmer ground and approached her with a look of deep concern on his round and jovial face. "Yes, darling, you look inches taller," he puckered his lips to kiss her, brushing her cheek with his bushy handlebar moustache. "You look very nice," he repeated, following her into the foyer, where she opened the door to a walk-in shoe rack. He watched her pick out a glitzy pair of shoes and strap them on in front of the mirror. The musky smell of her perfume had invaded the area, giving him the beginning of a small headache.

"Where are you off to this fine morning?" he persisted, looking at her ankles.

Perla inspected her feet from every angle with an unhappy look. She picked out another pair and without looking at him, she said, "Off to the Lido, dear. The girls and I have a full schedule today. Starting with the morning yoga class."

Feeling lightheaded from her perfume, George sat back by the fireplace and lit up his red Edward's tobacco pipe. He puffed a few times to start it up, making an effort not to wince at the thought of the other women Perla referred to as "girls." Following a series of decades spent taking antidepressants, giving birth to heirs, and trying to cover the passing of time with plastic interventions, *abominations* would have described the *girls* better. Thank goodness, Perla was not an eccentric wife, he thought, blowing out a thin layer of aromatic smoke. She took care of herself without falling into the extreme. Just a little Botox here and there never hurt anyone. As for the collagen injections, well, she had to keep it up for the sake of their daughter. Athena's entire career depended on her pout, which in her line of work, of course, had to be accounted for genetically.

From his armchair, George watched his wife with gravity. She was a reasonable woman as far as vanity went. Walking out the door in broad daylight, sporting a diamond necklace made for a Hapsburg princess was not like her.

"Do you think it wise to wear the Sophie necklace to the Lido, darling?" he asked without looking directly at her. "What if you lose it? Or worse yet, what if someone decides to steal it?"

"Oh, George, don't be silly. How would I lose it? I don't intend to take it off."

"You plan to wear it in the pool?" he pressed on, chewing on the end of his pipe without realising it.

As she nodded absentmindedly, George became somewhat agitated at the thought of his wife floating in the Lido pool wearing his dead mother's jewellery. He got up and placed his pipe on top of the fireplace mantle.

"Darling, this was Maman's piece de resistance," he said, taking a few steps toward his wife. "She only wore it to special functions."

"Yes, your mother was rather modest in her use of accessories," noted Perla, her lip curling a little at the end.

George thought there was another meaning to what his wife had just said but found he could not quite put his finger on it. He was sure she meant to take a blow at poor Maman.

"Well, never mind that now," he frowned. "I don't think it's a good idea to take it out of the safe and wear it to the pool. It's too heavy for that sort of activity."

"Don't worry, George, I won't drown from the weight," said his wife on her way out the door. "When do you expect me to wear the bloody thing? If the Lido is where I go, then the Lido will get an eyeful of *my* jewels," she emphasized the possessive pronoun. "Women and diamonds are not made to be locked up, dear. They are . . . exquisite."

With the last word in, Perla disappeared through the front door, leaving George perplexed. He took a few steps back and leaned against the grandfather clock, squeezing the key between his fingers, and wishing it had been the safe key instead. It wasn't like Perla to be so blunt and flashy. Did she want the whole world to admire her jewellery as if she were one of those mindless teenage heiresses the tabloids loved to photograph? The thought of it was ridiculous. She was a mature woman who would have looked better with a tiny cross around her neck. Not to mention, people who came from old money knew it was distasteful to flaunt their wealth in broad daylight. Even though he was alone in the room, George shook his head disapprovingly. Jacqueline Kennedy Onassis would have never worn the Sophie necklace to the pool.

\* \* \*

It was just like him to want to save every object of value for a special occasion that never materialized, thought Perla as she firmly applied more tanning enhancer around the Sophie necklace. Did he expect to take his possessions into the afterlife? Yes, let's bring it all into the mausoleum, she thought. Perhaps that was why he had it built in the first place. So he could bury the art, the jewellery, and the wife with him as the Egyptian pharaohs had done in their pyramids. She imagined spending the afterlife with George and his treasure, listening to the grandfather clock count the passing of eternity. Perla suddenly felt claustrophobic at the thought of it. If she was to die, she hoped there would be no afterlife at all. Only life. Wonderful life, basking in the sun and waiting for Leborio. To look at this beautiful man every day of one's life would be like bathing in the fountain of youth.

There was a children's story she once heard when her kids were small. In the story, a young prince set out to find the secret to eternal youth and immortality. He traveled the world in search of a magical creature that could help him find a way to live forever as a young man. His quest was long and full of trials, and with every sea he sailed, mountain he climbed, and bridge he crossed, he moved farther away from his home. One day, he stumbled on a flight of fairies, who offered him youth and eternal life in exchange for his company. The young prince agreed to this. Many years went by without the prince ever aging. The fairies spoiled him with love offerings and made up new games to entertain their guest. Yet, one sad day, the prince woke up to find a hollow longing in his heart—a longing to behold his parents once again, fight by his brothers' side, and look at his childhood sweetheart one last time. Despite the hypnotizing chants of the fairies, the prince turned his back on youth and everlasting life and set out to find his home. But nothing was as he remembered it: his kingdom had been conquered by another, his parents were long gone, his brothers were old men who no longer remembered him, and his sweetheart was gray and weathered from many years of unhappy marriage. There was a moral somewhere in that story, but Perla could not care less about it.

Oh, to be young again, she thought, I wouldn't trade it for the world. Her children were neurotic grownups who seemed to prefer their father anyway. As for George, living with him was as riveting as Egyptian afterlife in the basement of a pyramid. No, there will be no remorse for choosing youth and life over a decrepit existence.

* * *

Just as Perla Galanis was making her blinding appearance at the Lido Pool and Spa, Snejana headed toward the subway, walking through a gold-rimmed revolving door. She rested her well-manicured hand on the leather handle of a large, butterfly-shaped handbag. Not particularly tired after an uneventful morning shift, Snejana was planning to go home and get some sleep before ambushing Leborio on his way back from the Lido. She almost broke his balcony window the night before by throwing pebbles from the street, until a sleep-depraved neighbour poured a bucket of water over her.

"Go home, you daft cow! Can't you see he doesn't want to talk to you?"

Soaked to the skin, she squeezed the water out of the thick, black braid coming down around her long neck and wiped her makeup and tears from her face. Even though she knew he cared for her and that he was a very heavy sleeper, Snejana couldn't help but feel wretched. He hadn't called on her in a few weeks. Of course, he must have been so very busy, being a guru and working for Placido Pector. But she missed being with him. One of these nights, she would catch him on his way up. Maybe even tonight, she thought, descending into the subway station. That was if she managed to escape her already suspicious mother.

Deep in thought, Snejana barely noticed the shorter woman standing next to her on the train platform.

"What a nice purse," she heard her say and turned to find a curly redhead dressed in a purple chiffon dress, looking at her with the luminous smile characteristic of children.

"Thank you," the brunette smiled back, revealing a set of unusually big teeth. "It was a gift from my boyfriend," she added showing off both sides of the butterfly-shaped handbag.

The redhead winced at the sound of this last word. "It's very nice," she heard herself repeating, unable to say anymore.

Could it be possible? the redhead wondered. Then she dismissed the thought. No! The girl would be too young, even by his standards. But the handbag, it was one of a kind. It had to be the very same one. The redhead sighed, thinking of all the clever things she could have said and done to get the girl to talk. We always seem to have just the right line moments too late, she thought, watching the tall brunette walk away from behind the dirty window of the train.

\* \* \*

"My, my, aren't we all decked out this afternoon?" Rita towered over the chaise longue where Perla daydreamed of leaving her husband for the yoga instructor. "Any particular reason why you're wearing more bling than the Queen Mother?"

"Yes. I am celebrating."

"Celebrating what? George's coronation?"

"None of your business. And do get out of my sun space; I don't want to get tan lines in the shape of a giant pear."

"Suit yourself, Mrs. Robinson," hissed Rita as she walked back to her own pool chair.

She placed her towel away from Perla through the yoga exercise, and for the first time since she started coming to the Lido, Rita wore a sarong around her bottom.

"*Inhalamos*," hummed Leborio, to the beat of salsa music. "Inhale, lovely ladies." And the ladies took it personally, filling their lungs as if it was their last living breath. "*Exhalamos*," he continued, the words vibrating out of his throat and finding their way to a number of withered loins that magically came back to life.

Perla, Rita, and the others bent over into docile pretzels, stretching the monotony out of their limbs. Perla turned the Sophie necklace around her neck and pursed her lips tightly, afraid to chip her teeth in one of its diamonds. But the law of gravity dictated that the heavier stones would find their way to the lowest spot, and so she kept on pulling at them much like a dog pulls at a very stylish leash. No matter, she thought. It was all worthwhile to hear Leborio compliment her at the end.

"You look like a beacon of elegance today, Perla."

"Why, thank you, Leborio. I thought I'd wear something special today," she said, and added, "But I must confess it was quite uncomfortable during yoga. These sorts of accessories can be very heavy."

"I'm sorry to hear you had a hard time," he smiled, his eyes closing in intently on her neckline. "Next time let me know, will you? I will be happy to unload your burden."

Charmed by the young man's proximity, Perla fanned herself with a Lido spa brochure and straitened her hair with the tips of her fingers. He wiped her forehead with the back of his hand, scratching the outer layer of her makeup with the beads of his magnetic bracelets.

"Nice cuffs," she said, wanting to compliment him in return.

"I'm glad you like them. You know what they say about magnets," he said, jiggling his bracelets by her ear, causing Perla to shudder.

"No, I don't," she giggled. "What do they say?"

"They attract things," he whispered in her ear. Then, wiping his wrist on a white towel and leaving an orange coloured streak the size of a tennis cuff across it, he announced, "You're dangerously overheating."

Leborio put his magnificent arms around her shoulders and helped her sit under the shade of an umbrella. "There you go," he whispered, reaching behind her neck to support her. Out of reflex, Perla adjusted the Sophie necklace to match the back of her bathing suit, causing Leborio's hands to find their way back empty, into the tiny pockets of his scarlet Speedos.

"It must be the sun and the loud music," he said. Then, turning to the barkeeper, he made a gesture that prompted the man to cut the music off. "You must allow me to bring you a refreshing drink," he told Perla in a tone that did not welcome challenges.

This is how a real man speaks, she thought as she watched him walk away. Next to Leborio, her husband had the conviction of a eunuch. So much for his political aspirations, she thought, raising the corner of her mouth in contempt. A man like George would never stand a chance in a presidential election without a woman like Theresa Heinz to back him up. Not that there was anything wrong with a woman of means helping a man meet his potential, as long as it was the right man. The trouble with women was that they consistently bet on the wrong horse. Someone like Leborio deserved a better chance than teaching yoga by the poolside to a bunch of predatory housewives.

Perla was different, of course. Save the minor pickle of her being married to George, she really was no housewife. She led a very full life of her own, tanning, exercising, and shopping. And now that she had fallen in love again, she felt completely rejuvenated. Although Leborio was in fact younger than her son Denis, around him, she felt as if she were the younger one. It must have been his dark and profoundly masculine beauty that made her feel like an innocent adolescent stepping timidly toward her first great love.

She watched him move from across the deck and imagined being in his arms. If only they could get away somewhere together, get to know each other better, and leave George, Rita, and the whole lot of them behind. But, where would she tell her husband she went, all by herself? In any case, it was too early to proposition such a thing to a distinguished spiritual master like Leborio Borzelini. Being a man of honour, he might feel offended by the question.

"I've been meaning to ask you something for a long time," she said, when he returned. "And I hope you won't think me too bold," she added, lightly touching his wrist.

"Oh, but I have a soft spot for bold women," he said, raising his eyes above her bejewelled neckline.

Moments away from a blush and a giggle, Perla took a sip from the mystery cocktail Leborio had brought back from the bar. "What made you decide on this life path?" she asked. "I mean, a man of your intelligence could have anything he wished for, I imagine. So why the Lido? Why yoga? Why not something more profitable?"

He raised an ironic eyebrow and smiled. "Well, you see, I was brought up to value the human spirit above all riches," he began, dimming his voice just below casual timbre, on the verge of confidentiality. "I haven't told this to anyone in many years, Perla. There are so few people one can truly trust, especially when there are titles and fortunes at stake," he said, looking to see if anyone was listening. "But you," he added in a softer tone, "you remind me of this picture my late mother used to keep by her bedside. It was the golden-haired holy angel. Now, please don't laugh at a sentimental fool such as me, but from the first moment I saw you, I thought of nothing else but my mother's angel."

Not certain what to make of this, Perla assured the guru she would never dream of laughing. "Go on, please! This is most captivating," she begged.

"Very well then," he conceded, casting a glance away from Perla and into an invisible horizon. "I will tell you what I have told no other. I will tell you how I came to live here, in this wretched, backward place," he started, his voice barely rising above the sound of a whisper.

"The story begins many years before I was born. My parents were descendents of a certain blue-blooded family, whose name I will not disclose out of concern for your safety. It suffices to say they were keepers of a great secret, which, if ever revealed, would change the meaning of history as we know it."

He paused, lowering his gaze and shaking his head softly. For a moment, the symphony of honks ceased on the boulevard behind, giving way to the poignant lament of violin strings and carrying a sad czardas melody over the concrete fence separating the Lido from the city. Leborio looked into Perla's eyes in passing and then lowered his head again.

"In order to do this," he continued, his voice vibrating with emotion, "my father accepted to be assigned as the ambassador of one of the countries we lived in—the country where I first saw the light of day: the small but beautiful Costa Rica." He closed his eyes as if to remember, relaxing his face into a wide smile. "We left my country when I was but a child and came to live here, amongst what was left of a dying world system. Like the rats and the ruins, we too survived communism and watched it disintegrate into . . . this," he said, taking his hand out of the tiny pocket of the scarlet Speedos and flicking it in an all-encompassing gesture.

He paused again and looked away, appearing reluctant to carry on with his story. But Perla was hooked, and she wanted to know more.

"Oh, please, Leborio," she whimpered, placing her bejewelled hand over his. "Please, do go on!"

The spiritual master cracked his knuckles, and, in passing, rested his almond-shaped eyes over the sight of her neckline, where the brilliant necklace rose and fell with her every breath.

"You see, my dear Perla," he went on, "My father, the ambassador, groomed me from a very young age to guard this secret with my own life, even if it meant giving away my inheritance to our cause. And that is exactly what I did."

# CHAPTER 5

# NEON LOUNGE

In the daytime, Neon Lounge was just another old building in need of renovation, leaning against its equally feeble neighbour to keep its walls from coming down. Its colourless facade had been eaten away by multiple lost battles against climbing plants, graffiti, and dampness. The best Italian architects of their time had designed the houses on Old Court Street. Stonemasons, stucco masters, and mural painters had been imported from all over the pre-industrial Italian peninsula to build a street full of these villas, where members of the newly established royal court would live. Each house had been garnished with a lacing of wrought iron balconies fit for Juliet herself. Some had a flight of stairs contoured on either side by graceful railings in the style of Victor Horta. Old Court Street had been the splendid backdrop of carriage processions for the king and queen, visits of ambassadors, and royal weddings. Time and human political confusion had left it hanging for rejuvenation. Like a veritable Miss Havisham waiting for her groom to commit, Old Court Street waited for one of the many passing mayors, presidents, and dictators to commit to a restoration project and bring it back to its former glory. But, alas, the years went by without any improvement, leaving the street embittered and permanently damaged by elements of nature and human ignorance. Stripped of the glow the original few inches of mortar can give a building during the better part of its first century, the houses on Old Court Street appeared as desolate as a group of lepers holding each other up by the armpits to keep from falling. Neon Lounge was no different. Drifters sat on its doorstep during the day and shared the shade of its balconies with rats and stray dogs.

But at night, the building came alive with go-go dancers, deejays, bouncers, bartenders, and other such creatures of the clubbing scene. Its foundations shook with the beat of sophisticated electronic mixes, the kind that could not be downloaded off the Internet. Dancers dressed in glowing costumes, fire jugglers performed on the wobbly balconies, and bartenders stirred martinis with one hand and flamed Sambuca shots with the other. Outside, the line stretched around the corner as circumspect bouncers moved by unknown criteria selected a few to go in. This was not a building on its last legs. This was a gold mine of a nightclub with a cover charge surpassing the weekly earnings of most people.

Amalia stood still for a moment, glancing up at her husband's club. Appearances can be deceiving, she thought. No one knew this better than she did. After all, her whole life depended on the successful use of appearance. Placido appeared to be making money in a respectable manner. She appeared to spend it wisely. Placido appeared to be an adoring husband. Amalia appeared to believe him. They both appeared to be ever the doting parents to Armin, and he appeared to be growing, physically at least. Yes, appearances were the very foundation of the Pectors' happy household. And this was why Amalia took the time to make sure that appearances were maintained. She began walking toward the neon-lit door, making a clicking sound with the heels of her shoes.

* * *

"Shit, boss, your wife's walking to the front door," whispered the cross-eyed bouncer into his walkie-talkie. He pressed it against his ear. The answer pierced through the receiver and into his eardrum.

"How many times must I tell you that *shit* and *my wife* should never be part of the same sentence?"

The bouncer rubbed his ear. He pressed the button and muttered, "Sorry, boss. Should I let her in?"

"No. You should send her to the back of the line," came the answer. "Of course you should let her in, you ape! She is my wife. I think she earned the right to bypass the line. And don't forget to card her. That will put her in a good mood."

The bouncer clipped his walkie-talkie to his trouser belt and straightened his black shirt. He clicked his heels together and parted his lips slightly, allowing his upper teeth to show a little, lined up like tiny white soldiers.

"Good evening, Kim," Amalia nodded on her way through the door. "Still working for my husband?"

"Of course, Miss Amalia. Best boss in the city," grinned the cross-eyed giant. "Do you have a piece of ID on you?"

Amalia squeezed Kim's arm and returned a coquettish smile. "You made my night, dear boy. Did my husband teach you how to make me blush?"

Kim vigorously shook his head before closing the door behind her. Once she was out of sight, he opened his huge fist and stared at the small object he had extracted from her purse pocket. Old habits die hard, he blushed. The giant scratched his head with a mix of remorse and disappointment. A tampon! That was how low he'd sunk. To steal a tampon from the boss' wife. He'd gone to prison a petty thief and had come out an incurable klepto. If Placido knew, he would have Kim chopped to little pieces by an army of normally sized people. One way or another, Placido had half of the city on his payroll, and no one was too strong for him. Shaking the vivid image of Gulliver assaulted by the Lilliputians, Kim pursed his lips thinking about what might happen once Amalia got to the top of the stairs leading to Placido's office. He wondered how the boss and his mistress would get out of this one.

Amalia took her time going up to her husband's office. Like most women in her position, she had a hard time deciding whether she wanted to know or not. One way or another, a woman always knows when she is being deceived. But choosing to acknowledge the act of cheating is in fact more difficult than proving it. For the sake of family, comfort, and love, Amalia only flirted with disaster. She hoped to get close enough to scare her husband out of cheating but not get close enough to see it happening.

At the top of the stairs, she slowly turned the copper knob before opening the door. Behind a cloud of cigar smoke, Placido was towering over a seated Leborio, who was gazing into the computer screen.

"So you see my boy, every spreadsheet is protected by an alphanumeric password," she heard him say before he looked up and saw her. "Dollface, what a pleasant surprise!" he welcomed his wife, putting away his cigar. "I'm afraid you've caught me in the act."

"What act would that be, dearest?" she inquired, looking around the room.

"Smoking, of course. Now I know I've promised not to do it, but it's been a hectic day, and there's nothing like a good Cuban to release the stress."

He kissed her on the cheek and pulled her a chair from the corner of the room while Leborio nodded and smiled in his best effort to appear affable. Placido took the minx throw off his wife's shoulders and gently caressed the back of her neck with his big, raspy hands. Amalia concealed a small shudder, looking up to see if Leborio had seen it. If he had, he was hiding it well, gawking at the computer screen with interest. She glanced down at the chair her husband had pulled her and placed her handbag on it. Then, she walked toward the curtain-covered bed by the back wall and pulled the fabric away with one swift motion. It was hard to tell whether she was disappointed or relieved to find the bed dishevelled but empty.

"You ought to make your bed, dearest," she said, looking into the small closet next to it. "Although I never quite understood why you need to have a bed in here. After all, this is your place of work. And when at work, a man must not idle about in a bed."

"I'll call one of the girls to come and tidy it."

"I bet you will," she hissed.

Placido's jovial demeanour froze into a ruthless gaze. Amalia swallowed with some difficulty, knowing at once that she had over-stepped the boundary of appearance. Before she could backpeddle her way out of the course of an unpleasant argument, Placido put his hand on Leborio's shoulder as if to teach the younger man a lesson in conjugal negotiations.

"If my wife wants to find my bed neat and tidy, then she should phone me before coming here," he said. "Now, I don't mind surprises, and I certainly go through a lot of trouble to humour and support my wife's whims. But when she comes into my office and forgets the very purpose of her visit, which I take to be the feminine desire to please her husband by surprising him with her enchanting presence, then I expect her to abide by that custom." Placido paused, staring Amalia in the eyes long enough to make her knees tremble. Then, turning to Leborio again, he continued, "You see, my son, husbands and wives each have their shortcomings and flaws they must learn to accept. My philosophy is that a wife must be wise, and a husband must be discreet, which I grant is nearly impossible these days, when women are more foolish than ever and men are surrounded by temptation," he added, taking a prolonged drag out of his cigar and blowing out a perfectly shaped smoke circle. "But at the end of the day, if you can come home to a loving wife and forget about what the devil brings your way, the effort seems worthwhile. The secret of a happy and long marriage is mutual respect, my boy," he gestured holding the cigar between his thumb and index finger, like a teacher holding a piece of chalk. "Without it, it is hardly worth being married at all."

In the silence that followed, he took one last long drag out of the barely smoked cigar before he put it out and walked out the door without so much as a look back, leaving Leborio and Amalia to breathe the cloud behind him. Standing as straight as a pushpin in her dark red pencil dress, Amalia watched Placido disappear into the blinding neon lights of the club. Appearances must be maintained, she thought, mentally reciting the Pector family creed. But for how long? Will her life always be like this? Or will her husband's appetite for younger women and illegal business eventually fade? Most men his age had weaker libidos. They worried about setting a good example for their children and feared spending their lives behind bars. But not Placido. He feared nothing. He conquered everything. The only token of love and appreciation he offered his wife was his discretion and his money.

"I deserve more," she caught herself say aloud. She had almost forgotten about Leborio, who silently clicked away on the computer mouse.

"He does care for you."

"Does he? Sometimes I wonder," she heard herself say.

Leborio said nothing. She stared at him for a moment, looking for a reaction that did not come. His eyes were dark and chilling, like the eyes of some soulless creature. The corners of his bow-shaped mouth barely moved as he spoke, "You have a good husband, Amalia. You shouldn't spoil it."

Perhaps he was right, she reflected, thinking about the beautiful home they shared. The house had been custom-built, with large rooms and high ceilings. Though she had filled it with expensive artefacts, Amalia could still hear the echo of her own voice on the telephone or of the television programs she watched while waiting for Placido to get home. She played with the platinum ring on her wedding finger.

Then, something inside her revolted.

"I barely remember how it feels to be loved," she blurted.

Raising an eyebrow Leborio ventured to ask, "Was he ever . . . different?"

She considered it briefly and then shook her head. "No. *He* wasn't. But I know love when I see it," she sighed, folding her hands together. "Many years ago, before I met Placido, there was a young man who loved me madly. I was a showgirl at the Intercontinental back then. I even had my own matinee act. He came to watch me every day and brought me flowers. White lilies. They're my favourite, you know. Placido sends me red roses," she added, her dark eyes looking into the floor. "In all our years together, you'd think he'd notice. But he never once asked me what my favourite flower is."

"Men have strange ways of showing their love," said Leborio, clicking away at the screen. "Just because a guy knows your favourite flower doesn't mean he loves you."

"Oh, but he did. He did. I don't know if it was the angle of his face looking up at me on the stage or the glow young love sheds on a man's face, but in all my life, no one has ever looked at me like that again. I was surrounded by a battalion of almost naked women, the most beautiful dancers in the whole city, yet the only thing he saw was me," she said, closing her smoky brown eyes. "Placido has never looked at me that way. Is she more beautiful than me? Is that what it is? Younger? She must be. "

Leborio stood up and cracked open a brand-new bottle of blue liqueur from a small bar next to the desk. He filled a martini glass to the brim. He dropped a few ice cubes into it, causing the drink to spill over onto the carpet, and handed it to Amalia.

"So what happened to the young man who was madly in love with you?"

"He wanted to marry me," she said ruefully, taking a gulp from the blue liqueur.

"Why didn't you marry him?"

"Don't know," she said, taking another mouthful of blue liqueur and grimacing at the taste.

Once, a few years ago, she had seen him on the street. He'd walked between two bodyguards and disappeared into one of the corporate buildings downtown. She remembered he had looked right through her without a sign of recognition. Amalia passed her fingers over the fine lines framing her beautiful brown eyes and added, "I suppose he took over his father's business after all."

"Does Placido know about him?"

"No. What good could come out of that?" she shrugged. "Besides, our relationship was purely platonic. Holding hands at the local gellateria—that sort of thing. Placido was the first man who ever knew me intimately. I didn't want him to ever doubt that."

"Come now, Amalia," the guru gently pushed her toward the window ledge, leaned against it, and put one of his magnificent arms around her shoulders. "A man loves differently than a woman. Surely, you know that by now."

Careful not to seem impolite, Amalia pulled back and closer to the window frame.

"Your husband cares for you in his own way," added Leborio. "Remember that the very reason he must carry on like this is so that he may provide you and your son with the lifestyle you have grown accustomed to. He needs you to support him, so that he may support you and Armin."

His soothing voice had caused the peach fuzz on her arms to rise. Amalia put her drink down and stepped away from the window. She stared at him, unable to look away. He was so beautiful, so well put together, with his sleek wavy hair, chiselled jaw, and close shave. Yet she felt uneasy. For the first time that evening, she took note of the half a dozen dark bracelets wrapped around his wrists and the tight-fitting burgundy tunic he wore. It had shiny black buttons shaped to look like rune stones. The ensemble made him look like a sorcerer, a dark warlock, or some other practitioner of black magic. This was what the devil must have looked like, she thought. Easy on the eye but hard to look away from.

Amalia wondered if her husband had been right to place his trust in this strange young man. There was something about him that left her feeling unsettled. It was the way he spoke to her, as if she were a brazen horse that needed to be tamed by the strong but calm voice of an experienced trainer. The image of Placido's arm resting on Leborio's shoulder seemed unnatural to her. She picked up her minx throw and covered her shoulders, weighing the implications of what had been said. Fixing him with serious eyes, Amalia spoke carefully. "You're right about one thing. His son is important to him. It's true what they say about blood being thicker than water," she said firmly "Don't you ever forget it! Placido already has a son."

"Are you referring to Armin?"

"That is his only son, so yes."

Leborio raised an eyebrow and smiled. "Now I don't mean to pry, Amalia, but could there be any chance Armin might have aristocratic blood running through his veins? He does look rather blue-blooded from the profile," he noted with a wink.

Amalia said nothing. She ground her teeth and decided to leave before crossing the line of good taste. Enough boundaries had been crossed for one day, she thought as she came down the stairway. Instinctively, she reached into her purse pocket for the keys to the car and found that there was a missing object. Not a terribly important one but one of intimate use. Leborio, she thought. He had stolen her tampon. She just knew it.

She opened the door to the soundproof room and took the back way out of Neon Lounge, sidestepping a rummaging rat on her way to the car. Behind her, the unseen side of the building, contoured by a neon green halo, appeared to yield to the darkness surrounding it.

# · CHAPTER 6 ·

# PRIVATE AFFAIRS
# INVESTIGATORS

The black switch phone on the corner of the desk let out two painful rings before Iris, diving over the neatly arranged waiting chairs, grabbed the receiver and greeted the caller in a seemingly busy yet aloof tone.

"Good afternoon. Private Affairs Investigators, Iris speaking."

The voice hesitated at the other end, coughed a few times, and then whispered, "Are you a detective?"

"I'm sorry; you'll have to speak up. I can hardly hear you."

"I said, are you a detective?"

This time, Iris hesitated. Was she? Well, she didn't think of herself as a detective. Detectives wore beige raincoats and Sherlock Holmes hats, spoke into recorders, and took compromising pictures of husbands cheating on their wives. They also accepted any paying assignment, even if it meant destroying a marriage, breaking up a family, or putting an end to a good deed. She wore a purple chiffon dress that matched the flowers on her desk and only took on assignments that mended human relationships. Or at least intended to. In theory.

After three weeks of being gloriously available via phone, e-mail, fax, or in person, the redheaded investigator was beginning to doubt the success of her enterprise.

"I am an investigator, sir," she said, picking up a pencil and a paper pad. "Is there something I can do for you?"

"I sure hope so," said the man, this time using the full capacity of his voice. "I need someone to look into an old affair."

Iris didn't like the sound of it. In her experience, old affairs were better left in the past. She asked him for a more detailed description before turning the offer down. The man cleared his throat a couple of times and then settled on a hypothetical situation.

"Let's just suppose a man has a son, whom he raised since the day he was born," he started. "And now let's suppose this man has reason to believe the boy is not his son but rather the product of his wife's previous relationship. Would you be able to find out if the boy is his?"

"That depends, sir. Is the man still married to his wife?"

"Yes. Let's say he's been married to her for nineteen years."

"Happily married?"

"I suppose."

"And does the man love his son?"

The man told Iris that too depended. It depended on whether the boy was his son or not.

"All right," proposed Iris. "Let us suppose that something wretched were to happen to the boy. A bus would run him over, for example. What would the man do?"

"Why, he would have the bus driver chopped into little pieces, the son of a bitch. Or anyone else for that matter, if they were to harm my boy!"

"So that settles it," chirped the investigator. "He is your son, because you love him and would do anything to protect him. That is the definition of a father. And your reaction is the reaction of a loving dad." She took the silence on the other end as a sign of agreement.

"Good day! First consultation is free of charge. Please spread the word to your friends."

"What? What does that have to do with anything?" the man was bellowing so loudly, Iris had to move the phone away from her ear. "Now you listen, lady. If I need shrinking, I'll call a damn doctor. What I need is the truth. Put one of your male investigators on the phone right away. A man will surely know the difference."

She squeezed the pencil between her knuckles. "I'm sorry, but we don't have any men in our employment at the moment."

"Why not? Who ever heard of a detective company with no men?"

"Actually, this is not unheard of, sir," she said, her voice shaking ever so slightly. "Some of the most capable detectives in history were women. There is an entire detective series written by a Scottish writer about a ladies' detective agency. I highly recommend reading it. But that's beside the point. My point was that women are just as capable as men, and in some respects, they are better equipped to resolve delicate situations."

"Unless they refuse to take the case altogether."

"For good reason," replied Iris. "No good can come out of what you are asking me to do. You have a happy family. Why risk losing it over something that may or may not have happened almost twenty years ago?"

"Because I must know the truth," said the man with finality. "Do you know how it feels to wonder why your son is a lazy little shit whose only chance at graduating from junior high is if they were to award him a diploma based on seniority?"

Iris said nothing and so the man continued. "I always thought he'd come around, and one day, he will be able to amount to something in this world. But now I see he just lacks ambition all together, as if my genes are not even part of his system."

"And you decided that he is not your son based on his lack of ambition? Is that your proof?"

"No. I have reason to believe my wife had dealings with another man just before we married. And there is a very reliable source at the bottom of it," he huffed. "Goes to show you the nerve women have! No offense," he added quickly. "She's been accusing me of infidelity for years, and now I find out she's been playing me for a fool all this time. If this is true and the boy's not mine, I need to know. The stakes are very high. I've built a business empire from scratch, and I'm not about to leave it to my wife's bastard—if that's what the boy is." Iris thought his voice wavered on this last point.

"I'm sorry. It just sounds like the sort of case I don't like to support," said Iris, and immediately thought she should have used *we* instead of *I*. But it was too late.

"Then put one of your colleagues on the phone."

At a loss for words, Iris looked around the empty office. The late afternoon sunshine penetrated through the vertical blinds, shedding zebra-like stripes over the school bus yellow wall.

"I'm afraid we don't have any available agents at the moment."

The man started laughing. "You're alone in there aren't you? This is your business, and you are the only employee."

"I am very good at what I do, sir. No other employees are needed at the moment."

"Bullshit. You probably can't afford it," said the man with a jovial laugh. "Well, little Miss, I can. I can afford hiring you as many employees as you need. Just do me this one little favour and look into my case." Lowering his voice, he continued, "Can you picture a nice little secretary with square spectacles like those librarians wear, answering your telephone for you and taking messages? Or the bright criminology student who will infuse your investigations with fresh ideas while she works the evening shift for her part-time job? You could help put her through university just by hiring her. What about the conferences in London? Everyone knows London is the capital of the secrets industry. You could hire a retired teacher to keep an eye on things for you while you go to the London conference on private and public investigations. Think about it!"

Iris did just that. It would have been nice to have a few employees, and there were plenty of people in need of a job. She knew she would have made a fine boss. Once a week she could bring doughnuts and coffee for everyone, and they could sit down for an update and discuss all current cases, give each other helpful pointers, and poke fun together. Yes, it would have been nice. But it would also have been unethical to accept a morally questionable assignment for the sake of money. No, she said to herself. Iris Bendal would never sacrifice her principles for money.

The investigator started to refuse, but the man interrupted her, saying, "What would it take to get you to agree?"

"Not money, sir. But there are plenty of other businesses that might be happy to thrive from your offer."

"Yes, I suppose you are right. It's just that most detective agencies are already on my wife's payroll. She's had detectives follow me for years, and I'm afraid you are the only one she hasn't contacted yet. Of course, you would have to agree never to work for my wife. Otherwise, it would be a conflict of interests. That's the name for it, am I right?"

"If you were to be my client, then yes, that would be the correct term. But because it is very unlikely that you would be, there is nothing to stop me from working for whomever I see fit."

"Of course," he seemed to accept her decision. "Shame you don't want to reconsider my offer. You came highly recommended by one of my men. He said if anyone could get to the truth, it was his old friend Iris."

"And who might that be?"

"Does the name Leborio Borzelini mean anything to you?"

If this conversation would have occurred in a more personal setting, Placido might have seen Iris cringe, but as it happens, cringes are imperceptible to the human ear. Leborio! Iris wondered what Leborio had gotten himself into this time. Iris Bendal would not sacrifice her principles for money, but loyalty and curiosity were another matter.

"If at any point I feel you are concealing anything from me or questioning my methods, I will resign with full payment. If at any point you disrespect me or involve yourself in my affairs, I will resign with full payment. If you should ever attempt to bully or control the course of my investigation or any of those working for me, I will resign with full payment. Agreed?"

"Agreed," answered the man cheerfully. "Although may I point out the last demand is sort of useless, because you don't yet have anyone working for you."

"That is none of your concern," Iris said primly, as she tried to compensate for accepting the job. "I'll need some additional information on your son and wife. Come in the office tomorrow morning, and we'll take it from there. Nine o'clock. Don't be late."

"Ten," bargained the man. "I like to sleep in when I can."

"Fine. Oh, and one more thing. Come alone."

"Can I bring an associate?"

"Absolutely not. Alone or not at all."

"Okay. It's a date, little lady."

Before she could stop herself, Iris heard herself ask, "Do they really have detective conventions in London?"

"How should I know? I've never been to London. Besides, I made the whole thing up."

Iris tapped her pencil. Well, she thought, at least he was honest, if deferred. No point in questioning him now—I am already on his payroll.

"May I get your name before I let you go?"

"Of course, I expect this to be confidential. The name is Placido. Placido Pector."

Iris closed her eyes, and for the second time that afternoon, cringed.

# DENIS THE MENACE

Sunday morning at the Galanis residence was never an easy time, reflected George, lighting up his tobacco pipe by the fireplace. Not for the servants who ran up and down the kitchen stairs cursing the Dutch architect, who, in a case of displaced nationalism, decided to express his innermost longing for home by modeling the layout of the kitchen after the most impractical of designs: that of an Amsterdam townhouse. This forced the cook to take up residence in the upper floor of the kitchen space and yell orders to the staff below, while the butler, who always tripped on the last step of the stairs going up, cursed in a fashionably English accent. George found it unusual that despite not speaking a word of English, his butler sounded British-posh. Sunday morning was not easy for Regina, the hairless cat. Born in China and imported to the eastern lands of Europe before she took the shape of an overgrown rat, Regina was Perla's most faithful companion. From where he sat, George observed the cat patrolling the living room and patting the couch with her declawed paws in a clear state of agitation.

"The stew had better be ready on time," George heard Perla yell to the kitchen staff through the small walkie-talkie he had bought her after he was nearly driven to the brinks of insanity by Perla's shrieking orders. "And tell the butler to have the wine chilled in the cellar, not the fridge. Last time Denis noticed the slightest smell of food lingering in the bouquet. We don't want a repeat of that episode at my table."

Sunday morning meant George had to spare Gino, his Italian barber, and shave all by himself yet again. George consoled himself in knowing that Gino disliked Sunday mornings as much as he did. He glanced over his newspaper as the hairstylist worked at backcombing Perla's hair twice as hard as he usually did.

"Make me tall, Gino. I want my son to notice my hair." Perla stretched backward and yelled, "And make sure the silverware is polished. Denis is very particular about that."

"Bla-bla-bla," whispered George under his breath, and then he too yelled in the general direction of the kitchen, "And bring out the fireworks while you're at it. Denis simply loves fireworks."

"Shut up, George. I will not have you mock our son under my roof."

"It won't be under your roof, dear. And do you know why? Because you don't have a roof of your own," replied George—or rather, he fantasised replying. Instead, he wiped the shaving cream off his face, applied a generous serving of aftershave and cognac, and walked over to the grandfather clock. The big old timepiece ticking away to the beat of mortality reassured him that this Sunday morning too shall pass.

Denis arrived just in time for afternoon tea. He delegated his jacket to the butler, kissed his mother on the cheek, shook his father's hand, and picked up the newspaper on the mantelpiece on his way to the family room. He sat by the bay window and buried his nose in the business section of the paper.

"My stocks are down today," he remarked matter-of-factly while flipping the pages. "Your hair looks charming, Mother."

"Why thank you, Denny. Gino changed the—"

"Have you seen the price of oil this week?" Denis turned to George without giving Perla a chance to finish her account of Gino's pursuit for coif perfection. "The price of a barrel in the States is cheaper than one liter of our lousy oil."

"To be honest, son, I'm surprised a man your age still finds the oil fluctuation remotely interesting. I have seen this happen a thousand times before and so have you."

"It doesn't make it any less interesting," jumped in Perla, anxiously watching her son. She sat down and Regina promptly jumped in her lap.

With his head still buried in the paper, Denis shrugged. "What else would you have me do, father? There are very few things that get a man my age, as you point out, excited."

"Oh, come now, Denny. You're still a young pup."

The men gave Perla a synchronized look of disapproval, the sort of look given to a yappy Chihuahua dog. Regina purred in her lap, suddenly cuddling to her mistress.

"How about taking a holiday?" suggested George, staring at a black earpiece that was flashing small blue lights at random intervals. "You haven't taken a day off work since . . . well, I can't remember you ever taking a day off."

"I travel all the time," argued Denis.

"For work. Business trips don't count, son. You need some time to yourself, away from the office and away from that earpiece of yours," George pointed at his ear. "Time to relax and smell the flowers. Maybe you'll even meet a nice girl."

Denis rolled his eyes and walked to the fireplace. He tapped the marble mantelpiece with his long fingers, making a hollow thumping sound, not unlike that of a heartbeat. There was an unspoken charge in his voice.

"I don't have time for that sort of thing, Father."

George pressed on, "When will you have time then? You are already in your forties."

"He doesn't need to meet anyone, George," Perla said. "He has lots of time for . . ."

One look from Denis muted her instantly. "Mother, you lost the right to have an opinion on my personal life years ago. Never presume to comment on it again."

Perla shrunk in her seat, clasping the cat closer to her chest, and for a moment, no one said anything. The steady ticking of the grandfather clock marked the silence. Exchanging glances with his wife, George Galanis stood up and put a pudgy hand on his son's shoulder.

"All right, Denis. Why don't you and I go for a walk to the garage? I bought a new car that I want to show you."

"Oh, yes. Papa bought a Maybach," blurted out Perla.

"Indeed," nodded George. "Although, it was going to be a surprise but never mind that, dear. We'll only be a few moments, so you can go ahead and set the cook loose."

On their way out, the men caught a glimpse of Perla's mouth opening widely, like the beak of a magpie. They shut the door just in time to avoid hearing her scream into the yellow walkie-talkie.

Outside, the grass separating the house from the garage was wet. It was too early in the day for sprinklers. George and Denis walked silently toward the immense hall they called a garage, watching not to step in puddles, and brushing off raindrops falling from the surrounding trees as the wind made them quiver.

The sky behind the gray haze of city smog was presumably blue. A few clouds of an indistinct shade moved westward at a surprising speed. It wasn't going to rain anymore. But perhaps it was going to storm. The two men pushed the doors to the garage, revealing a small fleet of cars parked neatly side by side. At the centre, glittering like a black diamond, was George's new Maybach.

"I need to speak with you about your mother," George began, shuffling uncomfortably. "I don't know who else to turn to, and I'm afraid I need some counsel."

Without looking at his father, Denis circled the car once and opened the door, revealing its opulent leather upholstery. He sat in the driver's seat of the black Maybach and waved his hand in a gesture that encouraged the older man to go on.

"She's been behaving very strangely lately," said George gravely. "I know she can be quite eccentric, but this is a different kind of strange. She goes around dressed like a teenager, spends all her day at the Lido pool, and comes back home to do yoga exercises until the late hours of the night."

Playing with the buttons on the dashboard, Denis suggested, "Maybe she's suffering from menopause. I hear it can take a toll on a woman's body and mind. You should tell her she looks beautiful."

"I do. I tell her she looks nice all the time."

"Nice is a little detached, don't you think? A car can be nice. In fact this one really is," he remarked, passing his fingers over the beige steering wheel. "A flower arrangement can be nice as well. But when it comes to humans, no one likes to be described as nice. It just doesn't cut it."

"Yes, but that's not all," George whispered. "The other day she went out to her yoga class wearing the Sophie necklace. In broad daylight."

Denis took his hands off the wheel and came out of the car. George watched him walk up to the hood. He seemed to weigh the implications for a moment, and then decided, "She's having an affair with a younger man. How much did you pay for this car?"

"For God's sake, will you leave the car for the time being?" George said. "These are serious presumptions you're making. What do you mean she's having an affair? And how do you know it's with a younger man?"

"Why else would she go out looking like a Christmas tree in the middle of the day?" shrugged Denis, without waiting for an answer. "She feels she must compensate for the age gap and adorn herself with jewels. The shinier the better. They might blind the guy into overlooking the wrinkles, the age spots, etcetera." He paused and then said, "Come to think of it, it must be one of the gigolos at the Lido. I hear Placido Pector wants to introduce gigolos on the local market. There's no monopoly yet on the eastern side of the continent, and now that communism has fallen, there's a new demand in female high circles for gentlemen companions."

George looked completely baffled. Not only had he just been told his wife was having an affair but also that apparently there was an entire social phenomenon to explain this catastrophic indiscretion. This would have never happened ten years ago, he thought, shaking his head. It was hard to believe one came to regret the change in such a short time—especially one who had fought so ardently for change, freedom, and democracy. His political career was officially ruined now that his Jackie Kennedy had turned into a regular harlot.

"How can you be so sure?" he muttered. "Placido Pector? What are you talking about? How do you know all this?"

"One of my . . . lady friends," explained Denis, adjusting his Bluetooth earbud. "I see her once a week, at a very convenient price, if I might add, and sometimes we talk a little to set the mood. She told me that Pector is expanding his business and that he's running some sort of . . . shall I call it, *pilot episode* at the Lido."

"My God!" lamented George in a small voice. "How could your mother do this to me? To us, really!"

"Well, to you mostly. I don't have any political aspirations," replied his son, and then added, "Do you smell something?" he flared his nostrils, sniffing the air around him. "Bacon. I smell bacon. Are we having bacon for brunch?"

"I'll have her thrown out of the house this very afternoon!" threatened George, waving his arms in the air as he circled the car frantically. He paced around, thinking about ways to get even. With further consideration, the punishment increased. "I'll have her thrown out of the mausoleum too! She can spend eternity next to some clown half her age," he said, stomping his foot by the garage window.

"You'll do no such thing," said his son firmly. "It's unexpected that she's doing this now, when you are no longer fooling around on her."

"I have never!"

"Yes, you have. But that's beside the point."

George looked out the window of the garage. Outside, the sun had come out and the handyman was polishing Perla's Benz into a spotless shimmer. George wanted to buy her an Aston Martin, but she insisted on being driven in a Benz, because the car looked shinier.

"What can be done about this?" he heard himself ask.

"We'll hire someone to take care of it," said Denis. "They'll clean the whole thing up."

"What do you mean? Kill the poor bastard?"

"That depends on who he is and on how badly you want to run for president. But no, that might not be necessary. You might just be able to pay him off."

"Do you know anyone to do this?"

"I'll look into it." His son placed an arm on George's shoulder, in a comforting gesture.

"What should I do in the meantime?" asked George, lowering his gaze like a guilty child.

"Pretend you don't know anything and send her somewhere to make sure she doesn't get into anymore trouble. Women seem to forget the men they love when they are not around to see them."

"What if she won't want to go?"

"Send her somewhere she can't refuse. Send her to visit Athena. Isn't she filming in Portugal?" I can give her a call and see if she'd be willing to help us. I don't see why she wouldn't," he added, tapping the rims of the car with his shiny black shoe. "My sister loves acting, especially when it's off the screen."

"Yes, she does." George looked down again, his thick moustache framing a barely noticeable frown. "And I suppose Perla won't be able to say no to visiting her own daughter. What if she brings the gigolo along?"

"She won't," said Denis, dismissing the idea with a sluggish hand gesture. "Not around Athena. What man in his right mind would go for the beat-out Ford truck when he can have a Maybach?"

"My wife is not a beat-out Ford!"

"She ain't a Maybach either." Denis took a last look at the car behind him. "Trust me, she won't bring him anywhere near Athena. Very few men on this planet don't fantasize about my sister. Isn't that a queer thing to say for a brother?" he asked rhetorically just before he voice-dialled his sister's telephone number.

"Yes, it is," George said slowly. My son is a very queer man indeed, thought George, staring at the blue light on his earpiece. If that girl hadn't died, Denis would have lived a family man's life. Instead, he was a lonely, reptilian-looking executive. Life is all about give and take, George reflected. You win some; you lose some. At the end of the day, what you win always seems less than what you lose.

# CHAPTER 8

# A DELICATE MATTER

The offices of Private Affairs Investigators were situated at the corner of Aviation Boulevard and Renaissance Street, a narrow cobblestone road paved by German tradesmen during the time of the monarchy. Such opportune location came at the price of a wobbly door, pivoting between the half paved in asphalt belonging to the Aviation Boulevard sidewalk and the bumpier half belonging to Renaissance Street. The triangular building looked like something out of an amusement park. Its proportions were those of a wedge of processed cheese, made to fit tightly in a round box, next to seven other identical pieces. Its purple paint and yellow shutters stood out like a colourful band-aid on a child's bare knee. Before Iris Bendal took on a yearlong lease, it had been a paediatrician's office. Although Iris tried her best to dim the explosion of colour around the agency, it still looked to be an unlikely place to conduct investigations. Placido Pector had dubbed it "Lego World" that very morning, when they met to discuss the case of his son's legitimacy.

The meeting had been brief and to the point. Placido handed her an envelope with pictures of his son and wife, answered a few questions about his son's daily routine, and discussed finding a discreet way to complete the paternity test. Moments later, he stood up, cast a sneering gaze at the agency decorum, and left. Nothing wrong with a little cheerfulness, thought Iris, looking around at the rainbow-coloured chairs that might have once belonged to the seven dwarfs. She arranged a handful of sharpened pencils inside a rotary organizer, spreading them apart like flowers in a vase. She would spend the afternoon phoning her contacts at the neighbouring policlinic to see if they had what it took to run the paternity test locally.

A high-pitched motion-detecting bell interrupted her thoughts and announced an unexpected visitor, and she rushed out from behind her desk with a welcoming smile. A tall, small-boned man in his early forties stood by the door looking a little puzzled. The man was dressed in a French beige suit with a newspaper under his arm. His single-breasted, three-button jacket was tailored to fit him like a glove.

"I'm sorry," he said, "I must have gotten the wrong address. I was looking for a detective agency called Private Affairs Investigators."

"No, no, you're in the right place," smiled Iris, as she adjusted the cinch belt to her jacket with one hand and put out the other to introduce herself. The man stared at it for a moment before shaking it.

"Is that an oven bell?" he asked, pointing toward the door, while he wiped the hand he had touched Iris with on the leg of his trousers.

"Oh, that," laughed Iris, a little flustered. "As a matter of fact it is. I installed it myself for when I'm busy at my desk. I find it has just the right pitch. Not too loud, not too quiet."

"You don't have a receptionist?"

"Of course I do," she continued smiling. "She is away today. Personal obligation—you know how these things are."

The man, who had not yet disclosed his name, paced around with the air of a health inspector before he asked if there was a less chromatically distracting chair he could sit in. Iris invited him into the office and magnanimously offered him a dark green leather chair that would have fit nicely into a beauty salon from the seventies. It had two stirrups hanging by metal bars, where presumably one's feet were meant to rest. The man placed his shiny shoes on the peddles, causing the shinny stirrups to move away from each other.

"We're still in the process of moving," she explained.

"If you don't mind me asking, who owned this place before you moved in?" he asked, bringing his knees together and placing his newspaper in front of him, on the desk.

"A doctor."

"I'm going to venture and guess he was a paediatrician?"

"Gynaecologist," said Iris with a mischievous smile.

But the man did not laugh. His gaze fell upon the shinny stirrups. He quickly took his feet off and sat up higher. Nothing was said for a moment. Between short blinks, he tapped his fingers onto the shiny surface of her desk.

"Now, what brings you to our offices this fine afternoon?" she asked, grabbing a small paper pad and a pencil. Watching him attentively, Iris could see his small, round eyes move slightly as he weighed the pros and cons of answering her question.

The man did not reply immediately. He crossed his legs, smoothing the fabric on his slim-cut trousers. When at last he spoke, his voice was calm and assured. "What brings me to you is not, in fact, a mystery. I do not need an investigation but rather a tactful resolve to a family conflict."

Iris nodded her head in approval. This was the right way of thinking about family affairs. Human beings were far from perfect, and sometimes their mistakes ruined the fine balance of a happy home. In her view, people could change given the right circumstances and a sensible hand to point them in the right direction. As she thought

*C.R. Preston*

about this, her eyes inadvertently fell on her own hands.

"My father, you see, is a man of high standing in our community," started the man. For the first time, Iris noticed a small light flash out of what appeared to be a Bluetooth headset. It was not any bigger than a hearing aid, and it fit just as tightly into the shape of his outer ear.

The man carried on, touching his ear self-consciously, "Despite an ingrained naiveté he's always possessed, as some men born into privilege often may do, he is a good-natured man with a dream. His dream is to fulfill the political aspirations he's had his whole life and to do it with my mother by his side. Of course, her presence would be implicit to a political career, but that is not the only reason in his case," he said, lowering his gaze. "He loves my mother dearly and clumsily."

"Sounds like a fine husband to me," smiled Iris encouragingly, looking up from her notepad.

"Thank you," said the man. "He is. As for my mother, for the most part, she's been a good wife," he explained with a little less conviction. "Even though my sister and I were raised by nannies, I can't say she didn't put an effort into our education. She tried, and she tries harder now, as she's approaching old age."

Iris scribbled a few words down, fixing the man with a set of curious eyes. Seemingly unaware of her gaze, he looked away and stared past a yellow filing cabinet, through the large windows. He asked sharply, "Why does it take women the better part of their lives to reach simple conclusions?" Then, almost immediately, added, "Like the importance of one's child in one's life?"

Disregarding the etiquette of rhetorical questions, Iris corrected him, "People. Why does it take people such a long time to reach simple conclusions?"

Her comment brought him back. Vaguely amused, the man conceded, "I stand corrected. That is what I must have meant." Then, referring back to his question, "Personally, I blame it on hormones.

Mind you, hormones can't be held accountable for everything. My mother is well past menopause now, so I'm afraid there's no reason for her to behave like a love-struck teenager. Which brings us to the heart of the matter." He paused for a moment. "Mother is having an affair," he announced. "However, that is not the reason I came to see you."

What a relief, thought Iris, recalling her earlier conversation with Placido Pector, and his determination to prove something at the risk of causing harm to his family. This man was different, she thought, wondering about his name and why she did not know it yet. Only a few men could wear a well-made suit with such decency and nonchalance, as if he knew that wearing an expensive suit did not entitle one to preferential treatment.

"So what is it I can do for you then?" she asked, reaching for her pencil again.

The man brought his hand down from his ear. "My goal is to prevent further damage to our family and to my father's good name," he said, folding his hands over his knees. "We have decided on a solution to end this affair. My sister, who is working in Portugal at the moment, will soon require my mother's immediate presence."

"Did something happen to her?" Iris inquired concerned.

The man shook his head, "No, nothing happened to my sister. It's all part of the plan and she's going along with this," he explained. "Out of sight and out of mind, the affair will fizzle on its own. This is where you come in," he leaned closer to her desk. "I am presently busy with work and am not able to fly off to Portugal at a moment's notice. Even if I could, my mother knows me well enough to find my sudden interest in anything but work to be unusual. We don't want to tip her off on our plan of action now, do we?"

Seeing he did not get an answer, the man continued, "I was hoping you'd be available to set off to Portugal as my eyes and ears. Just to make sure my mother does not find a way to be reunited with her lover or communicate with him for that matter."

Iris said nothing. It sounded like the decent thing to do, to help a straying woman stray no more. But how does one prevent two people from seeing each other if they so desire? And more importantly, how does one censor communication in the age of the Internet?

"Money is not an object," he added.

It sounded like something Placido Pector had said to her during their brief meeting that morning. Suddenly, remembering Placido for the second time, Iris slapped her hand against her forehead. This was why one needed a secretary, she thought bitterly. She had already agreed to solve his case, and she could not do that from Portugal. Or could she? The thought of killing two birds with one stone seemed appealing enough. Of course, she would need to get creative in order for that to work. Iris ran her fingers through her hair pretending to fix her bangs.

"Just a fly," she grimaced. The man picked up his newspaper and rolled it into a cylinder, scouting the room for the insect. His weaselly eyes moved thoroughly, from corner to corner. While the man kept on the lookout for imaginary flies, Iris arrived to the only logical conclusion. If she was going to take this case, she would have to conduct both investigations from Portugal. Placido might not like it, but he was in no position to impose rules on her.

"All travel and living expenses would be paid for, of course," the man tried again. "Money should be no problem."

"I wasn't thinking it would be," she said gravely. "My concern is making a commitment to prevent something that as a stranger to your mother I would have no control over. How can I stop her from seeing this man if she so desires? And does anyone have the right to do so?"

"You strike me as a sensible person," he said, measuring her from across the desk. "The man she's involved with is very young. From what I can gather, he's a hotel gigolo out to take advantage." His voice became softer, almost pleading. "We're not talking about a woman's right to choose here. We're talking about preventing a disaster. Do you believe the right thing to do is stand by and watch in the name of freedom of choice?"

Iris did not reply. Instead, she covered her mouth with one hand, in a pensive gesture. She liked to think that she respected the choices of others. Her views on moral issues were mostly traditional. Things were either right, or wrong, with various shades of gray in between. This had not changed with the passing of time. Only society had. And so, her social views were liberal. She felt that human beings, and more specifically women, deserved a right to their own mistakes. After all, they had been denied that for a very long time. But this fundamental right ought not to have encouraged one to do wrong. Some mistakes were bigger than others, and the later they happened in one's life, the harder it became to right them. Iris could not stand by and watch a friend cheat, much less throw everything away on a whim. She was guided by the same principle in her professional life. Yes, the man was right, she decided, reaching for the pencil once again. She will find a way to help his mother.

He waited quietly and then spoke again. "I have no doubt you will use your judgment and rise to the occasion. After all, it is for a good cause. You will help keep an old married couple together and perhaps prevent a foolish woman of a certain age from making a devastating mistake."

Sitting up in her chair, Iris weighed his proposition with a look of concern. In theory, it sounded like a fine assignment. It was its practical application that worried her. She couldn't honestly guarantee that she would be able to keep the lovers apart. As much as she wanted to help, taking a trip to Portugal just to attempt to complete an assignment was a pretty expensive gamble. And Iris was not the gambling sort.

"Besides," added the man, "you will be compensated whether you succeed or not. All I'm asking you to do is try."

She looked up at him with a reserved smile.

"Are you up for the challenge?" he asked.

She agreed on ethical grounds. It was exactly the sort of delicate matter she had created the agency for. There were plenty of detectives out there who dressed in trench coats and disguised themselves behind wigs and sunglasses to spy on cheating spouses and take compromising pictures from behind a tree. Those pictures would then be handed in a yellow legal-sized envelope to people who did not know yet just how much their life would change after opening it. This was not what she wanted to do. Iris wanted to walk up to the cheating spouse dressed in a chiffon skirt and strike up a conversation that would cause them to reassess their values and rekindle their commitment to their families, without them ever suspecting that Iris was any more than one of those people we meet in passing but whom nonetheless change our lives forever. Yes, setting off to Portugal to herd a straying wife back into the bosom of her loving family would give her an opportunity to test those skills beyond the bounds of theory.

• CHAPTER 9 •

# MUMMY DEAREST

Perla Galanis was in the bad habit of checking her e-mail before heading off to bed. Most evenings, scrolling over forwarded messages containing PowerPoint slide shows of beautiful waterfalls shown to the soothing sounds of classical music, helped her relax. Then there was also a romance novel Web-site she liked to peek at in the privacy of her office. But on the night she received her daughter's e-mail, she never made it past her inbox. Squinting at the screen of her computer, Perla clicked the letter open and began to read.

*Mummy Dearest,*

*I've been meaning to write to you for a few months now, but you know how my schedule is these days. The movie I was filming in Malta was suspended during the writers' strike, and I was forced to accept an independent project, a nuisance really, with a script built on a true story about three little kids who saw the Holy Virgin some place in Portugal.*

*I'm playing the part of the virgin, of course. My publicist thinks it will be very good for my career. Every actress needs a role where she's wearing no makeup in order to be taken seriously by the critics. Anyway, it's really hot over here, and the three children who are playing the parts of the three children are depressing me. Real Portuguese kids have a look in their eyes that reminds me of puppies. They don't even speak English. I'm thinking of adopting one for a few years to see what all the fuss is about. My publicist thinks this, too, will be good for my career.*

*Next week, we're taking a trip to the place where the miracles happened; I forget what it's called. And, we'll have a whole day to mingle with the townspeople, who were all too happy to play extras in the movie. So while the other actors are doing that, I thought I'd take up my biographer on the offer he made me for a one-hour special (prime time, of course) on the incredible life of Athena Jeudi.*

*This is where you come in. I need you, Mummy. They need you to come and say nice things about me, like how talented I always have been, how pretty, etc. So, pack up your Louis Vuittons! First thing tomorrow morning a courier messenger will deliver your plane ticket. Come dressed to impress, Mummy. Can't wait to see you!*

*Hugs and kisses,*

*Athena*

By the time Perla finished reading this e-mail, her tan had mysteriously vanished, and her cheeks had developed a greenish shade of livid. She fell back in her seat and swivelled away from the screen, staring into the beige wall in front of her. First thing tomorrow morning she would be off to Portugal. Indefinitely, she thought, her heart pounding. Chewing on her cuticles, she tried to think of ways she could get out of this. But none came to mind. Her daughter rarely asked her for anything. She couldn't very well refuse her without a good reason.

She paced the room like a trapped feline, followed closely by her cat. The timing for this trip could not have been any less fitting for her. Things were going well with Leborio and leaving now didn't feel right. What if Rita snatched him while she was away? With trembling hands, she poured herself a glass of brandy.

Perla would have liked to tell Leborio that she would be gone for a few days. But she knew she wouldn't even have time to make it to her yoga class in the morning. Besides, she thought as she swallowed the last mouthful from her drink, it wouldn't be wise to tell Leborio about Athena. Not that Leborio would be so shallow as to prefer her daughter, but one could never be careful enough in such situations. These days it seemed the entire male population was in lust with her daughter. They named her the most beautiful woman alive four years in a row—which, in Perla's opinion, was a bit much. Granted Athena had a few striking features, but her mother thought she was a touch too scrawny to be a femme fatale. Nevertheless, it was wiser to keep her out of Leborio's way for now.

Perla's daughter, Athena, presented a few advantages over her mother, of which age, freshness of skin, fame, beauty, confidence, and marital availability were only a few. As perceptive as Perla thought Leborio to be, she preferred not to throw him in the way of temptation. But temptation lurked everywhere. Leaving him unattended to teach a herd of hormonal cows how to inhale and exhale was just as risky as bringing him along for the trip and finding a way to hide him from Athena, she thought, climbing the stairs to the bedroom.

After a sleepless night spent listening to George's symphony of snores and pondering the implications of Leborio being tempted under the Portuguese sun or by the Lido poolside, Perla packed up Regina, Gino, and a small fleet of Louis Vuitton luggage. She kissed George's extended forehead in passing and entered the black stretch limo waiting at her doorstep to take her to the airport. Her husband waved with a sombre turn of the wrist, watching her disappear behind the tinted glass.

The moment of truth had arrived. He walked up the stairs into their bedroom, and anxiously dialled the combination number to the safe. The door opened with a muffled click, revealing an empty chamber. The Sophie necklace was nowhere to be seen. With a heavy heart, George took out his phone and pressed the green button.

"Yes?" His son skipped the usual greeting.

"You're on," George said. "She took the Sophie necklace with her."

# CHAPTER 10

# ARMIN GETS A JOB

The next day, sitting on a red granite bench outside the Central Secondary School, Iris Bendal sipped the last of her herbal tea while watching Armin Pector's red Ferrari back into a cardboard box filled with empty plastic jars and office utensils she had packed in bubble wrap for sound effect. She tossed the empty paper cup in the garbage and got up just in time to catch a glimpse of the boy ducking into the passenger side.

"Damn it!" shrieked Iris, walking up to the car. "Don't you watch where you're going? Look at what you've done!" She grasped the box. She concealed a smirk when she saw he had covered his head with both arms and was now bracing for an impact that did not seem to come. "What are you doing?" she said, as his head peaked out from behind the leather seats. "What are you hiding from?"

The young man stood up slowly and scanned the windows to the surrounding buildings.

"I'm sorry," he whimpered. "I thought someone was shooting at me."

"Why would anyone want to shoot you?" she asked, not really allowing for an answer. "I mean, besides me. I kind of want to shoot you right now, because you've ran over my box. Do you always back out without checking your blind spot?" She took a few steps toward him. Her words seemed to have a calming effect on the frightened young man, and she watched him sigh in relief as he finally got out of his Ferrari.

"Are you all right?" he asked, closing the car door behind him.

Iris gazed in the direction of the box, where the back wheel of his car rested on top of the collapsed cardboard with the careless pride of a European explorer stepping on New World ground. She walked over and reached down to the box, struggling again to pull it out from under the car. Her slender arms yanked at it a few times, without any luck. Afraid to damage her purple chiffon dress, she looked up at him through the loose strands of red hair that had come undone from the effort.

"Are you gonna help me or just stand there?"

The boy was watching intently with a concerned expression on his milky white face. "Wait. I'll just back my car out."

"No!" she yelled out. "You'll back into it."

"I meant to say I'll drive forward," Armin squeaked

"Oh, do what you will. It's no good to me now!" She made a capitulating gesture with her hand.

Soon after the mischievous sports car had been safely parked away from the box, Armin introduced himself apologetically, leaving out his last name. There were very few people who didn't know who his father was and how much he was worth. Iris guessed he wanted to play it safe until he knew just how much the damage amounted to at market price.

"I'm very sorry about your box. What did you have in it? Perhaps I can cover the cost or replace it for you."

Iris scrutinized him, appearing somewhat irritated. He couldn't have been very bright to assume the contents of a cardboard box could be replaced. Some boxes could indeed contain replaceable items like crystal glasses, office supplies, and computer parts. People used those boxes for moving things around on residential streets or in front of office buildings. But there were other boxes that contained objects of infinite value. Those were the boxes that ventured outside storage boundaries, all the way to the posh part of downtown, close to the parks, and far from the subway stations. Such boxes held items one could not presume to replace so easily. No, the boy was not very bright at all. The brightest thing about him was his oversized red sneakers

"Tell you what," she spoke at last, "I will tell you what was in the box if you can guess."

She noticed the boy's doe eyes sparkle at once, sizing her from head to toe. He shifted on his feet, moving a little closer to her. Another minute and she could swear he'd have his arm around her shoulder. Just as he was about to make his first guess, Iris spoke again. "But there is one catch. You can only guess once."

She stressed the last word, knowing the young man would feel encouraged to make an informed deduction.

"I will do as you say," he smiled at her, revealing a set of teeth that were slightly skewed to the right. "But first you must allow me to express my apologies and get to know you before I can come up with a verdict. Allow me to invite you for lunch," he intoned magnanimously. "There's a nice bistro across the street."

She nodded graciously, squinting her green eyes at him, and for the first time, she smiled.

The bistro was not very crowded at that hour. A few schoolgirls made up to look much older than they actually were sipped cappuccino on the patio and overdramatized mundane events from their dating life. Iris noticed one of them nodding her head at Armin as they walked by her table.

"Do you know her?" she asked.

"A little. She's the daughter of a family friend," explained Armin, adopting the mildly defensive tone of an unfaithful lover who just ran into the other woman.

"Well, don't you want to go and say hello?"

"Not really. I don't know her that well. She was in love with my . . . brother. My older brother. Everyone is in love with him."

"You have a brother?" asked Iris, certain that it was a fib.

"I suppose I do," he replied, scanning the room for a table.

"That's an odd thing to say. One either does or does not have a brother. One does not suppose that one has a brother."

"Never mind," he smiled, allowing Iris to catch another glimpse of his oddly shaped teeth. The two larger ones at the front aligned away from the centre of his nose. On most people, this would have looked unattractive, but in Armin's case, she thought it added character to an otherwise weak face.

"We should probably sit at the other end of the room," he suggested. "You know how loud teenagers can get. Every sentence out of their mouths begins with 'Oh My God!' Irritating."

Indeed, thought Iris as she listened to Armin. Teenagers can be very irritating. Nevertheless, one must press on, in the interest of professionalism. She was determined to bring Armin where she needed him to be. Just as she had discussed with his potential father on the morning of their meeting, Armin responded to only one stimulus: women. And she was one of them—a very pretty one at that.

"So, Iris, what do you do for a living?" he asked moments after they sat at a small table close to the window. It was one of those questions that people asked each other when introduced. Iris thought he should not have risked asking it, unless he was confident he could also answer it once the polite exchange would turn the spotlight onto him.

"I own a business."

"What sort of business?"

"Something very unusual actually. A private investigation agency."

"Wow, that's mighty cool!"

"I beg your pardon?"

"I mean it's very good of you. To run a private investigation agency. It must be fun. And exciting."

"It is, of course, not without excitement," smiled Iris, batting her eyelashes at the unsuspecting boy. "Not for the faint of heart, I'm afraid. But who can blame them? It can get very lonely working on cases that require travel and discretion. Not to mention the risks involved. One could always get in a heap of trouble poking into other people's secrets."

"Actually, it sounds like the sort of job I'd like to have when I . . . am finished with my current obligation," he said, playing with the stitching on the tablecloth. "How many detectives work for you?"

"I'm in the process of hiring right now. I'm afraid I'll have to postpone making a decision until I get back. A difficult case requires my immediate attention abroad. Too bad I can't take an assistant to Portugal with me any more," she sighed.

"Why not?"

"No reason," frowned Iris, counting down to the moment of sudden enlightenment. It came slower than anticipated.

"Oh, wait! Does this have anything to do with your box?"

"I beg your pardon?"

"The box. The box I ran over. I bet it does! What was in the box? Resumes? Curnicumul vita?"

"Curriculum vitae," she couldn't help correcting him. "No, no such luck. The content of the box was far less replaceable." She leaned in, closer to the boy's diamond-studded ear, and, after making sure they could not be overheard, she whispered, "It contained samples."

She watched his glazed eyes widen for a moment before he scratched his head with an index finger.

"Hmm. It contained what?"

"Samples."

Armin smiled again, this time rubbing the tip of his tongue against the crests of his two front teeth. He raised an eyebrow and nodded his head a few times, like a talk show host encouraging a confession out of a guest. Seeing he had no idea what she was talking about, Iris burst out, "Oh, for goodness sake, the box contained cheek and nose swab samples from potential employees. To work as a detective you have to be tested for—" she wanted to say drugs but decided to not take any chances. "Diseases. Don't want to hire someone with a low immune system, who's going to get sick every day and hinder the outcome of an investigation."

"Oh" she watched his eyes open wide as the proverbial penny dropped. "Like Q-tips?"

"Similar," she conceded. "But the samples are no longer . . . legible. And I can't very well phone people to come and have a do-over. 'Good afternoon. This is in regards to your morning interview. I'm afraid there was a minor accident involving your sample. Would you be available to come in this evening and say *ah* again?' They would tell me exactly where to go, and rightfully so," she shook her head ruefully. "No, there is no way to fix this. I am on my own."

The boy placed his cold but humid hand on top of hers, in what could legitimately pass for a gesture of sympathy. Concealing a small shudder behind a polite smile, Iris pressed on. "I mean, what could I possibly do? My next investigation was going to require my assistant and me to go to Portugal. This is why I was hoping to find someone today," she frowned. "I interviewed a few people earlier, but without the samples, I'm afraid I'm right back where I started."

She picked up a tiny teaspoon and stirred the foamy drink the waitress had placed in front of her. "Where would I find another man adventurous enough to want to be an investigator, to travel at a moment's notice, to share lonely hotel rooms with me? Not every Joe is cut out to be James Bond or Simon Templar."

From the corner of her eye, she could see him stare down at her legs, and instinctively pulled on the chiffon to cover her knees.

"Listen," he started, "I can't promise anything, but I might be able to swing this off for you. I just have to check with my . . . supervisor and see if it's all right to take some time off. Then maybe I could come with you to wherever your investigation leads to."

"Oh no, I couldn't possibly accept your offer. This is dangerous stuff. What would your family— your older brother—think if you just took up such a dangerous career? I mean it would change everything, the way they perceive you, the way your brother thinks of his little Armin," she said, pinching his milky white cheek. "No, I can't do that to you. I can't turn you into a feared and intimidating man. You are too cute the way you are."

"But what if I don't want to be cute anymore?" the boy pulled back.

"No, no. My mind is made up, young man. You can't ditch a prior commitment to come with me to sunny Portugal. Why, that would be just wrong. What would your supervisor say?"

"My supervisor can shove it!" he blurted. "He probably won't even notice I'm gone. My . . . brother will be there to help him. Tell you what—I'll even pay my own way. Money is not an object. Come on, I really need this!" he seized her hand. "Please, Iris! Let me swab my cheek for you."

Iris reached into her big yellow purse and pulled out a brown plastic container. She sat it on the table and opened it with one hand. Inside, like a matryoshka doll, was a smaller container labelled "sample."

# • CHAPTER 11 •

# THE CAVE

When Leborio and his cousin Umberto came out of the Neon Lounge, it was already 4:00 AM. Umberto, looking like he'd been ran over by a train, pushed the heavy oak door with his left hand. Leborio paid no attention to his cousin and walked through it with the regal absent-mindedness of Hamlet on his way to his soliloquy. On the other side of the door, Kim, the giant bouncer, opened his crossed eyes after a lazy yawn just in time to see the dark brown oak come at him. Half a decade of rigorous tae kwon do training set itself into motion, and one swift block with his forearm sent the door flying back into Umberto's face.

"Bloody hell, man," Umberto yelled, and charged forward to hide behind his cousin. "I thought you got paid to keep people out of the club, not lock them in it!"

"Why don't you look where you're going, idiot?" yelled Kim, waving his large fists in the air. "I really ought to smack you."

Sensing the germination of a long and pointless conflict, Leborio lazily glanced back at the two men and said, "That's enough, you two!"

He put up his hand and adjusted the cuff to his tunic. "Kim, how would you like to join us at my flat? We're on our way there now."

The giant straightened up, his crossed eyes opening incredulously. "Thank you for inviting me," he began in a ceremonious tone. Then, shaking imaginary lint off his shoulders he asked Leborio, "Is there anything I should bring?"

"We're not going on a date," said Leborio. "I'm just asking if you want to come and play with us."

If this question had been asked twenty years earlier, nothing would have made Kim happier. Now on the eve of his thirtieth birthday, he found it somewhat unsettling. Playing with two other grown men held only one meaning for Kim, and his mother had warned him about such men. She said they could be lurking anywhere, even by the boss' right hand.

Keeping an open mind, Kim thought Leborio was rather attractive for a dude. Viewed from certain angles, he could see that there was something feminine about Leborio's big, black eyes. But there was no way his cousin would get to play with Kim.

The giant furrowed his brows. He had been working at the Neon Lounge for more than a year and had watched Leborio walk through the door he guarded thousands of times. Some nights, if Leborio was in a social mood, he would nod at the bouncer, a small gesture of acknowledgment that made the oversized man feel terribly important. Kim wasn't sure about Leborio's exact job description, but he could tell the position must have been pretty high up, something like the boss' right-hand man. Every night, he watched him leave the lounge accompanied by beautiful women and important men, such as the boss himself. Now, on this very night, Leborio had asked Kim to join him! If this did not herald the coming of great things, Kim wasn't sure anything else would.

He walked quietly behind the other two men, feeling a little guilty about accepting the invitation given his hostility to Umberto. He had never liked the bigoted bastard, but at that very moment Kim couldn't have been happier to be in the company of a neurotic Christian. It was a known fact that the Church still frowned on homosexuality, and no devout Catholic would ever consider eternal damnation for the sake of his XXXL buttocks.

The three men walked in silence down the main boulevard that cut the city in half. Half of the city could be crossed by foot. The other half was better crossed by cab—with the doors locked. Leborio led the group, swinging his hips ostentatiously, like a male gorilla in full mating season. Umberto dragged his feet over the sidewalk, sidestepping the potholes. He seemed too tired to notice Leborio or the subtle yet precise glances into the fancy window shops, where the irresistible reflection of a certain dapper young man made the creatively displayed Bvlgari jewelry fade into the background. Preoccupied by visions of his own perfection, Leborio did not say a word until Kim spoke.

"When you say play, what exactly do you mean by that?"

"Huh?" Umberto verbalized the general feeling of confusion brought on by this question.

"You said you wanted me to play with you. You two, that is," the bouncer mumbled. "What did you mean by play? Did you mean sports?"

"God, no!" laughed Leborio. "No one would benefit from my athletic abilities before a good night's sleep. Or should I say, good day's sleep?" he shook his head, looking up at the misty morning sky. "There will be no sports played this fine, cracking dawn."

"Oh Leborio, I wish you wouldn't take the Lord's name in vain," interjected Umberto. "Every time you say his name in casual conversation, he cringes."

"Does he now?" Kim heard Leborio laugh again. "I'm sure he cringes a lot more every time you open your mouth."

"Why do you have to joke about that? You know very well what happens to those who take the Lord's name in vain."

"But I don't. And I should know better than you. After all, I'm part of the industry."

"No you're not. You're a glorified yoga instructor."

"I'm a guru," spoke the spiritual master with heightened dignity. "That places me in God's— would *network* be the right word? Entourage. I'll settle for *entourage.* "

Umberto covered his ears in sheer horror and began humming a church hymn while purposely falling behind the other two.

"We're almost there," announced Leborio. "Would you quit humming the national anthem before the neighbours hear and label me as a fascist?"

As if to spite the devil, Umberto raised his voice a few decibels. Kim briefly contemplated ending the phonic pollution with a swift hit to the eject button, otherwise known as the Adam's apple. Appealing. But it didn't do to hit his host's cousin for no good reason.

"I don't think he's humming the national anthem," whispered the friendly giant instead. "It sounds more like 'Amazing Grace.'"

"Really?" asked Leborio, using the most repeated word in the lonely rhetoric of people who, through some odd turn of events, find themselves in the company of inferior intellects and out of the company of kindred spirits.

* * *

With a following of two men, one of whom had to stoop and sliver to fit through his doorway and another who hummed his way into the flat upholding a crescendo of muffled yet brave vocals as proudly as the slave choir of *Aida*, Leborio wondered for a moment in what way his life was a happy one.

In the way of comedy perhaps.

He was luckier than most, he thought. Out there, in the world, there was someone who would find this laughable entrance into The Cave to hold its own micro-happiness. Not everything had to be macro. Not yet, at least. But the man had plans to make it on a grand scale sooner than everyone thought. Soon, he would live in a great big house, a palace of his own making, something even his Excellency, the Costa Rican Ambassador, would envy. Someday he will find his place in the world – a first class spot – a place of progress and great consequence. Somewhere a man of vision like himself would require no particular skill in order to be successful.

Of course, he would miss The Cave. But every epic hero had to leave his home behind and follow the path of his adventure. The Cave, with its damp darkness, had been lovingly named by Leborio's boyhood buddy, the *real* offspring of the Costa Rican Ambassador. As young children, they spent many days hidden away from the blazing summer sun, in the cool comfort of the dark flat where Leborio and his mother lived.

The only room that always faced the sun was the black-tiled kitchen, and so they very seldom ate. And when they did, the preferred cuisine was always a single bowl of tomato salad, topped with a feta cheese piece the size of a Rubik's Cube, which they broke off with their forks while planning the next neighbourhood prank. They ran through the hallway into the living room, where the four walls were entirely covered in books, "for insulation," as he often explained, embarrassed. He claimed the books kept the room cool in the summer and warm in the winter.

The light coming from a few wobbly study lamps was no more than a weakening glimmer. Leborio professed this sharpened his night vision and made sure to turn the lights off behind him as soon as he left the room. It was a trick he had learnt from childhood, when his father skipped town and left his not-so-young bride to cover utilities by translating foreign authors by the flickering light of a candle.

Sitting in the dark had its advantages, as Leborio had come to believe. It provided the Spanish guru with many colourful stories of exceptional feats. Some days he would be training to be the first human in history whose eyesight surpassed that of a feline. Other days he would be transcending the physicality of his own existence by entering the deeper state of meditation that can only be achieved in complete darkness at the end of a billing period. In this life, one must never justify the need, but rather ennoble the justification of the action itself, he reflected. His flair for the dramatic never failed to add magic to ordinary troubles.

"Nice house," said Kim, squinting to see his surroundings. "Not at all the sort of home a boss-in-training would be expected to have," he added candidly.

Leborio watched him walk over to the far side of the living room, attempting to look into the next room. With an agile leap, Leborio's magnificent arm came down like a turnstile.

"That's my room," he said. "Very few people are allowed in there."

"I understand," mumbled the bouncer. "We're not there yet."

Used to having people work hard to earn his graces, the guru ignored his last remark and sat in front of an old, beat-out computer. Umberto, who seemed to have run out of singing breath, sat at a similar machine. The three computers looked as if they had made it through a nuclear disaster, and after having lost important pieces of original hardware, had been lucky enough to receive prosthetic downgrades from their less fortunate CP brethren.

"Turn it on," yelled out Umberto to the puzzled guest.

Kim sat at the least aesthetically acceptable computer of the three, meant for rookies of The Cave entourage, and awaited instructions.

"We're networking," explained Leborio, from behind the more respectable machine.

"Here? Networking?" sighed Kim. "But I'm no good at video games."

"That doesn't matter," decided Leborio. "I'm unbeatable anyway. The question is will you beat cousin Umberto?" Then, he turned to Umberto with a smirk, "Sorry, brother. No pun intended."

# CHAPTER 12

# PLANE TICKET

Snejana shook the last bits of sleep off and headed over to Leborio's. As she sat in the cab, she replayed the telephone call in her mind.

"Top o'the morning to you, Big Bird," he said. "What are you up to?"

"Sleeping."

"No time for sleep. The early bird gets the worm and all that."

"What do you want, Leborio? It's the crack of dawn," she said.

"I miss you, Big Bird. In fact, I am positively burning with desire for you. Just to fall asleep with you in my arms, oh, it would be heaven. We can spend the day together after. Come by at once, will you?"

"What, now?"

"Well, I don't know how I'm going to feel later. You know I'm fickle."

It was about time, she thought, as she walked up the steps, pausing only to check her face in a small compact she pulled out of the butterfly purse. All was well. She snapped the mirror shut and let herself into Leborio's apartment.

Wide-eyed and bushy tailed, Snejana almost dropped her purse from the shock moments after she walked in. She recognized Umberto, Leborio's cousin, sitting at a computer, but the large, cross-eyed man sitting at the third computer wasn't someone she knew. All three men were locked in a deadly cybernetic battle against the Hittites.

"Make yourself at home, Big Bird," said Leborio. "This is Kim, and you know Umberto." His eyes never left the screen. "We're starving. See what you can find in the fridge; we're not picky at this point."

"Is this why you got me out of bed at this hour?" she started, feeling the sting of tears. "To cook for you like a kitchen maid? I'm not your servant."

"Oh, don't be silly," Leborio said, turning away from the computer enough to favour her with a smile. "I had no idea these guys were coming over. My cousin showed up at the door after I phoned you. What was I to do, turn him around? Don't you think I'd rather spend this fine morning cuddled up in bed with you? But we must be gracious hosts, Big Bird. This is your golden opportunity to make an impression on my friends. What kind of hostess would you be if you didn't treat them to one of your home-cooked meals?"

Seeing herself invested into the role of the dotting matron, Snejana locked herself in the kitchen and phoned the only person she knew would be able to tell her a thing or two about omelettes.

"Hi, mom," Snejana whispered into the receiver. "Quick question: how many minutes should one let an omelette cook for?"

"Snejana, is that you? Why are you whispering? I can't hear you?"

"I can't talk very loudly. Just tell me how to make an omelette."

"Where are you?" her mother's voice was getting louder, indicating anxiety. "My poor child, are you sleepwalking again?"

"I'm out."

"At this hour? Have you gone mad?"

"Well, the early bird gets the worm and all that. Anyway, are you going to help me?"

"Why do you need to make an omelette? You don't like eggs."

"It's not for me."

"Oh, you stupid girl!" moaned the mother. "Are you waiting on that spiritual nebula that calls himself a guru?"

Snejana was beginning to regret calling in the first place, but at this point, she couldn't have done it for nothing. She insisted on the recipe.

"Are you his servant now? Is that why I struggled to raise you the way I did? So you can make a pretty female slave to a misogynistic pig?"

Snejana wasn't certain what misogynistic meant. "I'm not his slave. He loves me, Mama. I don't expect you to know anything about love, being that you drove father away, but the least you can do is allow me to be happy. Not every man is a pig."

"There I agree," sneered the woman. "Not every man. Only this one."

"Will you tell me how many minutes I have to cook it for?"

Simina remained quiet for a moment, breathing into the receiver. At last, she spoke in a dismal tone, "Four to five minutes on low heat, you fool. Make sure you do his laundry for him too."

"Thanks; I will," Snejana said hanging up the phone mid-air.

Forty-five minutes later, the warriors were served individual plates of Snejana's first-ever omelette, next to evenly distributed dices from a garden tomato she found on the windowsill. The omelette itself looked curiously compact, and a fork tip could not penetrate it any more than it could a chunk of dried banana.

"Big Bird, are you trying to poison us? This is worse than Umberto's peanut butter and jelly sandwiches. What . . . is it?" The spiritual master turned the plate at a forty-five degree angle, letting the shrivelled omelette slide off the plate and shatter on the hardwood floor. Welling up with tears and frustration once again, Snejana looked at the ground in shame. She didn't understand what had gone wrong. What did her mother do different to make her omelettes melt in one's mouth? Cooking had to be a talent one was born with, she reflected, feeling rather desolate that she turned out to be a failure in the kitchen. It was at this precise moment that the doorbell rang, and Umberto got up to answer it.

"You got a package," he said, dropping it in Leborio's lap.

"Great. I hope it's food. The eatable kind," he said, preemptively handing Snejana the tissue box to wipe her tears. He tore the large envelope open, pulling out a single sheet of paper. "Oh, no such luck," he announced. "It's a plane ticket to Lisbon, made out in my name."

Snejana stopped crying and immediately began computing the possibilities and implications of this new turn of events. Umberto raised an eyebrow, while Kim asked somewhat rhetorically if Brazil was not a little far to travel.

"Brazil, yes. Luckily, Lisbon is the capital of Portugal, about two hours away from here by plane."

"Who sent the ticket?"

"It doesn't say," Leborio looked up, answering Snejana's question. "But it's a one-way ticket, so they obviously want me to stay."

"Are you gonna go?" Snejana cut to the chase.

"I don't see why not. Let it not be said that Leborio Borzelini missed out on any adventures life threw his way."

"So you don't know who sent it, you don't know when you're coming back, but you're going anyway."

"Big Bird, what is this, a Stasi interrogation?" he rolled his eyes. "Can't you be happy? Something fun has happened at last! Portugal awaits us."

"Us?" her voice softened up. "You want me to come with you?"

"Why of course. Two's company, three's an entourage. I never travel without one. It would be in bad taste to arrive without a clear purpose and without companions. We're all going to Portugal."

"Even me?" Kim's crossed eyes gawked incredulously between the guru and his cousin.

"Especially you, my new friend. I have taken a swift liking to you," smiled Leborio, sizing up the giant.

"We're all going to Portugal!" repeated Snejana, hopping up and down, spreading hugs and kisses between the men who were now chanting with her. She threw herself at Leborio, who instinctively ducked to dodge the impact, sending her into the bear-like arms of the giant. Kim spun her around a few times, lifting her off like a rag-gedy doll. Watching the celebrations from the opposite corner of the room, Umberto gave his cousin a look.

"With what money? You have a free one-way ticket, but we don't. How are we supposed to travel with you?"

Kim stopped spinning Snejana and gently put her back on the ground. Catching her breath from all the excitement, Snejana turned to Leborio for an answer. He seemed to ponder the question for a few moments before putting forward a new course of action.

"We'll have to do some creative fundraising," he proposed, turning to face his friends. "To start with, how much can each of you come up with?"

"I have enough saved to buy myself a ticket," volunteered Snejana.

"I could get a ticket," said Umberto morosely. "But then why would I waste my money on that?"

"Brother," sighed Leborio, fixing his cousin with a reproachful gaze, "must you always spoil the fun with negativity? Surely, the Lord has a prosperous life in store for you," he said with finality. "How about our new friend?" he turned to Kim who fiddled with the small bullet-sized object he held in his pant pocket.

"I had a little ... hmm ... a little saved up," he stuttered, "but my mom is not well."

As the giant shuffled his feet helplessly, the others remained silent. Leborio lifted up his arm and placed it encouragingly on his shoulder. Trying to comfort Kim, he felt like a kid standing on his toes to touch a basketball hoop.

"I try to help out as much as I can," Kim explained a little embarrassed. "She needs medicine. Some of it is expensive, and there's no one else to pay for it," he went on in a low voice. "I've been working overtime at the club, but it's not enough to cover my mama's pills."

"Say no more!" nodded Leborio. "I shall think of something."

Leborio closed his eyes for a moment and used his spiritual training to conjure up a vision of the secret benefactor. Benefactor was such a dramatic term, he thought. It implied a significant improvement of one's lifestyle, and this, after all, was only a plane ticket. Not even a return one at that. How very Dickens of whoever sent it. It had to be a person of some means, someone who could afford the luxury of his company. Could it be Placido? He dismissed the thought almost immediately. Placido would have sent a return ticket and a detailed explanation of the sort of job expected from him. And he wouldn't waste his money on currier but would rather send a boy from the club to deliver the package. Dismissing possibilities one by one, he decided it must be one of the old hags from the pool. But which one? He'd only started working Perla over, and she appeared to be bashfully invested in the role of the virginal adolescent rather than that of the sugar mama. As for Rita, the mere thought of her rippled bottom made him shudder in horror. He couldn't be that unlucky. Not when he had a destiny to fulfill.

Leborio sensed Kim wanted to be part of his jolly adventure, but he guessed the bouncer's monumental size prompted him to be on the pragmatic side. As far as he could tell, Kim had never picked up his belongings on a whim, like a gypsy, to embark on a on a purposeless journey. He appeared to be the kind of man who worked hard to do his duty to his mother, even if it meant getting in trouble from time to time. In Kim's case, trouble meant he emptied pockets, wallets, and purses whenever possible. Leborio remembered he'd slipped once, a few years back and got caught and booked for petty theft. Though the conditions of Kim's probation were mostly lifted by now, he still had to phone an officer every Saturday night from his place of employment. Lowering his voice to a whisper, Leborio stood on his toes again and suggested that if they were to leave right away, Kim could get back in time for his Saturday phone call. This, however, brought to attention another significant obstacle.

"What about the boss?" asked the giant. "Who's gonna work the club?"

"Who indeed," repeated Leborio in a flat key, making it hard to determine whether he was being sarcastic or genuinely worried. "Placido is a man of opportunity," he shrugged, bringing his arm down. "He made his fortune following his gut into the pockets of the local whales. Well, gentlemen, I believe we have found our own whale on the Portuguese shores, and we should be absolutely raving mad to pass on such an opportunity," he said, waving his hand in the air for emphasis. "Placido himself would never forgive us if we didn't seize the moment," he added solemnly. "Once we get to Lisbon, I can send him word of our whereabouts. But for now, we must hurry, or we'll miss the plane. I for one am tired of guiding the elderly ladies of the Lido pool on their spiritual path. Kim," he turned to the giant, "aren't you tired of guarding that door every night as if it were the gates of Hades?" And without waiting for an answer, he added, "There's more to life than that. You know it. You can feel it in your gut, can't you?"

Kim touched his growling stomach and hesitated for just a moment. Then he said, "Would you like help packing?" The plane was to depart in the afternoon, and there were still arrangements to be made.

# CHAPTER 13

# STAMP OF APPROVAL

S o, brother, are you going to contribute?" asked Leboiro focusing on Umberto's reaction from the comfort of his armchair.

It was unusually difficult for Leborio to determine when his cousin winced. When he didn't speak, Umberto barely moved his mouth to conceal a nervous grimace he had acquired when they were children. He had a pleasant face, with a poignant, straight nose and clever eyes of a light brown shade that reminded Leborio of amber. His chin was perfectly shaped, giving Umberto's features a dash of nobility. If he had been darker, he would have looked very much like his cousin. They both stood six feet tall, with broad shoulders, making it especially hard to tell them apart in the dark. In fact, Umberto was often confused for his cousin, to Leborio's dissatisfaction. There was only one Leborio Borzelini, he thought, staring at his cousin in contempt.

Once, when Umberto was only nine years old, they fought over trading stamps for their collections. The most valuable item in the pre-teen stamp market was The Belize, a triangular postage stamp depicting tropical fish. Umberto, who wanted to be an explorer when he grew up, managed to trade his most valuable item, his pocket compass, for a clown fish Belize stamp that a boy in his class owned. Overjoyed, the boy ran straight home after school and told his little cousin about his great conquest.

Young Leborio turned up his nose at the news. "What's so special about a fish stamp? I'd much rather get my hands on a turn-of-the-century stamp."

"I like fish stamps," pouted Umberto, disappointed by Leborio's reaction. "At least they're colourful. And Belize sounds like the kind of place I'd like to live in. Besides, who cares about old stamps? No one's gonna wanna trade you."

"Good. I don't want to trade. I want to collect. An old stamp has so much history you can't help but care for it. Does your friend have any old stamps?"

"Probably not," chuckled Umberto. "But we can see if his grandpa is interested in trading with you."

Umberto invited his cousin to join the negotiations in case his classmate should have old stamps to trade. Excited about acquiring The Belize, he also invited some of the other kids to witness the historical moment.

"Now, make sure you keep your cool," he told them. "I don't want to seem too excited, just in case he decides to bring the price higher."

His friends kept their composure until the stamp album was opened, allowing them to catch a first glimpse of the clown fish picture. They stared in awe among a series of, "Oh wow!" "Oh my," and "Cool!" While Umberto laid out his pocket compass on the table, his cousin watched the other kids marvel at The Belize. He'd already seen a stamp he'd liked, an old French Napoleonic head in a yellow bistre tone, looking back at him from the page opposite The Belize. Leborio suspected it would be a lot more valuable than the picture of the clown fish and that in the long run, the French stamp would really count for something.

"Hold up!" he said to the boy with the stamps. "There is a stamp I'd like to trade you for, and I'm going to make you an offer you can't refuse."

"Oh, yeah? Like what?"

"My bike. I have a twelve-speed bicycle I'm willing to trade for your Belize."

All eyes and ears turned to Umberto's little cousin.

"The Belize?" said Umberto. "But you don't even like The Belize."

Without meeting his eyes, young Leborio put out his hand to the boy with the stamps. "Do we have a deal?"

The stamp boy shrugged his shoulders to his baffled classmate, and shook his cousin's hand.

"I've always wanted a twelve-speed bike," he excused himself.

Leborio took the clown fish stamp and put it in his small collecting book. He took one last look at the Napoleonic head and allowed himself to be swept away by questions and requests to show The Belize, while Umberto's eyes welled up in disbelief. If he had dared look his cousin in the face, he would have noticed how the shadow of a smile had faded into a half frown, leaving the boy with a confused grimace set between his nose and his chin.

Later that night, there was a phone call reporting that Umberto's father, who was an airplane pilot, had crashed and burned over a place called Snake Island. The three of them were about to climb the staircase in the boys' bedroom and make their nightly escape through the attic window when Umberto's mother came in sobbing. She was so upset that she paid no mind to the girl who was not supposed to be in their room. Young Leborio ground his teeth, watching the girl try to comfort his cousin.

"He's with God now," she said, stroking Umberto's blond hair.

"How do you know?" wept the boy.

The girl lifted his face up with her small hands and gave him an assuring gaze.

"God is good and just. He will look after your dad," she said, softly kissing his wet cheeks.

Though Leborio knew it was the right thing to do, the sting of jealousy burned him like a bad rash. With one irrational leap, he pushed his cousin to the ground and pulled her out of the house, kicking and screaming.

It wasn't until the funeral, a few days later, that Leborio noticed something strange had happened to his cousin's face. The children made up, the way children do, without any fuss or explanations. And like most children, they silently clasped at the germinating seeds of resentment. Twenty years later, Leborio knew his cousin believed two things: that God was the measure of all things and that Leborio was responsible for the departure of the only girl he'd ever loved. His face still locked into a half frown every time he smiled, laughed, or cringed, making it hard for his younger cousin to read him.

"Contribute what?" Umberto said, interrupting Leborio's thoughts.

"Well, everyone contributes something. Snejana will pitch in money. Kim will be our ... defender."

"Do you mean your bodyguard?"

"You can't deny it has a certain ring to it. Besides, it doesn't hurt to bring someone to protect us while we're away from our turf."

"And what do you contribute?" asked Umberto.

"Some contribute money and skills; others contribute experience," grinned Leborio, crossing his legs and casually inspecting his velvet loafers as he did so. He was one pipe short of looking like a retired captain.

"I don't remember you ever having been to Portugal."

"Life experience, brother. I don't need to have gone to Portugal to know it. Look around!" he gestured toward the four walls surrounding them. Top to bottom, they were all insulated in books. "I've read all about Portugal," he said. "History, geography, ecosystem, music, food, art—you name it. I've read it all."

"Swell for you."

"And that goes for most countries in the world," added Leborio, with a flourish fitting a grand spiritual master.

"I'm sure there's a trivia game somewhere waiting for you to win it."

"You laugh, brother, but there's something empowering about knowledge. Most people look to others for guidance. All I have to do is search for the answers in here," he tapped on his subtly advancing forehead.

"What I do for answers of the useless information variety," his cousin interrupted, "is Google. A lot faster and more accurate than this," he gestured toward the guru's noble forehead. Leborio paced around the four walls of his precious library, weighing the implications of knocking his cousin out with one swift blow to the half-smirk. For whatever reason, he decided against it.

"You've been saving money since we were kids," said Leborio, creasing his monobrow. "What are you saving it for? Every story needs an adventure, brother. Even yours. Don't you think our trip to Portugal is the best way to spend it?"

"No," replied Umberto.

"Then what are you going to do with it?"

"I'm going to continue saving."

"For a house with white shutters and a picket fence?" laughed Leborio, and when he got no answer, added, "With the money you're making on a deejay salary, it will take you two lifetimes, brother."

Umberto cut him short, "I've been investing."

On the subject of investments, Leborio was invariably quiet, not because he knew nothing of it but because the concept of using something of value over time to create a durable share of profits completely eluded him. It required a steady income, which Leborio preferred to spend on self-maintenance; the patience to watch money grow, which was something that Leborio could hardly pace himself to do; and most importantly, the willingness to take one's share and walk away. Sharing was what sheep did, thought Leborio. Men owned.

"She won't care, you know. The house won't make a difference," he said in a prophetic tone. "In case you haven't noticed over the past couple of decades, she and I have been moving forward and toward each other."

His cousin gave him one of his asymmetric smirks and made his way to the door.

"How is that possible if she just got back a few weeks ago?" he asked facetiously. "Oh, let me guess! You've had a telepathic relationship."

Leborio reconsidered the logic of his previous statement and held up his hand in a gesture of dismissal. "Whatever," he muttered. "The hero always ends up with the girl. Don't you know that? You can't change the ending of an epic story by buying a house."

Looking down, Umberto raised his eyes slowly, like a guerrilla fighter before the battle. For a moment, Leborio thought his cousin would jump at his throat and braced himself for the impact in the least noticeable way.

"Perhaps not. But every story needs a setting, *brother*, even yours," said Umberto, shutting the door behind him.

Leborio got up from his armchair and quickly walked to his balcony. He disliked other people having the last word, mostly because they lacked the creativity to make it memorable. As an exception, Umberto's reply had not been a bad one. "I'm curious; what are you investing in?" he yelled out as he hung from the balcony railing. "Penis enlargement solutions?"

His cousin looked up at him from the street and once again robbed the guru of his grand finale. "No. I own a large collection of turn-of-the-century postage stamps."

# CHAPTER 14

# JOURNEY TO PORTUGAL

"So are you going to tell me about this case?" he asked, tapping the backrest of the seat in front of him with his running shoes. It was hard to tell whether the intended colour of the shoes had been white or red. The creamy white leather of the sides stood out against the bright red tip that rounded off to replicate clown shoes or to accommodate a severe case of elephantitis.

Iris had started on her journey to Portugal hoping to kill two birds with one stone and was getting ready to dismiss Armin's question in a manner that would have been at best less than polite. What could an eighteen-year-old boy wearing Ronald McDonald running shoes understand from the puzzle in front of her? A text message from Denis Galanis containing the name of the hotel where Perla was going to stay, a map of a city on which Iris had marked the address of a medical lab where she intended to complete the paternity test, and a printout of the e-mail Athena had sent containing the press clearance for the movie set. Iris and Armin were going to pose as Biography Channel reporters who were doing a special on Athena Jeudi. But this could all very well backfire, so the less Armin knew, the better.

Sitting in economy class on the only flight of the day heading out to Lisbon should have been exciting enough for him, she thought. He fiddled with the headphones for a few minutes after the plane took off and ate all his peanuts, staring longingly to the front section of the plane.

"First time traveling economy?" she asked rhetorically.

"Yeah, actually," he gave her a vacuous look of discontent. "I always travel first class. The peanuts are better."

"You can't be serious," she said, searching through her purse for a tabloid magazine, a candy bar, or any such trifle that might be successful at distracting her companion and keeping him from wanting for conversation. She had a lot of planning to do without having to babysit Armin. Though this was exactly what her assignment came down to: babysitting the "cargo" and delivering it to a medical facility with the adequate equipment to complete a paternity test. Bringing Armin along for the ride was the only way she could honour both investigations.

"Why are we traveling economy?" he whined.

"Well, Armin, we are keeping a low profile. Traveling first class would attract too much attention."

"Oh, that makes sense. We're like … spies," he said, as his expression changed from puzzled to excited. "Should we have code names? Or hand signals? And do we have any gadgets? I always wanted Bond's gadgets."

"You and every other living male," she replied while tracing down on the map the exact distance from the airport to the hotel. "No, Armin. We will not have code names, although if you keep it up with the questions, we might have hand gestures."

The boy huffed indignantly and turned his attention to the window, where green patches of land peeked through the cottony white clouds. He appeared to be lost in thought.

Iris found that her mood improved after mentally covering every angle of the double investigation she would be running. Noticing Armin was pouting silently next to her with the grave dignity of a martyr, she decided it would be wise to improve his disposition before landing.

"Such lovely scenery, don't you think?" she said, looking out over his shoulder and getting close enough for her perfume to seep through the invisible wall of air conditioning between their seats. "I'm sort of excited. I've never been to Portugal. Have you?"

"Not yet," he said coldly. "I usually go to Mauritius on spring break." And almost immediately he added, "Spring vacation. From work. The work that I do."

She tried not to laugh. Young people were so transparent nowadays. There was something to be said about being brought up under a communist system. It made one very vigilant. She would have never slipped like this when she was Armin's age.

"Speaking of work, are you ready to be briefed?" Without waiting for a reply, she went on. "The case we are handling is very hush-hush and information is only given on a need-to-know basis," she whispered in his milky-white ear. "The first thing you're going to need to know is that we will work in the presence of celebrities, specifically, movie stars," she paused for effect. "Do you have any problems with that? Because if you do, you should probably tell me now."

"I guess not," he said matter-of-factly. "No. I don't have a problem. But I would like to know more."

"Fair enough," she nodded. "I will be impersonating a TV reporter, and you will be my camera man. The woman we are interviewing is Athena Jeudi."

"The actress?"

"Yes. She and her family will be the subjects of our investigation."

"Why? What did she do?"

"I'm afraid that information is classified," replied Iris, making an effort to keep a straight face. "But I'm sure that an observant guy like you will have no problem figuring it out after a few days." She winked as Armin blushed under the grown-up sound of the word *classified*. She could see him sit a little taller in his seat.

Iris had never seen a sunnier place than Lisbon. On dreary winter days, to chase away the gray, she closed her eyes and thought of the little fishing town her grandparents would take her to when she was a child. They were from San Jose, as was her father, but now cars and people overpopulated the city. They took little Iris to the fishing town where her father used to spend his vacations before leaving for Europe. In her mind, there was no place sunnier than Costa Rica. Until today. The brilliant sun sprang from ground up, shinning a dry, warm light into the perfectly blue lens that was the Lisbon sky. It was as if they were two pots in a hydroponic room, flooded with light from every direction. Nothing but solar energy surrounded the city, which was built on superimposed terraces. Beautiful people filled the streets, dressed in bold colours and walking with purpose toward destinations she would have liked to know. Not exactly your typical port city, thought Iris, recalling the pathological laziness of Mediterranean folks at high noon. The cab passed a circular building reminiscent of the Coliseum. Clad in soccer billboards and artesian fountains, this must have been one of the town's landmarks. She reached for her map, and tracing their itinerary with her finger, she settled on a red dot of unquestionable importance to the city.

"Colombo mall," she said. "It figures that the biggest landmark of a city should be a mall."

"Why do you keep using a paper map? Don't we have a GPS? It's not that bold of a gadget, you know," Armin shook his head. "You'd think that jet-setting agents in today's world would have at least a basic means of orientation."

"Columbus sailed the world with nothing but a compass. We don't need a GPS to find our hotel."

"Colombo find America," replied the otherwise quiet cab driver, as if he had waited for the right moment to burst out the only English phrase he knew and had memorized.

"Actually he didn't. Of the Western explorers, Americo Vespucci found it first. Hence the name: America."

The driver may have not understood the explanation, but something in the tone of the redhead caused him to become agitated. He repeated the phrase in a less friendly tone. "Colombo find America!"

"No, he didn't. If he did, it would be called Columbia, not America."

"Be quiet!" whispered Armin. The short cab driver pulled the car over to the curb and opened the passenger door, gesticulating for the woman to get out. He opened the trunk, took the two suitcases out, and firmly placed them on the ground.

"Colombo find America. Yes?"

Armin turned to Iris, his eyes pleading for a reasonable answer.

"No!" she replied firmly. "*Obrigada, señor.* Armin darling, would you be a dear and grab those suitcases? We only have another block to go, and I'm sure we could both use a walk to stretch our legs."

Hotel Almeida was not one of those flashy places where businessmen liked to rub shoulders with socialites and savour the view from the top of the ladder they sold their souls to climb. Its miniature lobby and gold-garnished draperies gave it a rather quaint appearance. A cluster of Swarovski crystals descended from the centre of the ceiling, glimmering over the embroidered tapestries of the sitting area, where scenes depicting Vasco da Gamma's journeys were woven in spice-coloured shades. The receptionist, dressed in a vintage Valentino suit, didn't need to smile because the clientele was steady and selective. He looked over the frames of his spectacles right at the wind-blown redhead and consulted a guest book he kept behind the marble counter.

"Good day, madam. What name was your reservation made under?" he asked in perfect English.

"Bendal. The name is Bendal."

The man stared down at the boy's running shoes with a visible look of disproval and discreetly scanned the lobby in embarrassment. If anyone would see that, the hotel would have to automatically drop a star from their rating. For the sake of damage control, he nodded and handed her an envelope. "This contains the card to your room and a safe key. I trust you'll enjoy your stay with us."

"*Obrigada,*" said Iris, placing the envelope in her purse.

"Oh, madam," said the man, pointing to Armin, "Does your bell-boy need help with the luggage?"

"I'm not her bellboy!" snarled Armin. "I'm her associate."

"Yes, thank you. Send the luggage up with one of your men," said Iris.

As soon as Armin and Iris arrived in the room, Armin headed toward the veranda. "Check this out!" she heard him say, as he walked out into the sun through the sheer white curtains. "There's an infinity pool on our balcony. How cool is that?"

"It's not a balcony; it's a veranda. And don't get too comfortable. We're here to work, not suntan."

"Come on! Would you just come out here before you say that?"

Reluctantly, she stood up and made her way through the white brocades framing the door to the terrace. At that exact same moment, a warm gust of sea wind blew over Lisbon, causing the curtains to part, revealing Iris in her fanned floral print chiffon dress, her auburn hair swept like a sunny twirl, and her bright green eyes sparkling with wonder. The next time she was cold, Iris would close her eyes and think of Lisbon, of this perfect day with its perfect sun.

"Incredible!" she said, overjoyed by the beauty surrounding them. "What a truly magnificent view!"

With his eyes fixed on her, Armin nodded his head. "Magnificent, yes," he mumbled and blushed.

# CHAPTER 15

# HOTEL ALMEIDA

From the moment their plane landed in Lisbon, Armin had found it impossible to concentrate on anything else but the dry afternoon heat and the phenomenon of wind blowing through skirts. And rightfully so, because catching a glimpse of the event required a fair bit of concentration. It was a little bit like bird-watching—skirt-watching had to be consistent. Murphy's Law stated that at exactly the very same moment one might turn his neck to stretch or look out for speeding cars while crossing the street, the wind would sneak up on skirts, dresses, and undergarments and cause them to rise like hot air balloons. Just in time for one to catch the last act of the performance, the wind would then cease to blow, leaving spectators teased into ambition. Armin was determined not to miss the next one, and he failed to notice the statuesque brunette walking out the elevator adjacent to the one they took on their way up.

Out of the corner of her smoky eye, the woman caught a glimpse of a most unusual occurrence: a member of the male species had not turned to gawk at her but instead looked right through her as if she were a regular, plain Jane. Gay, she thought, but the uncertainty dampened her mood. She walked past the reception area, where the Valentino-wearing employee of Hotel Almeida bowed to her the way Columbus must have done for Queen Isabella.

Queen Isabella—there's a part I'd like to play, thought Athena, wondering if there had been any scripts written about her. Of course, for that to work, Isabella of Spain would have had to have been an extraordinarily beautiful woman. Had she been? Athena had not the slightest clue. Back then, women were born into their titles. They didn't have to work for it like Athena did. Take the *People's Magazine* Most Beautiful Woman of the Year title. It was the result of thousands of hours spent in makeup, hair styling, and self-reflecting in the mirror. She deserved it, because she really was the most beautiful woman on the planet. Every man who had ever laid eyes on her could swear by it. Well, every man except that one who passed her in the lobby a few minutes ago. Maybe he didn't get a good look. Or maybe he was nearsighted.

She puckered her famously generous lips around the filter of an unusually long cigarette, and allowed the man in the Valentino suit to reach out in slow motion and light it for her, looking as flustered as a teen boy during his first rock concert.

As she leaned back, an unmistakable voice permeated the lobby. "There you are, Atty."

"You've got to stop calling me that in public, Mummy," she blew the smoke out, looking around to make sure no one heard. "Imagine if the press got a hold of that one. I would forever be dubbed Atty."

"And what's wrong with that? It has a nice ring to it."

"Atty is no JLo, Mummy. The only ring it brings is that of the oven bell. Atty, the housewife. It's got a very '*Honey, I'm home*' sort of feel to it, doesn't it?"

"Oh, you're being ridiculous! A name is just a name. As long as you have a good one, where's the sense in changing it?" reasoned

Perla, falling back on a hand-embroidered Rococo armchair in the lobby. "Athena Galanis is a fine name for a woman. Don't you think?"

"Clearly not," replied Athena Jeudi. "What are you doing out of your room anyway? I got you a suite facing east so that you can tan all day. Didn't you find the veranda attractive?"

"Yes, very," granted the mother. "I thought I'd check and see if any new guests arrived."

"Are you expecting anyone?" Athena's voice went a pitch higher.

"Oh no, of course. Not me," smiled Perla, fixing her hair with her fingertips. "It's just that those Biography Channel people should be here soon. Didn't you mention it?"

"Yes, I did," Athena said, lighting up another cigarette. "Well, don't sit here and welcome them with a red carpet. It's the other way around. They court us. They wait for us. Not us for them," she explained. "Please, Mummy, it makes me look bad. Just go back to your room and play with that miserable rat of yours."

Perla held up her hand in a gesture of horrified outrage, "I wish you wouldn't say that. Regina is a wonderful creature! She's part of the family. Your family, the one you hardly visit, mention, or acknowledge for that matter," she cast a reproachful glance at her daughter. "Now, if you gave her a chance, you'd see what an intelligent cat she is. Did you know she likes to watch the shopping channel, and whenever there's a makeup promotion for one of the lines you endorse, she meows to alert me? She follows your career with such interest that it can only be evidence of her affection for you. Regina is as much part of our household as Gino is," she added, gently lifting her coif with the tips of her long fingernails.

Athena shook her head, "Great. Not only am I related to a hairless cat who likes to watch the shopping channel, but I'm also a relative of a comb-happy Italian hairstylist. What's next? You're going to adopt a couple of orphans? Wait! Actually, that's not a bad idea," she paused and puffed on her long cigarette. "I've been thinking that I should adopt a few kids this year. Everyone's doing it. Don't you think it would be good for my image?"

"Sure," huffed Perla. "You can't even stand a cat, so the next logical step is to adopt a few children."

Athena rolled her eyes and exhaled a bluish cloud of smoke through her perfectly shaped nose. "Have you seen your cat lately? I swear it could be a close relative of the Grim Reaper. I bet it's feeding on human brains as we speak."

\* \* \*

As much as Regina would have liked to feed on human brains, at the exact moment Athena was describing the cat, a pair of cautious feet stopped in front of the door to Perla's suite as a dexterous pair of hands gently fiddled around with the lock. A loud moan came inside the apartment, the kind that dying patients of fatal outbreaks give in movies just before they succumb to bleeding out of every orifice as part of a horrible death.

Iris, who didn't scare easily, leaped backward straight into the Venetian mirror hanging on the wall. Luckily for Iris, who had been known to be a little superstitious, the mirror did not fall. What on Earth was that creature? And why didn't the client mention the small detail of a werewolf accompanying his mother on the trip? Denis had told her about Gino, the hairdresser— not to be confused with Perla's secret lover—but he said nothing about a growling creature guarding the room.

 She dusted off her white linen dress, a souvenir her father had brought back from Greece. Too bad he hadn't been assigned to Portugal, she thought, wondering in what way diplomatic clearance would have made her investigation easier. It probably wouldn't have solved her breaking and entering problem, and it wouldn't have taken care of the Hound of Baskerville crying out behind the door.

Judging that enough time had gone by for Perla to return at any minute, she cut her losses and proceeded with plan B: sending Armin to the lobby to keep guard for new faces, especially of the tall, dark, and handsome persuasion. A woman of Perla's age would not sneak around like a teenager to meet her lover in a cockroach-infested motel. She would want him close, in the comfort of her own hotel, where she could turn him on and off like a bubble bath and keep an eye on him so that he doesn't spill over into the neighbours suite.

As she was texting Armin with the new orders, proving there was something to be said about modern technology, even if one preferred to lead an investigation the old-fashioned way, the door closest to Perla's suite opened, revealing a tall, dark, and well-gelled man dressed in a white scrub. Without much consideration, the man ran to Perla's door and having gained momentum, kicked it. From where she stood, Iris observed his pain-driven howls and reflected that he might have made a decent soccer player but not much of a rugby player.

"Bloody hell, Regina! Stop it!" A soothing, if brief, moment of silence preceded a growl more ferocious than any leading up to it. The man resumed his kicking position, looked down at his slipper, and thumped over the carpet in sheer frustration. "You wretched, rabid, fowl bundle of hideous flesh! I'm gonna break your wrinkled little neck." The volume of the next meow seemed to take the exchange over the boundaries of civilized dialogue. In fact, Iris was sure the creature was swearing at him.

"Some day! Some day, Regina, you will pay for your ... arrogance. You'll end up as someone's meal. Just you wait!"

Iris quickly turned away when she saw him limping back to his room. She pretended to use the phone, concealing her face behind her hair. But the man had already taken notice of her.

"The cat must be in heat. It's been going on for half an hour," he said.

You'd think, thought Iris, smiling at the man who knew the cat's name. Could this be him? He certainly fit the part, with the shiny dark hair and the white gigolo ensemble. "I heard it, but I confess I assumed it was a crying baby," she said.

"No, no crying babies here. Just an ugly, hairless cat," he explained, smiling and leaning casually against the wall. "Is your suite close by?" he inquired.

"Mine? Oh no, I got off at the wrong floor, Doctor . . ."

His brow furrowed briefly. "Gino," he put out his hand. "Doctor Gino, at your disposal, Miss . . ."

"Oh," she said, dropping her phone back in her purse. Denis had mentioned him. So this was the hairdresser, she thought, sizing him up. "Just call me Iris, Doctor Gino."

"Lovely name. It suits your hair colour."

"Is that your cat in there?" Iris asked.

"Oh no, God forbid! It belongs to my . . . patient."

"You're traveling with your patient?" she marvelled, making an effort to keep a straight face. "I don't mean to pry, but that is so kind of you Doctor Gino. I find most medical practitioners nowadays don't care for their patients outside working hours."

"What can I say? I'm an old-fashioned man," Doctor Gino said modestly.

"Is your patient very ill?"

"Not very. Her condition is more of a psychological nature."

"So you're a psychiatrist then? How exciting! Our very own Freud."

"I do work with the human head," he said, smiling.

Iris raised an eyebrow, thinking that to say hairstylists and shrinks work with the same medium, namely the head, is to compare the Queen of England with a Ukrainian folk dancer because they both wear crowns.

"Fascinating!" she said, pressing the button to the lift. "Will you be staying for a while, Doctor?"

"It all depends on my patient, you see. I'm not sure how long she plans on staying."

"Well, I'm sure you and I shall run into each other again," Iris said as the elevator door opened.

"It was a pleasure meeting you, Iris. Perhaps you and I may have a drink together."

"Of course Doctor Gino. I know where you're staying," she smiled as the doors between them closed.

But I don't know where you're staying, Gino thought after she disappeared behind the doors to the elevator. Lovely young woman! Way out of his league, he thought, but not out of Doctor Gino's. Doctors could get any women they desired just because they owned a nicely framed piece of paper saying they were able to memorize the Latin name of body parts and their corresponding chemicals. What did women like about that? Perhaps being in school for so many years showed commitment on their part. The money was good, and they were mostly gone. Yes, if he were a woman, Gino would have married a doctor too. But would he have slept with a doctor? Forgetting to limp, he smoothed the wrinkles on his white hairdressing scrub and walked back to his room with a hopeful spring of the step. This Portuguese trip might turn out not to have been a complete waste after all.

The elevator bell disturbed his thoughts, and he turned around, smiling, to see if the redhead changed her mind about having that drink.

When the elevator doors opened, Perla was pleasantly surprised, "Oh Gino, you're out here," she said, trilling the last word. "Good! I want you to have another look at my hair and make sure it looks fabulous."

"Of course Mrs Galanis," he said, as they entered Perla's room. He got his comb out of his pocket for the fifth time that afternoon. "Are you expecting company?"

A swarm of butterflies circled in the pit of her stomach, thinking about what Leborio had confided to her before she left for Portugal. According to his story, the blue-blooded Costa Rican was very likely the only son of an ambassador to have ever become a guru. She'd always known there had to be more to Leborio than met the eye—even though no one could dispute that what did meet the eye was indeed very pleasing—and his noble origins confirmed she had the sharp instinct of one who has met her soul mate. And what a soul mate! Leborio Borzelini, a man like none other. Well, perhaps a little like the Knight Templar from the romance novel she was reading. Real men, she reflected, scoffing at the thought of boring old George.

Although she was dying to share her secret with a human soul (Regina had known for a long time), she had promised Leborio to keep his secret. Besides, she didn't completely trust Gino after being unable to find the town he said he was from on a map of Italy. She found Milan, Rome, Florence, but Teheran was not anywhere in sight.

"I'm giving an interview about my daughter to the Biography Channel. The reporters are on their way, and I want to look my best," she explained.

"That's wonderful, Mrs Galanis. You must be so proud of your daughter!"

Still wounded by Athena's comments about the cat, Perla didn't reply. Her daughter could be such an insensitive woman, she thought. It was almost as if the only thing she cared about was her looks. She wondered where on Earth she got that from. She and George were not vain people.

Perla sat in front of the mirror, watching Gino inflate her hairdo by another inch with his tight comb. Not too bad, she thought, focusing on the contrast between the platinum blond hairdo and the caramel skin shade she sported courtesy of the tanning enhancer kit. She looked the part of the movie star's mother, and even that of the politician's wife, provided the politician was of the liberal kind.

# CHAPTER 16

# ENTOURAGE

O h, look—that man looking this way is holding up a sign with your name on it," pointed out Snejana, who was the first one to come out of the arrival gate and was hauling Leborio's sports bag with one hand, clasping a butterfly-shaped handbag with the other.

"Indeed he is," remarked Leborio, visibly pleased. "He probably recognizes me."

Umberto covered a snort. "From where? The Lido Pool and Spa?"

Leborio shot him a frosty glance and pulled out his gold-plated pen from his shirt pocket. "People know of me, you know," he said, as he herded his entourage toward the short and sturdy driver with both of his magnificent arms wide open.

"I believe you've been expecting me," Leborio said, extending one of his bracelet-adorned hands for a shake. "I am Leborio Borzelini."

"*Muito prazer, signõr*. I never would have thought," the man said, picking up a suitcase.

"And why is that?"

"I was told I would pick up only one passenger," he said, looking first at the others and then back to Leborio.

"You mean to say you were only given the name of one passenger. That is my name. I like to travel with an entourage."

"No problem, *signor*. My car is big," said the driver amiably.

As Snejana and Kim helped the driver place Leborio's luggage in the trunk, the guru put his gold-plated pen away and sat his convex—and quite sweaty—behind by a window seat, magnanimously showing his cousin into the other.

"Big Bird, why don't you go sit with the driver so Kim can fit onto the other bench?"

With a forlorn look on her face, Snejana obeyed. Umberto checked to see that the partition glass was up, and then shook his head, "Why do you treat her so badly? She's a human being, not a dog."

"And so she is, brother," Leborio cracked open a bottle of water from the limo bar. He gulped down more than half of it before stretching back into his comfortable seat. "Women are sweeter when kept under control," he went on, in a neutral, textbook tone. "Like children, they will push boundaries to test you. If I allowed her to feel in control, she would never forget the sweet taste of power and always try her hand at it. The world has seen enough of liberated women, who are as callous and as harsh as sandpaper. I'm really doing poor old Big Bird a favour. Besides, we're making the driver happy," he added with a wink. "He gets to peek at Sne's legs instead of Kim's sweat stains."

"Sure you want me to sit here, boss?" asked Kim pulling himself into the limousine.

Umberto rolled his eyes again, his face locked into a half-bent grimace. Why did he even come? He supposed he came out of curiosity and because it was the Christian thing to do, given the way Leborio treated the poor girl. Yet it never ceased to amaze him how he invariably ended up next to the one person he loved least. He couldn't wait to get to the hotel and get away from his cousin and his poisonous reasoning. He understood God made people like him for the same purpose he made darkness: to make the light shine brighter. How could one become confused about taking the right path when Leborio's was so clearly wrong? Yes, God made Leborio to show Umberto his own righteous path. Yet, why did he allow innocent creatures like Snejana to be the victims of this darkness? He suspected premarital sex had something to do with it. But there were various degrees of sinning, and it was plain to see that, despite not being very bright, Snejana did not deserve the sort of evil Leborio had to offer.

Over the years, Umberto spent many nights tossing and turning, trying to find a reasonable explanation for Leborio's nature, for his being able to get away unscathed from every cruel act he committed, and for his very existence. But there was nothing rational about it. In fact, he had gradually come to believe there was something mathematically wrong with the system behind his religion. This very thought caused him to cross himself in shame, as he did on that first afternoon in Portugal. Through the tinted windows of the limo, he looked up at the cottony white clouds and asked the same old question. How could God and Leborio coexist in the same universe? Then, bringing his first three fingers together, Umberto touched his forehead, his chest, and his shoulders.

Snejana sniffled as she dried her large eyes in the rear-view mirror. Perhaps it wasn't so bad sitting at the front of the limo, she thought, shifting her long legs around in the passenger side and leaning her butterfly-shaped purse against the airbag envelope. The driver seemed like a nice man, smiling at her at every stoplight and shifting gears with the grace of an artist applying brushstrokes on his canvas.

"My name is Alfonso," he said, wiping his forehead with a tissue. He didn't speak much English, but then again, neither did she.

It took her less than five minutes to arrive to the conclusion that dear Leborio had probably been generous to let her sit at the front where she could see the beautiful city of Lisbon without the inconvenience of tinted glass.

The city looked wonderful, like the sort of city she could live in. She kept count of the nail parlours, and there were at least half a dozen she could visit. Once they settled in, she would definitely get her nails done. Or maybe she would wait and see who Leborio's mysterious benefactor was. It had to be a woman. She was sure of it. Would this woman be beautiful? And would her nails be manicured?

Behind the tinted glass, Leborio's black eyes stared into the sun. He watched it disappear behind the exuberant Manueline cathedrals and reappear from behind Moorish villas made of rammed earth and adobe clay. They drove by a labyrinth of narrow streets and tiny squares. Layered staircases marked the seven hills of the city, connecting the dots that led up to the Roman walls of a castle that looked like a fortress. Every once in a while, Leborio caught a glimpse of the ocean peeking out from behind Lisbon's red rooftops.

Scratching his head—the second most impressive search engine after Google—the grand spiritual master recalled this was the city from whence explorers had set out to conquer new worlds, carrying the gold of the old world aboard their ships. This was the city where civilizations collided over a span of thousands of years. Okay, so it wasn't Constantinople, but by god, it was Lisbon! And he was in it. How good it was to be alive driving toward one's destiny.

He'd always known his destiny could not possibly have waited for him in the city he came from, a city where great beauty could only be found among what was left of the past, struggling not to drown amidst the sea of grotesque and kitsch brought on by the winds of change. He had never belonged to the backward civilization he had been born into. Not to the Lido, not to the Neon Lounge, not to the Cave. Well, perhaps a little to the Cave. But his life, his real life, was meant to begin in a place like Paris, Chicago, Barcelona, or Lisbon—

cities whose mere names carried the intrinsic energy of importance.

The limousine passed a street corner where a marble statue of Vasco da Gama stood, glistening in the sun like a giant diamond. Leborio stared up at it and then closed his eyes in silence.

"You all right there, chief?" Kim asked, gently nudging Leborio's knee.

"Keep still," whispered Leborio. "I am picturing my future."

"What does the future look like?" asked Umberto under his breath.

"Like Vasco da Gama," answered Leborio mechanically.

In the depth of his trance, the Spanish guru beheld the image of the Portuguese explorer with his mind's eye—white, flawless, and majestic. Locked to memory forever, Vasco da Gama's statue was swiftly decapitated and given a new head: that of Leborio Borzelini. Next, the guru's higher self inspected the outcome, dissatisfied. There was still something missing. Perhaps the guru's leather pants? Nah, that couldn't have been it, he decided, after picturing the explorer scorching in black, skin-tight trousers. Something else. Something more distinctively Leborio. Oh, yes. Off came the arms and in their place a magnificent pair of well-toned pipes stood out from the voyager's robes. Vasco turned a few times in a slow-motion pirouette, allowing the guru to admire the upgrades. Leborio smiled, pleased with the outcome.

"You're cutting his head off, aren't you?" interrupted Umberto.

"Quiet!" hushed the giant. "The boss is meditating."

"He's not my boss, and he is not yours either, so stop calling him that," Umberto curled his lip. "He couldn't meditate if his life depended on it. What he usually does is cut the heads off people who were important enough to have a statue erected to their memory and replace them with his own. It's part of his great plan for world domination through visualization," he added, turning away to look out the window.

"Huh?"

Immune to the mayhem around him, Leborio chiselled away with the great concentration worthy of a spiritual teacher. Moments later, the car stopped, and the driver opened the door and held it out for Leborio.

"We are here, *signor*. Have a pleasant stay."

And without further ceremony, he placed the luggage at the door of the Hotel Almeida, got back behind the wheel of the limousine, and drove away into the sun. Before Leborio's three companions could take the initiative to pick up the luggage, a bright-eyed Portuguese bellboy teleported himself and the suitcases to the front desk. For a brief moment, Umberto's half smile became whole.

"What are you smiling about?" asked Kim.

"Clearly, the bellboy did not know what the limousine driver did: Leborio Borzelini tips no one," he whispered, walking through the door.

"This, my friends, is the definition of good taste," declared Leborio as he entered the lobby of the hotel. "Now let us find whoever is in charge of this magnificent place."

"Why?" Umberto snorted to hide his laughter. "Do you want to mentally decapitate them too?"

"And why not, brother, if it can get me to own a place like this?"

Leborio did not like to walk around the lobbies of expensive hotels without a purpose. It made him feel a little like walking into Prada dressed in street clothes. He scanned his surroundings as quickly as possible and decided that the closest thing to an owner was the pompous-looking receptionist sporting a Valentino suit. Followed by cousin Umberto Bore, the girl who looked like an ostrich, and the cross-eyed giant, Leborio walked right up to him as if he'd been expected.

"Good day. I am Leborio Borzelini."

Looking over his silver spectacles, the man in the Valentino suit stared down from his gilded counter. Leborio repeated his name, pausing for effect. With the tip of his finger, the receptionist pushed the silver frames back on his nose, continuing to inspect Leborio with the amiable expression of someone who'd been sucking on lemons for a very long time.

"And that is very nice for you," he said, looking at the monitor behind the front desk.

"Are you not expecting me?"

"No. Are you here to fix the penthouse toilet?"

"I am a guest of a guest, you see," explained Leborio, patiently. "I believe someone of great importance has reserved a room in my name."

"Of course you are," said the receptionist with a little smile. "Perhaps if you give me a more detailed description of our illustrious guest, I could see about your reservation. What is the lady's name?"

You smug little vermin, thought Leborio, smiling back at the Valentino. You think you've got me all figured out, don't you? I'm going to get to my room, enjoy my stay, and meet my destiny. And once I do, I will teach stiff-nosed bastards like you a thing or two about manners. The spiritual master took a deep breath before he spoke again. "I'm afraid I couldn't say. It was an anonymous invitation."

"Well, what do you know? I happen to have an anonymous reservation made out to an anonymous guest. A single guest," stressed out the receptionist staring back at the guru's entourage. "Will the rest of your party need accommodations?"

Leborio was going to argue that they could all fit in one suite, but something in the way the receptionist was sizing up Kim told him all attempts would be futile. He nodded his head, certain his benefactor would understand the need for a second suite and gladly pick up the bill.

"Very good, sir. Here is a card for a respectable motel on the outskirts of Lisbon. Your friends should have no problem finding vacancy there."

"My friends are staying here, with me," Leborio started raising his voice. "Unless you'd like to explain to our anonymous, illustrious guest why my friends and I turned around and returned to where we came from."

The Valentino seemed to weigh his options quietly. Like a gray little mouse in front of the cheese trap, he flirted with disaster for but a brief moment. Once the moment passed, he put out his delicate hand and revealed a key card. Leborio pocketed the card unapologetically and walked up to the elevator followed by his entourage and a slightly confused bellboy.

It wasn't until they arrived at the door that Snejana made a very obvious observation. "There's only one key card. Does that mean we're all crashing here?"

Leborio swiped the card and shrugged. It was a large suite, decorated with Murano stained glass and Venetian mirrors framed by brocades of Chinese silk. There were two beds, standing side by side on long, wrought iron legs; a reclining sofa made out of embroidered velvet; and a matching loveseat by the door to the balcony. The apartment was fit to be a playground to the gods.

"Boss, you gotta come out here and see this," yelled Kim from the veranda. "It's the most beautiful thing I have ever seen."

Unaware that "thing" stood for the view, a small infinity pool, and a sun shower worthy of the Caribbean, Leborio refused to be distracted.

"Big Bird, give me a hand, will you?" he called out to Snejana, who was struggling to hoist a suitcase onto the luggage rack. The girl dropped the suitcase right away and walked over to him. With the corner of his eye, Leborio could see his cousin shaking his head in disapproval. He raised his voice enough to make himself heard by Umberto, "I want to lift one of the beds and hang it over the other," he said, carelessly pulling off the flawless bed sheets and tossing the mattress on the ground.

Standing with her hands on her hips, Snejana stared at him with a blank expression.

"I don't understand," said the girl, as he unscrewed the wooden spheres decorating the bedposts on the other bed, revealing four large metal screws.

"It's simple," Leborio rolled his eyes. "Help me pick up this bed and place it over the other. I want to make bunk beds."

He counted down from five in his head, and on the fifth beat, Leborio watched his cousin jump to Snejana's rescue. They hoisted the wooden frame up to their waists and matched the bedposts on all four corners. Then, leaving Snejana and Umberto to balance the bed frame, he pushed his weight on each corner, impaling the bedposts on the upper bed over the metal screws of the lower one.

"And this is actually one time the big guy would've come in handy," Umberto muttered while giving the girl a hand putting the bed sheets back on. "It figures Ferdinand is out on the veranda, smelling roses."

"You've made bunk beds!" a very surprised Kim blurted when he entered the room.

"And you've made nothing," noted Umberto.

"What are they for, boss?"

Climbing aboard the top bunk, Leborio took a moment to consider the question before answering. "For fun."

## • CHAPTER 17 •

# LUST IN LISBON

Sometime the next morning, Umberto Bore woke up to complete and utter darkness. Not the shadowy obscurity of night, when the human eye accustoms itself to see the shapes of objects surrounding it under the dimmed lights of the stars. But rather the thick, dark nothingness that makes up the visual world of a totally blind man. He rubbed his eyes repeatedly, hoping he could blame it on lingering sleep or on two giant eye cookies. But there were no eye cookies, and if there were, they were pretty average in size.

Lying flat on his back, Umberto had a hard time remembering where he was and suddenly panicked. He stretched out his arms and touched the silky covers of the bed, the smooth corners of the pillows, and the hairy surface of a man's back. He gasped in horror, pondering for a moment the possibility of having slept through Judgment Day only to wake up straight in hell. There must be some kind of mistake, thought Umberto.

"It's Leborio. He's the one you're looking for," he screamed to the hairy fella next to him, whom he took to be the angel of death.

"Shut your friggin' trap, you blistering moron!" the angel of death replied. "Don't make me smack you."

A level higher, the grand spiritual master opened his eyes to a beautiful summer morning. An early breeze parted the curtains for a moment, letting the sun shine its way into the room. Next to him, a very happy Snejana had been staring at him patiently.

"Good morning, sunshine," she kissed him.

"Indeed it is." he sat up and looked about the lavish room. "Now, this is how I ought to wake up every day."

"Next to me?"

"No. In an expensive-looking room."

The girl pouted. She moved her head away, leaving a red mark on the bulge of his bicep. Leborio rubbed his arm gently, inspecting it on both sides. He wanted to stretch across the bed but had a feeling Snejana might start to cry if he asked her to get lost. Instead, he dropped his weight over her and stretched until he heard her bones crack.

"Did you hear something?" he asked.

"Yes," she groaned. "My ribcage popped."

"Not that," whispered Leborio. "It sounded like the faint scream of a man. A few doors down perhaps."

"It was your cousin, I think."

"Umberto? Where is he?" the guru inquired.

"In there," she pointed, showing Leborio the wooden cube under their mattress. "Our bunk collapsed over theirs. And now they're stuck."

Leborio scratched his head and took another concerned look at his magnificent arms, which, by now, had regained their coloration. He wasn't about to strain himself and lift the top bunk off, and he doubted Snejana was strong enough of a woman. No. It had to be an inside job. Literally.

"They'll figure something out," he said, pulling the girl's hand on his way to take a morning shower.

Umberto, who had figured the angel of death sounded an awful lot like a certain cross-eyed giant, felt his surroundings with the tips of his fingers. It appeared they were enclosed in wood, tightly shut by at least two wrought iron bedposts, which, in the fall, had impaled the surface of the upper case.

"Wake up, Kim. We're trapped."

"No. You shut *your* trap."

"Or else you're gonna smack me," he said, bracing for impact. "Yes, yes, I know that. But we're still trapped. And we might be in danger of suffocation."

"Suffocation you say?" The giant reached over with the intention of wringing Umberto's neck just enough to shut him up or make him pass out, whichever came first.

Umberto kicked his feet up in the air like an unwilling lass. "No, no, no. Stop it! Do you really want to end up dead? Because that's exactly what's going to happen if you don't get us out of here at once. First, the oxygen will get thin, causing our brains to shut down. Then, we'll stop breathing altogether, taking this unfamiliar darkness with us as our last living image. Is that what you want? To be suffocated between two Portuguese hotel beds, like a giant sandwich?" Assuming the silence to be a vehement shake of the head, Umberto pushed it into the imperative. "Of course not. Now give me a hand to lift this bloody sarcophagus off."

Umberto grunted with all his might, pushing up onto the wooden ceiling. But the impaled top bunk didn't even move. "Well, give me a hand, will ya?"

The giant yawned, rubbed his eyes, and arching his hairy back once, popped out of the wooden enclosure like an oversized Jack-in-a-box. Pieces of wood fell to the floor, setting up an indefinite perimeter around the two men.

Cowering behind a broken headboard, Umberto was praying ardently for his immortal soul and even more ardently for his bodily safety. Curiously, to Umberto, the integrity of his body was tightly linked to administering retribution onto his wayward cousin. There was still much that needed to be done in the way of divine justice, and one could not quite picture doing it without an eye or leg or with a broken nose. Especially not the kind of justice he had in mind. After all, getting even with the Spanish guru for stealing his childhood sweetheart, ruining his chance at happiness, and generally being a jerk was no easy task when the things Leborio cared about, aside from money, were so few and far between. His cousin could only nominally think of one. But a fella would need nothing short of divine intervention to take her away from Leborio.

While Umberto prayed, Kim emerged out of the rubble, holding the weight of a king size mattress on his shoulders with the reassuring grace of Atlas. The giant spat out one of the screws where the decorative spheres of the original bedposts had been placed, and displeased with the rusty aftertaste, wiped his mouth with the back of his hand.

"Where's the boss? I'm hungry," he said, scratching his family jewels with the same hand.

"And you can't eat without him?"

The hairy Atlas considered the question, and, setting the mattress down, reached for a pair of brown leather sandals. He fastened them on and without a care for his grooming and stepped out in search for breakfast. He remembered about his pants just as the doors to the elevator parted, revealing a lobby full of sharply dressed men holding up cameras.

* * *

Snejana came out of the steamy bathroom, wearing no more than a white towel. Her uncombed hair was dripping, leaving small puddles across the floor. The sound of her wet feet flopping over the cold marble caused Umberto, who had collapsed on top of the mattress on the floor shortly after he finished his prayer, to open a curious eye. The towel dropped to the ground as she opened her suitcase, looking for a bra. In a sheer state of panic, the Lord's true subject ducked behind the broken headboard, panting like a steam engine.

"Hmm-hmm." Umberto cleared his throat.

"Oh, hey," she said, casually pulling a shirt over her head. "Didn't see you through all that rubble. How did you two get out?"

"Kim . . . he penetrated through . . . through the box."

"Leborio thought he would," she laughed, flipping her head upside down to dry her hair. "He's so clever, isn't he?"

"Kim clever?"

"No, silly. Your cousin. He is the smartest man I've ever met. Smarter than me, that's for sure!"

"You don't say."

Snejana fell back onto the loveseat, staring at the ceiling. The fresh smell of herbal shampoo carried off into the room, and tips of her wet hair brushed against the floor, as she drew lazy circles around her belly button with a long-nailed finger. Umberto swallowed with great difficulty, and stood up, forgetting about his prayer.

"I'm thinking of learning Spanish," she went on. "I find myself fascinated with everything Spanish. The music, the art, the passion. Especially the passion," she said, dipping a red fingernail into the small push button at the base of her belly. Umberto's eyes opened wide, as his breathing picked up frequency.

"Are you all right?" she gave him a concerned look.

Still hyperventilating, he turned the other way and reached for a small bottle of water from the minibar. "It's the bloody heat," he explained. "Even with the air conditioning, I can hardly breathe."

"That's why I'm only wearing the essentials," she said, hooking her index finger into the elastic band of her underwear and slinging it back with a loud slap. Umberto guzzled the water wondering how flexible one had to be to fit entirely into the minibar fridge. He could use a very cold shower, once the guru was done with the bathroom.

"It is quite possibly the sexiest language," Snejana went on, clearing out invisible lint from the same belly button. "Maybe Leborio can teach me. What do you think?"

"I think if there is a person who can teach others something he hasn't got the slightest clue about, that surely is my cousin."

She considered the reply for a moment and asked, "Have you known Leborio for a long time? I bet you have. You seem to speak like him sometimes."

"He's my cousin," said Umberto, in response to the verbal equivalent of a cold shower. "So, yes, I've known him all his life. But we are nothing alike. And we certainly don't speak like each other."

"Well, yes. I suppose he's got that Spanish streak about him."

The older cousin shook his head, "He's got nothing Spanish about him," he said. "Not one bone. Nothing. Nada."

The girl sat up, her eyes wide. "But surely, he is a Spanish guru. Why would he be a Spanish guru if he didn't know Spanish? I even heard him speak it. Why, just the other day he was talking about you and called you *cousin* in Spanish."

"Cousin in Spanish?"

"Yes. *Cabron.*"

Umberto shook his head, while Snejana pressed on, "How would he know that if he didn't speak Spanish?"

"He knows a few words here and there. When we were kids, we played with our Spanish neighbour. Well, not really," he corrected himself. "From Costa Rica but spoke Spanish nonetheless. So we learned a few phrases, mostly swear words and profanity," he said, crossing himself.

"Costa Rica?" she repeated excitedly. "Did you know Leborio

comes from Costa Rica?"

"Does he now?"

"Yes, yes!" she sat up and cautiously lowered her voice, "Not many people know this, so you can't say anything," she warned. "But Leborio is actually the son of the Costa Rican ambassador."

"Really?" Umberto raised his brow. "The ambassador of Costa Rica. And here I thought my mother's brother was a no-good gambler who abandoned his family for a gypsy woman."

"No, no, no." She shook her head with vehemence. "You've got it all wrong."

"Yes, I see. My uncle must have been undercover the whole time. Losing the house in a gambling debt and running off with a younger woman must have all been part of his cover. Especially the part where my folks took him in and then helped set up little Leborio and his mom with a roof over their heads. A small, but functional apartment in a fairly central area of the city. A place we now refer to as the Cave."

She nodded.

* * *

"Holy shit," muttered the giant, covering his crumpled happy face boxers with hands the size of snow shovels. Who were they, and how did they know he would be coming out in his underwear? He braced himself for the impact of over thirty camera flashes and thought about what his mother would say.

But nothing happened. The men put their cameras down, sighed in disappointment, and resumed their conversations. The giant tapped his little finger on the Close Door button until the doors were shut, and using the other hand, he scratched the happiest of faces on his boxer shorts. That was close, he exhaled, watching the buttons light up from floor to floor. *Ding*, the doors opened yet again before the fourth floor, revealing a slender woman with cascading dark hair and stunning blue eyes. The woman got by Kim and pressed the lobby button. She did not seem to notice him. Kim stared with his mouth hanging and missed his fourth floor stop, inexplicably drawn to her luscious long hair. He'd seen her somewhere before. Maybe at the Neon Lounge? Though a woman that beautiful would have had to be the boss' mistress, he reflected.

"Mind moving farther back?" she spoke without turning. "It won't be good for my image to be in pictures with a half-naked giant."

The doors opened into the lobby once again, this time to a blinding sequence of camera flashes. Kim prudishly covered the front of his boxers with his hands again and watched the woman float with absentminded grace between microphones and recording devices. Yes, he had seen her before, and yes, at Neon Lounge. She was the face at the centre of the Hollywood-themed upper-floor jazz room.

\* \* \*

The passageway cut through the limestone just where the hieroglyphics ended. It was narrow and dark, and the man could barely breathe. Delicate drips of sweat trickled artistically around his forehead and down his rugged neck. With one swift motion, he took off his sword and armour and crawled through the opening bare-chested. Brushing his sweaty torso against the coarseness of the stone, the man pushed through slowly and persistently. He could see a soft light glimmer at the end of the tunnel, and he could hear her gentle cries for help. At last, he pierced through the tapered burrow and into the burial chamber.

Amongst statues of past pharaohs and right next to the emerald-encrusted tomb where the depiction of a balding man with a moustache marked the centrepiece of the room, a firm-bodied woman with hair and skin of gold lay spread across the four corners of an embalming table, pinned by the arms and legs with shreds of silk.

"Madam, allow me to untie you." He bolted to her side, pulling a big dagger out of his leather trousers. With the back of his large, dirty hand, he gently wiped her tears of fear and sat her up like a doll. "Who would do such a thing to one so exquisitely beautiful?" he muttered in chivalrous anger. Her strength had left her while waiting to be rescued, so she pointed to the emerald tomb just before fainting.

"I will avenge you, my lady!" he thundered, just before beheading the statue of the balding man with the moustache. He picked her up ever so gently, engulfing her in his muscular arms, and he carried her outside to his white horse.

"Who are you?" she whispered, bewitched by his strength.

"I am your friendly neighbourhood knight templar, my lady. And the son of the Costa Rican ambassador—although I have told no one of it. No one but you. And I am at your complete service."

"Can you take me far away from this tomb?" she cried, covering her eyes with the back of her hand in true damsel-in-distress fashion. "My husband was going to bury me alive with him."

"Was your husband a Siva Hindu?"

"No. But he very much appreciated the Taj Mahal," she explained.

"Oh, you poor, angelic creature! How could anyone bury such beauty? Come back with me to my land, and I will protect you with my own life, while making passionate love to you and working out all day long to maintain my rugged good looks."

Unbeknownst to her, the mother of the movie star let out a small whimper in her sleep, causing Regina to rotate her pink hairless ears for a nocturnal check. Well, almost nocturnal. Heavy curtains guarded the morning sun from disturbing the beauty sleep of Regina's mistress. Planning her escape from under the clammy armpit of the woman, the cat glanced in the general direction of the nightstand and immediately wished for reduced night vision skills. Something about the cover depicting a muscular, dark-haired man wearing a half-revealing crusader get-up while carrying a platinum blond beauty clad in equally revealing garments made the cat think of lumpy custard. And she hated lumpy custard.

* * *

"Boss! Boss! You won't believe who I just ran into."

"Don't tell me. Let me guess—our breakfast?"

"Better. I ran into an angel."

"Then you should probably be speaking to Umberto," shrugged Leborio as he pulled on a pair of silk embroidered socks.

"No, no. You don't understand. Not a real angel," explained Kim, rubbing his eyes. "I just shared an elevator ride with the most beautiful woman in the world."

"Beauty, my friend, is such a subjective issue," the grand spiritual master sighed, "that one may very seldom declare it absolute. Not every woman is . . .," he thought of an incontestable beauty, "Athena Jeudi."

"Except for Athena Jeudi," blinked the giant. "And she's here, in our hotel. Look, I got her lipstick!"

"How did you get her lipstick?" asked Umberto from behind the bunk rubble.

But no one else seemed to care how he got it, only that he did. Moments later, eclipsed by a large contingent of journalists and paparazzi, Leborio watched the actress sign autographs despite the frantic efforts of the receptionist to remove the media from the hotel lobby.

"Out gentlemen, out!" urged the man in the Valentino suit. "The lady is a guest here. It is forbidden to take photos on the premises of the Hotel Almeida. The police are on their way," he threatened, waving his arms in the air. "Please get out. Now!"

With the coolness of a refrigerator, Athena flicked her hair over her shoulder and pouted for the cameras. She turned her back at the men, revealing two spaghetti straps that held up the dark and slippery fabric over her translucent skin. Then, her head turned to the cameras, kicking off an eruption of flashes.

"You dropped this," he said. Dressed in a gray samurai tunic with black embroidered vines, he proudly held up her lipstick. His eyes simmered like two dark coals, fixing the woman with all their manly might. Athena barely touched his hand grabbing the lipstick, and looking right through him, turned to pose for the cameras.

"Hot damn!" whispered Leborio. "Now that is what I call a beautiful woman. Do you think she noticed me?" Leborio asked Kim. And without giving him a chance to answer, he decided, "She must have. She was just playing hard to get. Women often do that. We have to pursue her, my friend," he smiled to the giant. "This woman is perfect for me. Did you see how well she photographs?"

# CHAPTER 18

# ARMIN PECTOR THE PROTECTOR

Iris gave Armin the signal to stop filming after she had listened to every cutesy-wootsy story about Athena's childhood. Perla told them about how Athena wanted to be a movie star from the moment she could talk, how she convinced her daddy to buy her a role in a children's movie, how she worked hard in front of the mirror to develop a wide range of facial expressions (Iris, who had seen a few of her movies, was only aware of one: the pout), and how her career had picked up after she changed her name, left the country, and seduced a Hollywood director. Iris had heard enough for one day. She could hardly wait to get to a phone and find out the results from the lab, which would take care of at least one of her professional commitments. Who would've thought finding the results of an expensive and complicated paternity test would turn out to be an easier task than catching a neglected housewife *in flagrante delicto*? This was not to say that Perla was innocent. The signs were all there: the ambitiously backcombed platinum hair, the over-tanned skin, the resplendent jewellery, and last but not least, the ever-searching eyes of a woman expecting someone. While Armin was busy packing the rented camera lights back into their cases, Iris decided to take her chances.

"Will you be staying in Portugal for a while, Mrs. Galanis?"

Caught off guard, Perla put on a big smile and shrugged her shoulders in an effort to appear nonchalant.

"Anything is possible when a mother visits her daughter. I might prolong my stay to keep Athena company if she wants me to. After all, Portugal is a wonderful place to spend some time in, don't you think? And the sun does wonders for my joints—not that I need it yet. I'm not that much older than you," she added, batting her faux eyelashes. "But we women must always pay attention to our bodies. They are the greatest gift we are granted in this life."

"If that were true, it would be a very sad life," noted Iris pensively. "To know one's body will eventually age, shrivel, and decay into a handful of dust is not much of a gift at all."

"Everything ages, my dear. Our job is to put that off for as long as we can."

"Of course, some things are better with age."

"Yes, wine and scotch," replied the older woman.

"And the human mind," added Iris, closing her notepad. "While our bodies wrinkle and lose their firmness, our minds get better with experience. So in the end, wisdom must be the real gift bestowed on us."

Perla sat up from her armchair, gathered her belongings, and began bidding the two of them farewell. Here I go, thought Iris. I've done it again, trying to fix people instead of keeping one eye on the ball. Hoping it wasn't too late, Iris gave it one more try.

"I can't help but admire your commitment to staying fit. What is your secret, Mrs. Galanis?"

Lighting up from within, Perla began reciting a long list of home remedies and exotic products she had come across. She could swear by a number of shopping channel cosmetics. At the top of this list was the tan enhancer kit, something she secretly credited with Leborio's arrival into her life.

"Last but not least, you must remember to exercise," she advised the younger woman. "I do yoga at the Lido every day, religiously, and I have to say it keeps me young inside and out."

Bingo! thought Iris. She knew of only one thing that kept the heart young. Besides, Dennis had mentioned he suspected Perla's lover had to be somehow tied to the Lido hotel because she spent unreasonable amounts of time there.

"Do you have a good instructor? I've been thinking about taking up yoga myself."

The older woman sized her up with a suspicious eye. "He's called a guru," she said. "The yoga instructor is called a guru. My guru is in very high demand, so I'm afraid I won't be able to help you. It's been wonderful talking to you two," she added, smiling at Armin who smiled right back without a care in the world. "But now I have to get back to my suite."

"Perhaps we may be able to continue our chat tomorrow," suggested Iris, hoping to get a reaction rather than a favourable answer. "We could work another segment into our documentary that would focus on Athena's excellent genes and how her mother manages to keep as fresh as a peach. I'm sure many women would like to hear all about it."

"I'm afraid I already have plans for tomorrow. Another time, perhaps."

"Morning or afternoon?" insisted Iris. "Maybe we can work our interview around your plans."

Perla shook her head. "No, no. That won't be possible. My daughter is filming in Sintra tomorrow. We will be out of town."

With that, Perla retreated to her room in haste. For a while, she paced restlessly around the room. Then, she picked up the phone a few times only to place it back on the nightstand. Eventually, Perla gave in. She generously applied squirts of perfume to her neck from an ornate atomizer bottle, grabbed her handbag, covered her hair with a neck scarf, and put on a pair of sunglasses. She tiptoed to the door, listening to make sure there was complete silence in the hallway. With one swift twist of the wrist, Perla turned the doorknob, cracked the door ajar, and made for the lobby, heading directly for the reception area.

The lobby was empty now. Perla sat on a couch facing the restaurant. A few pretty maids seamlessly glided about the coffee tables, dusting them off and refreshing the newspaper supply. Their pastel uniforms covered their legs up to the knee. A little short, thought Perla, shooting disproving glances in their direction. She wondered if Leborio had noticed them and felt her stomach turn in anxiety. Perla looked about her cautiously and then walked up to the reception counter.

"Good day," she greeted the well-dressed receptionist.

The man gave her a starchy smile and abandoned the computer screen with a barely perceptible tilt of the head.

"Hello, madam."

Without taking off her sunglasses, Perla leaned into the counter.

"I have two rooms with you," she said confidently. "I'd like to make sure my check cleared for both."

The man's nostrils flared out for a moment, taking in the poignant musky smell of her perfume. Almost immediately, his nose wrinkled disapprovingly and he took a step back. He asked for her name, and, pushing the silver frame of his spectacles up with his finger, he typed something into the computer. Perla looked about her again, turning back just in time to see the receptionist nod with a bemused expression.

"Yes, madam. Your checks cleared," he said to her.

Perla smiled in an effort to appear pleased, and anxiously tapped her fingers on the reception counter, revealing a set of very shiny red fingernails. The man in the Valentino suit looked down his nose at the surface of the wood and then back at Perla again. Slowly, her hand retreated to the strap of her Hermes handbag.

"And that is for both rooms," she repeated, uncomfortably.

She thought she caught a glimpse of a faint smirk before he replied, "Yes, madam." Then, lowering his voice, he added graciously, "Both of your rooms are being inhabited at present."

Perla sighed in relief and placed a handsome tip on the counter before heading back to her room, almost skipping with joy.

* * *

Hauling the filming equipment back to their room, Armin followed Iris down the hallway as if in a trance. She had wedged a pencil through her hair, pulling it back into a loose flip, and he could see the outline of her neckline through the strands. It was as delicate as Chinese calligraphy and just as mysterious. How could someone so strong have such a fragile neck? He could break it in a split second with a single arm. And so could anyone else. Unless he protected her. What an intoxicating thought! Like a powerful drug, the image of his own strength protecting this weak-limbed woman as if she were a child spread through his bloodstream, rushing to places he had spent the last of his pubescent years learning to control.

Armin Pector never felt more like a man than at that very moment. Watching her move in front of him, unaware that he could break her tiny wrists with one swift motion, that he could pin her down and crush her under his throbbing body as if she were a ripened fruit, made him feel an irresistible urge to protect her. He would protect her, possess her, and make her belong to him. Yes, decided Armin, he would have her as soon as tonight! But in order for that to happen, she would have to like him. He remembered something she had said during the interview with Perla.

"I, too, believe in wisdom and its enduring quality," he heard himself say to her once they walked through the door to suite 112.

"Huh?"

"Wisdom," he repeated. "I think it's the only thing we have in this life. The only thing that can help us become *somebody*," he said, emphasizing the last word.

"*Somebody*?" repeated Iris, absentmindedly. "Do you mean somebody of consequence?"

"Yes," he went on with a candid grin. "I'd like to be somebody important. This is why I am focusing on my mind," he said, tapping a knuckle against his head. "Wisdom is where it's at. The old woman was wrong to care so much about the body," he added. The word *body* made him think of hers, and he found himself guessing how it looked under the blue dress she wore today.

"What do you know about wisdom, junior?" she laughed, bringing his fantasies to an abrupt end.

"I might be young," he started. "But I've had a hard life, a life many men would shy from. And I have always had an old soul. The soul of a man trapped in the body of a boy. But now I am a man," he said decisively, straightening up as he caught his own reflection in a large Venetian mirror. "Did you know that men have the responsibility to protect the weak? Real men know this. And this is part of wisdom," he continued, without being very sure of how his thoughts connected. "This you understand only when you achieve manhood."

"And who is this weak you speak of that your *manliness* obliges you to protect?" she emphasized the word. She let her hair down with one hand and stepped into the light of the veranda, running her fingers through the tangles.

"Women and children," he followed.

"Which one am I supposed to be?"

Her smile was meant to be sarcastic, and yet it made him melt. Both, he thought fighting the urge to lift her off her feet and carry her inside. Before he could think of anything witty to say, she took out her cell phone and shooed him away. "I have an important call to make. Why don't you go and get us a couple of drinks from the lobby bar?"

Iris waited a few moments after the door shut, and then she picked up the phone and called the medical clinic. A Portuguese-speaking secretary placed her on hold. Being placed on hold in Portugal was really not that different from being placed on hold anywhere else in the world. Elevator music was a universal choice for telephone directories. We really do live in a global village, she thought, feeling rather sad that the old days of appealing to a human being on the other end of the line had come close to an end. She remembered the days she would phone tech support to help her connect to the Internet.

Now, they had Web sites directing people through the phone options of various companies to avoid dealing with redundant automated machines. As for tech support, it had been outsourced. Who knew if the Portuguese-speaking secretary was even at the medical clinic? Perhaps she wasn't even in Portugal. Perhaps she was answering calls from a tiny cubicle in Sao Paolo, booking appointments for a doctor in Lisbon.

* * *

Thinking along the lines of outsourcing, Armin slipped a colourful bill to an enthusiastic bellboy with the aim of securing him the two colourful cocktails he intended to use as liquid foreplay to seduce Iris. Then, he walked out of the hotel and into the flower shop across the street. Nothing like flowers to say romance to a woman. Without as much as looking at the colourful arrangements around him, he picked up a large red rose bouquet and handed the little old lady at the front counter an equally large bill. She took it, offered young Romeo his change, and imperceptibly shook her head as he walked out.

Of course, Armin did not notice her disproval. He also didn't notice the most beautiful woman in the world was watching him from the shaded window of her suite. The gay guy, as Athena had come to refer to Armin, crossed the street holding up a huge red rose bouquet. Did gay people buy each other roses? It seemed a little funny to imagine a man buying another man a dozen roses. Perhaps tickets to a game or a couple's massage would have been more appropriate. Intrigued, the actress threw on a silk robe and decided to find out once and for all why the young man with the rose bouquet was immune to her charms.

"I carry them for you, sir," offered the bellboy, holding the rainbow-coloured cocktails at about the same angle Armin held the rose bouquet. The two young men took a silent elevator ride to the fourth floor, each reflecting on a hopeful future. With the corner of his eye, the bellboy peeked at the other young man and wondered how he had come to be so rich. His milky white skin suggested he lived in a country where sun exposure was not an issue, a place where nature had four seasons, none of them being Portuguese summer. Against the fairness of his skin, a dim set of dark brown eyes framed by long dark lashes gave him the dramatic look of an eighteenth-century romantic poet. The bellboy could see Armin's wallet sticking out of his back pocket and thought how easy it would be to perform a magic trick if it weren't for the two colourful cocktails tipping over in his hands. He liked the job he had at the Hotel Almeida and would have never risked losing it by going back to his previous trade. By the looks of his patron, stealing his wallet would have meant as little as removing a piece of lint from his D&G T-shirt.

This was probably right. Armin's thoughts were invested entirely into creating the best possible conditions for the conquest of Iris. Ever since he had met her he could think of nothing else but proving himself to her. He knew she was clever and cultured and puzzling, and if she were a man, he would've been jealous of her simply because she belonged to that secret club of people he could not understand, the club his father referred to as the "more intelligent than Armin" sort of people. But she wasn't a man, even though she reminded him of one he could not quite put his finger on. She was an auburn-haired, green eyed, small-limbed woman he felt an irresistible urge to hold close to his chest and marvel at her motor functions the way a child marvels at a doll's flexibility when stretching her arms and legs.

"I'll take it from here," he told the bellboy once they got to the door of the suite. The boy nodded gracefully and handed out the cocktails, taking one last look at Armin's back pocket. Smiling from ear to ear, Armin walked in, balancing two drinks and a dozen roses, only to find Iris on the phone.

"I've been on hold for the entire time you've been away," she lamented. "Oh, good, you've got the drinks. Bring me one will you?"

She took one sip of the rainbow-coloured drink and spit it back out. "What is this? Are you trying to poison me?"

"It's a drink. A colourful drink. That's what you asked for, isn't it?"

"I don't take alcohol, especially not during the day," she said, wiping her mouth with a tissue. "I'll have the odd glass of wine if I can't sleep, but wine comes from grapes, not from Windex-coloured spirits," she added, holding the glass up to the bedside lamp. "You'll never catch me drinking liquor, so please be a dear and return those for their nonalcoholic equivalent," Iris asked, as Armin dragged his feet back to the door with his head down. "I noticed you brought in roses," she called out, "And I'm afraid you'll have to take those back too. I'm allergic to roses, you see."

Wishing he hadn't sent the bellboy away, Armin closed the door behind him once again, leaving Iris to her phone inquiries. His first instinct was to toss the drinks in the garbage and top them off with fresh red roses. Upon further consideration, he decided to down the drinks and drag the roses all the way to the lobby bar of the Hotel Almeida, where he plopped them and the two empty cocktail glasses on the shiny black counter.

"Who are the roses for?" said a sultry female voice. He turned to meet the most sought-after face of the movie industry.

"They were for my . . . companion," replied Armin, unsure of the nature of his relationship to Iris.

Her gaze lingered on her Martini glass for a moment. The faint sound of a piano carried a jazz melody from the other side of the lobby. She looked up at him smiling enigmatically, and fixed him with a deep stare. "They're beautiful."

"You can have them," he said, looking down at the marble floors.

She wiped the smile off with a cocktail napkin, and stood up in her swivelling bar stool. She was used to receiving flowers from just about every man who'd had the privilege of meeting her, but had never in her life been presented red roses with such indifference. He continued to look down, his chin almost touching his chest.

"Let me buy you a drink. It's the least I can do to thank you for these gorgeous roses," she said without even looking at the flowers. "Besides, it looks like you could use the company." She turned to the bartender and ordered two martinis. The man rushed over in the blink of an eye, holding out a napkin and a pen.

"I'm so sorry, so sorry to ask, but I am your most big fan," he started. "You can sign autograph for me, yes? I know you stay at Hotel Almeida, but I no see you at the bar before." Then looking at the napkin, he added, "My name is Luis. Can you say is for me?"

Athena rolled her eyes and conceded to sign the napkin, making it out to Louise. Fortunately, the bartender did not know enough English to realize he had been renamed as a woman. He lifted the napkin with the great care a priest handles holy relics and placed it in his shirt pocket.

"Don't you put it on eBay, now!" she said as he walked back to the counter.

"No, no, *senhorinha*. I keep this forever. I love you. I watch all your movies."

"That's great. Now, how about those martinis?"

The bartender turned around grinning from ear to ear and reached for a tall bottle of vodka.

"You're famous," noted Armin without any great infusion of enthusiasm.

"I guess you could say that," she smiled modestly.

He looked at her and nodded his head. "You're Athena Jeudi," he said matter-of-factly. "I used to have a crush on you."

"And what happened to make you change your mind?"

"Dunno. I met someone I guess."

"Your companion?"

"Yes."

The bartender balanced the two drinks on a silver tray and set them on the counter in front of them. She tasted hers and pushed the other glass closer to Armin. With his shoulders slumped and his eyes turned downward, he looked as wretched as a beaten mule.

"Drink up," she said, watching him barely sip from the long stemmed glass before he placed it back. His wrist wavered over the counter, small and pale, like a wilting flower.

"Strange how life goes, isn't it?" Her eyes closed intently on him. "One moment you have a crush on a famous actress and the next, you're in a complicated relationship with a man. Well, you know, it might just be that you didn't give yourself enough time to explore love with a woman," she lowered her voice and rested her hand above his milky white wrist. "Especially one that you fantasized about."

He nodded and mumbled something. Nothing was said for a few moments. Then, the colour returned to his face, and his eyes suddenly gawked out of their sockets. "A complicated relationship with a man? What are you talking about?" he jumped off his seat and out of his apathy. "Are you implying I'm gay?"

"Well, aren't you?"

"No!" he squeaked. "I'm here with a woman. The most beautiful woman in the world!."

Athena leaned back in her seat and crossed her arms over her chest in a defensive gesture. "I'm sorry. It's just that not many men are so . . . indifferent to me," she explained, flustered.

"Indifferent?" His voice sounded even higher now. "I gave you her flowers. I think I was being civil enough."

"Civil, yes. But I'm talking about being excited, the way the bartender was. You didn't have any reaction, and I must say I'm not used to it."

"Today just keeps on getting better and better," Armin shook his head. He gulped the martini down and grabbed two bottles of water off the bar counter.

"Thank you for that drink, and please enjoy the flowers," he said to a wide-eyed and extremely confused Athena. With that, he left the bar and went back up to the room.

"What happened to your friend?" the bartender asked, refilling her drink.

"He left," Athena said slowly. At least he wasn't gay, she thought, reaching for the drink. She should have known from his forlorn look, from the way his eyes were drawn at the corners, gleaming with angst, that he suffered from a soul-consuming malady all young men have to struggle with. And she could tell this one was young. He would make a fine diversion from the distinguished moguls who were constantly sending her gifts and courting her publicist for a five-minute meeting with Athena. Decidedly, she was in the mood for a young, hopeful romance.

Holding her head in her hands, Athena closed her eyes for a moment, picturing Armin's black hair falling against his milky white cheek, making him look as desolate as a romantic poet looking over the wasteland that use to be his beloved home. She had seen that look a million times before. He was in love. The only thing that took Athena by surprise was that she was not the cause of his illness, which was why the symptoms seemed to make him that much more attractive.

She lit up another one of her slim cigarettes, and puckering her lips around the chocolate-scented filter, she took a long drag. Who was the woman he was fixated on, and how did she manage to rule the heart of this most interesting young man? Athena blew the smoke out slowly, watching it go up toward the mirror ceiling. It had been her experience that beauty and persistence can conquer the heart of any man. She'd find a way to get close to Armin, just as soon as she got back from filming in Sintra. With that thought, she pressed her fleshy lips together until they puffed up like the petals on a blooming peony.

Her reflection in the bar mirror stared back at her, and she was pleased with the effect a tiny lift of the left brow gave her already stunning face. She leaned closer and turned the other cheek for a closer inspection. The corner of her mouth rose imperceptibly to sketch a smile of contempt. She almost felt sorry for mankind. They stood no chance in the face of such disarming beauty.

* * *

"Yes, this is Iris Bendal," she said, not without a tinge of irritation in her voice. "Yes. I see. Are you absolutely positive?" The person at the other end must have been certain indeed, because Armin heard Iris ask if she could secure a copy of the test results for her client.

"Great, I'll pick them up in an hour."

She passed her long fingers over the lime green dress she had changed into and tidied up a few imaginary wrinkles. She opened the taffeta floor-to-ceiling curtains with one swift motion and began humming a random tune.

"You brought water," she popped the lid off one of the bottles. "What a brilliant idea! I didn't even realize that was exactly what I wanted," she said, planting a jovial kiss on Armin's creamy white cheek.

Her lips felt warm against his skin, and he closed his eyes for a moment. When he opened them again, the sun was shining brightly through the window glass. That was precisely the problem with Iris, he felt. She didn't know what she wanted. But he did. Sometimes the simplest choice is also the best. He would make sure to be the water to all the other cocktails surrounding the object of his affection.

"Come Armin. We're going out," she said picking up her handbag.

"Where to?"

"I have some business to take care of a few blocks away from the Belem tower. I thought this would be a good time for you to visit it."

"What is the Belem tower?" he asked.

# CHAPTER 19

# ROAD TO SINTRA

Counting the passing of the hours in her hotel room, Perla began to realize that if she was going to see Leborio at all, she would need an accomplice. There was just no way she could do it alone. She didn't want to spoil the romance by showing up at Leborio's door, and the hotel lobby wasn't safe. Even if she managed to get away from Athena, she found it impossible to escape the Biography Channel reporters, who seemed to have an endless appetite for asking stupid questions. It seemed she needed the help of someone she could confide in, someone who could occasionally create a diversion, someone willing to cover for her. Because hairdressers have been the natural allies of women since the time of Queen Cleopatra, she chose to spill the beans to Gino while he applied her nightly hair treatment.

The not-even-close-to-Italian hairstylist took it like a professional. Pumping away cautious squirts of conditioner into the vortex that was Perla's hair, Gino listened quietly to a detailed play-by-play of the platonic love story between his mistress and the extraordinary pinnacle of human wisdom that was her guru. He stopped massaging her scalp as soon as she arrived at the part where the guru, whose age had been conveniently left out, took up residence in the Hotel Almeida. A brief, if unsolicited, picture of the old hag throwing herself into the faceless arms of passion made its way into his visual imagination.

Gino's pointy lips parted ever so slightly. He should've known from the way she had him go at that platinum blond mop of hers, as if the fate of the world depended on the height of her hair. He wiped his hands on a face towel and pressed his lips together. This was none of his business, he decided. And he would've been able to get away with politely nodding and pretending to listen if not for Perla's spontaneous question.

"So do you think you would be able to come up to Sintra with him tomorrow morning? Tell him to meet me in front of . . .," she hesitated, "city hall. Every place has one of those," she added. "I don't know if I'll be able to see him, you see, and I'm afraid that if someone doesn't explain the situation to him, he'll soon tire of the mystery and leave."

Gino said nothing. Seeing that the hairstylist hesitated, she went on: "Please, please Gino! You are the only one who can help us; the only one I can trust. My very happiness depends on you. Will you please help me?"

Gino considered the options—or lack thereof—for a moment. Here's hoping Leborio was a cool guy, Gino said to himself, and nodded reluctantly.

"Oh, thank you! Thank you ever so much, my faithful friend. I am forever in your debt," she cried out.

* * *

That very same evening, following Armin's pilgrimage to a white defensive tower of unimpressive height, as Iris was washing her hair in the marble-plated bathroom of suite 112, the phone on her night-stand rang intermittently. Armin, who was watching a Latin American tele-novella on cable, picked it up on the third ring. There was a long pause at the other end.

"Hello?" he said a few times over before hanging up.

In a matter of seconds, Armin lost all interest in daytime drama. He sprang to his feet, eyes flickering with suspicion. Making an effort to seem casual, he leaned into the bathroom door and asked Iris whether she was expecting a call. Through the thick glass door, he could see the shape of her body moving as enigmatically as a shadow puppet. She took her time to answer, unaware the young man's wheels were setting into a tumbling avalanche of uncontrollable doubts and emotions, trying to figure out the meaning of her silence. It was another, he decided. There must have been others, who, like him, awaited their moment. What if she already had someone? He'd assumed she didn't, just because she never said she did. He asked her once more, this time louder.

"I can't hear you. I'll be out in a few minutes," she yelled over the running water.

The phone rang again, and this time Armin, moved by a mixture of curiosity and jealousy, attempted to be cunning. He answered in as feminine a voice as he could muster up.

"Iris. Iris Bendal please," said a man at the other end in a voice that seemed familiar to the boy.

"Who's asking?" he insisted in the same soprano pitch.

The other man hesitated for a moment and then said, "Room service."

"Who's on the phone?" asked Iris, coming out of the bathroom while drying her hair with a hotel towel.

"It's for you," he answered in his normal voice and handed her the phone.

But the caller had hung up. She put the phone back without a great deal of thought. Placido would phone back at a later time—and a better time for that matter. Besides, a little bit of suspense never hurt anyone. He could use a few more days of soul-searching before getting the answer he so badly needed to know. To be perfectly honest, Iris did not trust Placido Pector to be a man of his word. Who was to say that once he got his answer he would even honour her fee? The word of a gangster never amounted to as much as a business transaction. No, she would deliver the test results in a legal-sized envelope and exchange it for a letter-sized envelope containing a check in the sum upon which they had agreed. To be safe, she would call the lab and ask for a copy of the results to be mailed to her at Hotel Almeida.

He watched her reach for a pair of dangling earrings.

"Who do you think it was?"

"Nothing important I suppose."

"What if it was?" he insisted.

The hook on her earrings closed with a small clicking sound. "I guess it'll have to wait until we get back from Sintra."

Though it discouraged further inquiries, her answer had about the same appeasing value as Iago's council to a hot-blooded Othello. His stomach tied up in pins and needles with unanswered questions and gloomy intuitions, Armin imagined a secret lover—or perhaps more than one, each living only to catch a glimpse of this cruel goddess with eyes that saw into one's soul. If anyone asked him, he would've said her eyes were green. But he had only seen such green on cats and Indian mystics. Iris, who had never thought much about how other people saw her, had noticed from a very young age that if she squinted ever so slightly, just enough to make her pupils shrink, she would considerably increase the odds of getting whatever she wanted. And, because what she wanted was usually to see inside people and fix whatever needed fixing, she got in the habit of flashing her eyes at everyone she knew.

She did this as they climbed aboard Athena Jeudi's private trailer, the next day. It worked on the driver, a sturdy man who could have been anywhere between thirty and fifty years old. He smiled back at her the way toothless widows smile at clay statues of baby Jesus. It also worked on Charlotte McMahon, Athena's publicist, who shook her hand reassuringly. Charlotte knew nothing of the investigation story and was thrilled to meet the two reporters from the Biography Channel who were to travel to Sintra with the film crew. The subtle squint worked particularly well on the film director, a man whose bald-by-choice look had started a trend amongst already balding thirty-somethings.

"I'm Iris Bendal, and this is my cameraman, Armin."

"Pleasure to meet you both," smiled the director, gallantly kissing the hand of the woman and unknowingly throwing Armin off the cliff of jealousy and into the pits of agony.

"I believe you're looking for our star," he said, pointing them toward the back of the trailer, where Athena, wearing her Virgin Mary costume, was busy trying on new stilettos. She lifted the hem of her robes up to the knees and walked in front of a mirror, visibly pleased with the results. With every glimpse she got, her perfectly arched eyebrows raised a little higher, causing the collapse to be so much more visible once she turned to face Iris and Armin. The movie star gave Iris a cold glance, barely making eye contact, and then turned her attention to Armin. Her eyebrows rose again, complementing the fullness of her pout.

"What do you know? It's the gay guy," she said, biting her lower lip. Then, turning to Iris without really looking at her, "And this must be the most beautiful woman in the world."

"You're too kind," blushed Iris.

"I'm never too kind," said the actress. "But I'm often sarcastic."

Before Iris had the chance to reply, the driver started the engine on the Mercedes trailer. Both women yelled aloud in a fit of panic.

"Wait! Mrs. Galanis—where is Mrs. Galanis?"

"Yes, we must wait for Mummy. Has anyone seen her? Where is she?" Athena turned to her publicist, "Charlotte, you must go find her."

\* \* \*

Perla checked her lipstick; she had gotten up unfashionably early that morning in order to be able to phone a cab and arrange for Leborio and Gino to be brought to Sintra. With all the details taken care of, she grabbed Regina and a small carry-on bag and headed for breakfast. The restaurant would have been nearly empty if not for a small group of well-dressed Italians sitting at a large, round table. Perla turned her head, going over every nook and cranny of the room with the precision of a Russian periscope. Two coffees and a croissant later, she got up and decided to wait in the lobby. This is where she was now, thinking she wouldn't have had to go through all this trouble if it weren't for the wretched Biography Channel people, who just would not let her be.

"Can I have the key to my room?" she asked the receptionist, taking a piece of candy from the mint bowl on the gilded counter.

The man in the Valentino suit turned to face her with his usual slightly bemused expression. Holding a tiny espresso cup made of white porcelain between his long fingers, he looked down at the hairless cat. His knuckles stiffened on the minute handle.

"Oh, good morning, madam," he said, carefully setting aside the cup. "Which one of them?"

Tucking Regina under her arm like an envelope purse, Perla made a face.

"Huh?"

"The room, madam? Which room?"

Perla leaned over the counter as the receptionist kept a close eye on the smooth and wrinkled head sticking out from under her armpit.

"Why don't you tell me which one of my keys you have?" she lowered her voice.

The smell of musky perfume carried over the gilded counter. The receptionist wrinkled his nose again, and took a step back. He checked something on his computer screen and then said, "I'm sorry, madam. It appears you haven't left either of your rooms this morning."

Perla let out a faint sigh of relief and stripped the shiny wrapper from the mint candy. Leborio was still in his room, and, if she was lucky enough, she might catch a glimpse of him on his way to breakfast. She might even pass by him casually, letting him see she was there and putting an end to this torturous game of anonymity. She reached in her carry-on and put the key card on the reception counter.

"Now I've left one of them," she said to the man in the Valentino suit.

She sat on the couch facing the restaurant, sucking on the mint. Eventually Leborio would have to eat, and then he'd see Perla sitting there, with a sleek carry-on at her feet, casually stroking her cat with an absentminded expression. While she was practicing looking distracted, she heard the clicking of a woman's heels and looked up to see her daughter's publicist running up to her, panting.

"Ah, there you are, Mrs. Jeudi!" Charlotte McMahon greeted her, gasping for air.

"How many times do I have to tell you people that my name is not Mrs. Jeudi?" Perla spit her mint in a napkin. "It's Galanis," her mouth opened widely. "Mrs. Galanis."

Charlotte put her hand up apologetically, still struggling to catch her breath.

"They're all ready to get going," she said at last and sneezed.

"That's great," huffed Perla, passing her a tissue. "I've been thinking," she said, watching Charlotte blow her nose. "It might not be such a great idea for me to come all the way to that forsaken town. The cat hates to travel," she added, lifting Regina up by the hairless pits.

Charlotte's nose wrinkled in anticipation of another sneeze, as she stared in horror at the small animal. She shut her eyes for a moment and took a big breath just before snatching Regina out of Perla's hands and taking a few steps back.

"Don't worry about the cat," she said, coughing in her sleeve. "I'll look after it. Now please follow me, Mrs. Galanis. There's no time to waste."

With this, Charlotte rushed back through the revolving door, coughing and sneezing her way out of the hotel. Throwing one last look over her shoulder, Perla left the lobby without catching a glimpse of Leborio.

* * *

Iris leaned against Armin and whispered, "What did she mean by calling you gay?"

"She was kidding. We met the other day, and it's a bit of an inside joke."

Turning her attention to the two guests, Athena dropped the hemline on her costume, fell back into a cushioned armchair, and curled her index finger at Armin.

"Go on," Iris nudged him, "Sit next to her. See what she wants."

"Why do you want me to go? Are you trying to get rid of me?"

"Armin, don't be ridiculous. Just go talk to the woman. See what you can find out."

"Find out about what? I don't even know what we're supposed to be investigating because you won't tell me."

"And for good reason. I told you, everything is on a need-to-know basis."

Armin stomped his feet into the hardwood floor of the Mercedes trailer. "Well, I need to know why you want me to talk to her," he hissed. "And because I know you won't tell me, I will tell you what I think. I think you want me to go talk to her so you can go talk to the director. Don't think I didn't see the way you looked at him and how he kissed your hand. Did he use his tongue?"

Iris fought off a fleeting chuckle. "Yes, he used his tongue to lick my hand, just like a cow. Now quit being an idiot and pull yourself together." She accompanied the scolding with an ever so slight squint, and added, "It is time you acted like a professional. Go infiltrate our subject like a real agent, and we'll reconvene at the end with the results."

His lip quivered for a moment before he walked the path of self-sacrifice and sat down next to Athena Jeudi. The movie star, who had done away with the white and blue headpiece of her dress, shook her luscious dark locks in a deliberate gesture that demanded either an immediate rerun or slow-motion editing. Unfortunately, the thespian's craft was lost on Armin.

"Is that your companion?" She laughed, emphasizing the last word. Armin nodded his head miserably. "Not much to look at," she sneered. "Just a regular pretty girl wearing a pretty dress. And if you ask me, her face is a little on the round side."

"I'm not asking you," he said sharply. "Someone like you could never understand someone like Iris. She is the most intelligent woman I have ever met, and she's got these amazing eyes, and she's just too cool to describe. That's why every guy who meets her instantly falls in love," concluded Armin, and to prove his point he stared at the bald director whose body language while speaking with Iris was much in the way of a bionic man positioned within range of a giant magnet. He looked back at the actress and added, "And I, for one, am of the opinion that a woman's face ought to be on the round side. It adds softness."

Out of vitriolic remarks, Athena bobbed her head like a wind-shield doggie and tugged at the hemline of her tunic until a pair of diamond-shaped knees glittered in the morning light. She crossed her legs slowly and lasciviously, exercising her own version of the slight squint.

"Surely someone like you would not feel so strongly about a woman unless she possessed some special quality—if yet unidentified. But I'd watch out for that one. I know her type. The more you chase her, the less she'll like you. You have to make her come to you. You have to force yourself to ignore her. And find a distraction," she added, lighting up a long-stemmed cigarette.

"Thanks for the advice, but things are fine the way they are," Armin began to get up.

"She doesn't seem to be that sweet on you. In fact," said the movie star, nodding off to the other pair, "she seems to be a little sweet on our director."

Before Armin could express his outrage, Charlotte McMahon pulled herself up the trailer ladder with one hand, holding tight to her chest something resembling a wrinkled frozen turkey or a very old baby.

"Be careful with Regina; she's very sensitive to sudden movements," they could hear Perla advise from behind the flustered publicist.

Forgetting about Armin for a moment, Athena stood up from her seat. "What is that bloody thing doing in my trailer? Mummy, I thought I told you how I feel about your cat. Get it out of here right away! And Charlotte, would you stop coughing like a dying French courtesan? What's the matter with you?"

"I'm so sorry," uttered Charlotte as she gasped for air. "I'm allergic to cat hair."

Regina stared at her with righteous indignation, seemingly certain she could not be held responsible for Charlotte's allergy any more than the bald director could.

"And I'm not going anywhere without my cat," said Perla, rather unapologetic about being late. She grabbed a dignified hold of the animal, which no longer enjoyed being held by the publicist. "I'm not trying to be difficult, but I've got nowhere to leave it, and I'm certainly not about to put it in one of those animal hotels. Regina is a very civilized creature, and she goes wherever I go. Now, Atty, I understand if you feel that strongly about her not coming along, but I'm afraid if she's not coming, neither am I."

For the first time that morning, Athena and Iris looked each other in the eye, suddenly united by a common state of panic. They couldn't allow the older woman to stay behind completely unchaperoned—well, not that the cat didn't count—while her mysterious gigolo was undoubtedly prancing about Lisbon. "That won't be necessary, Mummy," Athena spoke first. "I'm sure we can make arrangements for the cat to join us."

"No, Atty, I don't think it's such a good idea," Perla shook her head vigorously. "Why am I even traveling in my present state? I'm still jet-lagged, and I could use a day of rest. Besides, you don't need me to distract you from your work. It's probably better that I wait for you in Lisbon. A woman of my age should not be traveling so often."

"Splendid idea," interrupted Iris with a cheerful smile. "If Mrs. Galanis in staying behind, then so shall we. I mean, we were only riding up to Sintra so that we could get a chance to talk to her on the way. Now that she's no longer going, we could just finish the interview in Lisbon."

Athena's eyebrow rose again, this time in appreciation. She smiled at Armin, the corners of her mouth rising bemusedly. She patted Perla on the shoulder, "Fabulous! Hear that, Mummy? You can spend the day answering questions about me. That sounds exciting. Off you go, then!"

"On the other hand," Perla turned to Iris, "I always say age is a state of mind, and by those standards, I'm still a young woman. Can't go to Portugal and not see Fatima. We can do the interview on the way up."

"Sintra—we're going to Sintra," explained the director. "The action of the movie takes place in Fatima, but it was more cost effective to film in Sintra. More scenic, anyway."

Perla nodded in agreement, "Sintra, yes. I hear wonderful things about it. Off we go then!"

While the engine of the spacious Mercedes trailer revved up boastfully, the director, who had taken quite a liking to the redhead from the Biography Channel, helped her and Perla find a comfortable seat on a faux suede couch and began assuring the two women they would not regret the decision to visit the wonderful mountainous town. Charlotte, who had not yet caught her breath, handed out sparkling water and lemon slices. The director put on a pair of sleek sunglasses and tied a blue bandana around his naked scalp. It made him look like an archaeologist, although the only thing standing between him and the Valley of the Kings were the Brazilian flag flip-flops he wore instead of hiking boots.

"Did you know Lord Byron loved coming to Sintra?" remarked the director. "The breathtaking scenery inspired him, they say. He wrote much of his poetry there."

"Lord Byron was a bit of a gypsy if you ask me," replied Iris. "He loved living anywhere but England. Not that I blame him. British weather never did any wonders for the disabled, and our lord suffered from clubfoot and epilepsy. He travelled all over Europe looking for sunny spots. In fact, he's every Mediterranean town's claim to fame. Go to Cinque Terre, and they'll tell you that Lord Byron considered it his second home. Go to Venice and Genoa, and they'll call the late lord *Giorgio* on grounds of familiarity. In Athens, he's practically a local god, right up there with Apollo and Hermes."

"Hermes should be a god in my opinion," interjected Perla. "He makes the most exquisite accessories. Scarves in particular."

"That's because Byron helped the Greek independence movement fight against the Ottomans," continued the director, leaning slightly toward the redhead.

"Yes. Many believed that had Byron lived, he would have been crowned king of Greece."

"I'm impressed," the director looked up to the others. "Beauty and brains all in one package." He pointed at Iris. "That's not fair to the rest of us, Ms. Bendal."

"Yeah," jumped Armin, his face flushed with bile. "Especially when some people don't have either."

The other man turned to him with a curious look on his face, a look that Athena had only seen at the end of a take, just before he was about to yell, "Cut!"

The actress pursed her lips for a moment, then gazing at Armin, she spoke loudly enough for all to hear, "It's funny you should bring up looks and Lord Byron in the same context. From the very first moment I saw you," she said to Armin, "I thought your resemblance of him is uncanny. Don't you think?" she turned to the others.

"Yes, indeed," they all nodded their heads, while a self-conscious Armin pushed his shiny black hair behind his ears.

"And do you know what would be a great idea?" she went on, watching Iris' reaction from the corner of her eye. "If we could somehow bring the presence of Lord Byron into our movie. Think about it. We're filming in Sintra, and what is Sintra famous for? Lord Byron, of course."

"And pastry," added Charlotte faintly.

"Never mind pastry," Athena cut her off sharply, eyeing the publicist's plump figure in reproach. "What people want to see is the character of the romantic poet," she said, giving Armin a little wink.

"In a story about the Virgin Mary? A story that is supposed to take place in Fatima?" The director did not bother to hide his incredulity.

"Athena, my dear, you're the only woman I know bold enough to suggest that Lord Byron makes a cameo appearance in a story about the Holy Virgin's works on earth," he turned to the others and started laughing. "I mean, on one hand, you've got the Virgin appearing to three little children in Fatima during the Great War. On the other hand, you've got Lord Byron vacationing in Sintra during the early nineteenth century having a jolly opiate time with his writer friends. How the two hands can ever meet is beyond reason. It really ought to make for a very entertaining fantasy piece, don't you think?" he waved his arms in the air in an exaggerated gesture.

"Oh, Harold," she said as she put her hands around the director's shoulders, winking again at Armin, who this time scratched his head in confusion. "Don't be so narrow-minded. Don't you think the Blessed Virgin, in her all-knowing wisdom, knew all about lord Byron?" she whispered in his ear. Harold did not reply, stretching his arms across the backrest of the sofa instead. She stood up, gesturing to the others as to the audience in a theatre, "And if she did, she must have thought about it just as we have. The two most famous apparitions in Portugal: the great British poet and the Virgin Mary. It's only natural one would dwell on both. The Virgin herself must have felt his presence in this place," she put her hand to her heart, keeping a solemn silence for a moment. Then, like a whirlwind sweeping over the trailer, Athena moved from person to person, clasping hands and spreading excitement. "Yes, that's it!" she said to Armin. "She came to rescue his lost soul. Like in *Ghost*!" She held her mother's arm. Then, turning to Charlotte, she gestured an imaginary movie premiere sign. "Think of the appeal that sort of a story would have. We could write that into the script." She gave Harold an animated look. "We don't even need to write it. Make it a silent part. I'll do the talking. I could just do a bit of improv."

Harold passed his fingers over his bandana, a gesture that revealed he once had hair to play with. "That's the darndest idea I ever did hear, Athena, my dear. You're talking about changing the entire script on a whim."

"A whim that'll make you infinitely more famous and all of us wealthier," she said with confidence. "Seriously, who do you think is going to care about a story with no romance and no leading man? You know I'm right, Harold. You know I'm right."

The director chewed on a pencil, deliberating for a competent decision. He spit out a small piece of eraser. "And where would we find a suitable Byron?"

Athena turned to Armin and waved her cigarette like a magical wand, "How would you like to be in the movies?"

The driver stepped on the brakes not a moment too soon, causing Regina to go flying out of Perla's arms and claw herself onto Charlotte's bosom. Inertia also sent the Virgin into young Byron's arms and pasted Iris onto a window. With her nose pressed against the tinted glass, she caught a glimpse of a shiny black limousine speeding to wedge its way between the trailer and a fiercely steep ravine.

"*Merda! Filho da puta,*" cursed the driver, manoeuvring away from the other car, which seemed determined to catch up with the film trailer. The road winding up the mountain was entirely made of curves, and like all European mountain roads, it was hardly wide enough to accommodate a single vehicle. It was as if all European mountain folk had asked themselves "Why would two cars ever want to drive on the same road at the same time?" And because they failed to produce an answer, they went ahead and carved a path wide enough to be a bicycle trail.

Looking down from the window of the trailer, Iris could only see the bottom of the ravine, eclipsed every once in a while by a series of curiously shaped trees. The limousine aggressively pushed itself, cutting the trailer off at every turn, when it was clear there was no way of passing in front of it.

"What are they trying to do? Kill themselves?"

"Or us," said the director, leaning against the window for a better view.

"Paparazzi, probably," explained Athena as she put on a fresh coat of lipstick from her endless supply. "They'll do anything to get a picture of me."

"They must be very well paid paparazzi," noted Iris somewhat circumspectly, "to be able to travel in a limousine like that."

Perla turned her attention away from calming Regina after the recent trauma of having been airborne. Could it be possible? One look out the window told her it quite could, and her heart began pounding like a schoolgirl's. Now that he knew who had sent after him, dear Leborio could no longer contain himself. Surely, he wanted to let her know he was near and was growing impatient to see her. She put her hand up to the glass and touched it gently. Behind her, Iris Bendal narrowed her eyes and scribbled something down in her notepad.

* * *

Sitting comfortably in the leather seats of the black limousine Perla had rented for him, Leborio was indeed growing impatient. He could see the writing on the side of the trailer every time it turned a corner, and he was quite sure it was no coincidence that it bore the name of a famous movie production company.

"This road, is it only leading up to Sintra?" he asked the driver, who confirmed that it was. "Then we must get closer to the trailer. Can't you get any closer?"

"Any closer, *signor*, and we'll end up under it."

Sitting next to the mortified hairdresser, Leborio inhaled deeply and crossed his legs. His dark eyes fixed the wavering shape of the Mercedes trailer through the tinted widow.

"Is this not Allah's way of punishing me for choosing a life amongst

Christians?" Gino huffed anxiously. "If only I did not take Maryam, the dentist's daughter, out on a date when I was eighteen years old. If only a soldier had not seen us holding hands, thus making me a direct enemy of the revolution and forcing me to either marry the girl or flee Iran at once!" Gino's voice rose with each sentence, and he paused only to wipe the spittle from the corner of his mouth. "I should have become a mechanic or a construction worker and not a rich woman's house pet," he spat as he fought to right himself after another curve. "I should have married the dentist's daughter, Maryam. If I had, my big old teeth would have been healthier, and I would not have been having my last living thoughts next to a psychotic gigolo on his way to a godforsaken Portuguese town!"

"You want me to smack him, boss?" asked Kim, rubbing his large sweaty palms over the beige fabric of his safari pants.

"Yes, I believe all the man needs under the circumstances is a good old smack across the head," said Umberto. "I am at peace with myself and putting my faith in the Lord. If this is how He wills for me to die." His voice trailed off. He placed his interlocked fingers around his knees, pressing his thumbs down until all colour disappeared from them.

"What's the matter, brother? Is fear stronger than faith? Oh, quit fretting about like a woman for God's sake! No one is going to die. And no, Kim, there is no need to smack Gino. We'll catch up to the trailer any moment now."

"Do you mind me asking why it is so important to catch up to the trailer?"

"There's something aboard that trailer that I want," Leborio said.

Umberto's brow furrowed. "How can you be sure it's there if you can't see inside?"

After a pause, Leborio answered that it was destiny. It was destiny to run into the woman he desired on his way to Sintra. All the more reason to listen to that voice inside telling him he was meant for greatness. Everything about his life had the stamp of destiny on it: his brilliant mind, exquisite appearance, spiritual sensibilities, and unusual experiences. It was as if the world itself was a work of fiction created for the sole purpose of bringing a captivating character to light: the character of Leborio Borzelini, more charismatic than Bond, more resourceful than Batman, more haunting than Heathcliffe, and more cunning than Odysseus. And now, it was destiny that brought this beautiful woman wanted by every man alive his way. She was just the kind of woman next to whom he pictured himself. Leborio knew he had to have her.

Sure, the actress played hard to get the other day when they met in the lobby of Hotel Almeida, but Leborio knew it was only a matter of time until she too succumbed to his charms. In his experience, women were a lot like lab rats. All one needed in order to tame them was the right amount of stress and a little time to observe their weaknesses. Thanks to the limo driver, who was working on delivering the necessary amount of stress at that very moment, all that was left for Leborio to do was keep an eye on her once the trailer stopped.

Sitting next to Alfonso in the front seat, like a good girl, Snejana sobbed quietly through the meandering turns of the road to Sintra, knowing exactly whom they were risking their lives to chase. It was that cold-blooded actress all the men dreamed about. She had seen the way Leborio looked at her the other day. Her mother had been right about him. She should have listened to her. Not every girl had the good fortune of having a mother with psychic abilities, and like a fool, she had taken it for granted. It was too late to do anything about it now. Thousands of miles away from home, the girl felt powerless and humiliated.

Umberto elbowed Leborio. "For goodness' sake, man, do something about that girl crying her eyes out."

"Crying is not so bad, brother. That's how women have been eliminating toxins for centuries. If you ask me, that's why they live longer than men. They have a good cry and then get on with it. We men keep it all in until our hearts give out."

"What hearts?" Snejana cried out.

"Come now, Big Bird, don't dramatize things. After all, you're not an actress," he chuckled, sending the girl into a sobbing frenzy.

"You want me to smack her, boss?" whispered Kim. His proximity to the weeping girl had resulted in a splitting headache.

"Let me think about it, Kim. Good man!"

"Are you serious?" Umberto reached for the button that raised the partition glass between the front and the back of the limousine. But Leborio kicked his hand with the tip of his shoe and shook his head dismissively. "How can you be so cruel?" hissed Umberto trying to keep his voice down. "What you are doing to her is an embarrassment to me as your cousin, a man, and a fellow human being. What kind of twisted creature are you?"

"A lot of questions, brother. Why don't you ask them to your saviour?"

"Don't you dare take His name in vain!" threatened Umberto, shaking his fist in the air.

"I most certainly would not," Leborio replied serenely. "He made me in his image just as he made you. Well, it might be that he spent a little more time on me—no offense. My point is that God created both Jesus and Hitler, and he loves them both equally. So you see, in the end it doesn't really matter which road you take to Sintra, as long as you get there."

He turned to Gino whose head moved from one man to the other with the confusion of the late spectator at a tennis match.

"A fellow spiritualist from India told me once that God is on a mountain, and the ways that lead to him are different. A greater truth was never spoken, my friend."

Gino nodded, secretly urging Allah to take pity on his cowardly soul and deliver him safely to the firm ground of Sintra. It was a busy day for all deities involved. Between the trailer and the limousine ten different souls called upon four different gods – three of which could fall under the umbrella of the holy Trinity – and one just outside of it, for no good reason other than her gender. But there were thirteen passengers, which meant that three of them did not pray for mercy. Aboard the trailer, there was one whose curiosity left no room for fear. Aboard the limousine, one thought whatever God could do he could do better, while the other was on his way to becoming an atheist.

# CHAPTER 20

# SINTRA SHOWDOWN

No one should ever have to go through life without trying Sintra cheese tarts, Iris said to herself while stuffing her face with the delicious pastries in a quaint shop at the bottom of the narrow street where the trailer was parked. The drive up hadn't been that long, but the mountain air always made her hungry. As far as she could see from the double-arched window, other double-arched windows stared back at her from a colony of Moorish buildings. Painted more or less to match the not-so-broad spectrum of colours between plain white and ivory beige, the downtown quarter of Sintra consisted of sturdy structures built in the romantic style that might have resulted had the Moors and Christians decided to sort their differences through a build-off. The arched windows tapered at the base and stood out like keyholes against the various shades of white. Above, yet almost within reach, a few clouds set the surprisingly close sky into perspective. Was there any place in Portugal where the sun didn't shine? she wondered.

The movie crew had gone to prepare for the shoot. Coming out of the trailer, Iris smoothed her chiffon dress and told Armin to keep a watchful eye on Perla. She had seen the way Perla jumped to the window at the mention of the black limousine, like a princess watching from her tower the mortal combat between her beloved and the monster holding her captive. Her investigative instinct told her it had to be more than a coincidence. Perhaps that was Perla's lover concealed behind the tinted glass of the limousine. She thought it would be wise to have someone watch her, just in case she planned to meet this secret lover in Sintra.

"Just make sure you don't lose sight of her," she said, holding Armin's gaze. "Not even for a moment."

"So let me get this straight," Armin raised his chin. "You want me to follow the old cougar, while you go off on your own private tour of the city. What's there to stop you from, say, going on a date with dear old Mr. Clean?" he sneered.

"How could I go anywhere with him if he's with you directing the movie? He'll need nothing short of a miracle to direct a scene and go out with me at the same time." She tilted her head to one side in a reproachful gesture. "Old cougar? Really, Armin?"

Armin scratched his head, looking puzzled. "I thought we were here to investigate Athena Jeudi, not her mother."

"Her mother is the key to our investigation," Iris explained, without even having to lie. "Besides, what was that story of you having met Athena before all about? And how come I knew nothing of it? You can't go around meeting people we are investigating and not telling me."

Armin smiled, savouring every word as he spoke. "It's on a need-to-know basis. I didn't think you needed to know."

Iris fought to hold back a touché sort of smile. She gave Armin one last pep talk, highlighting the protocol and objective of his mission before setting him loose.

"Look, no one is going to suspect that you're on this mission. Not to mention you get to star in a movie. Isn't that exciting? Stay close to

Athena without letting Perla out of your sight. Don't wander off, act on your curiosities, or make conversation on any topics other than your role in the movie, Portuguese cuisine, and possibly the weather." In short, thought Iris, refrain from thinking for yourself and, more importantly, don't share those thoughts with anyone else.

"And you, what will you be doing?" he asked.

"I'm going to try and find out why that black limousine was doing it's best to run us off the road."

"But it must be long gone by now. It could be anywhere. How will you find it?"

"How hard can it be to find a stretch limousine in a town like Sintra?"

"It might be harder than you think," he said, looking around at the endless meandering streets. Each street seemed to lead out into a labyrinth of its own.

"We'll see," she replied, ufolding a colourful paper map.

Armin shook his head silently and checked the time on his cell phone. Sliding the phone back in his pocket, he glanced in her direction one last time and seeing she was busy checking her map of Sintra, he disappeared behind trailer toward the general direction of the movie set.

Shortly after, Iris was a little put out to discover Armin was right. As she found from her brief encounter with a group of American tourists and their tenor-voiced guide, the municipality had a population of nearly 2,000,000, a quarter of which lived in the town of Sintra—not a typical small mountainous town. Now it was up to fate to guide the investigator in the right direction, and there was no better way to do that than with pastry.

Shortly after Iris finished sampling a plateful of delicious pastries in the shop facing town hall, she saw a tall brunette clasping a butterfly handbag, the same one she'd complimented months ago while waiting for the subway. Only this time, she wasn't prancing about town with the uplifted spirit of a girl going on a date but rather holding on to the purse as if clutching onto a lifeline. The brunette stood in the centre of the piazza for a moment, looking as wretched as a cat in the rain. Her height made her stand out like a sore thumb—or rather whichever happens to be the longest finger on one's hand. She sat down on the front steps of town hall, slouching with her head over her knees. Iris was not going to let the opportunity to get to the bottom of this pass her by once again. She was going to solve the mystery of the stolen purse once and for all.

The matter of the stolen purse, as she had come to refer to it, was the very reason she had become an investigator. She had a knack for knowing the truth from a thousand lies, but sometimes the truth was not worth its own weight in gold. And like all abstract notions, truth did not weigh very much at all. Without evidence to support it, that is.

Evidence made the difference between right and wrong, between redemption and hopelessness, between helping an old friend find his way back to himself and watching him turn into a stranger. If only she would have pursued the matter right then and there. If only she would have proven to him without a shadow of doubt that she knew what he had done. If only she could have made him own up to his deed, perhaps he would have been less of an asshole, she thought, immediately checking to see if her unladylike use of epithets had been somehow overheard.

The last time they saw each other, she had her purse stolen in broad daylight in the middle of an airport. He had driven her there and held her to his chest for a moment, before she noticed that her purse was gone.

"My whole life was in it," she lamented. "And the pictures we took."

He did not seem moved by the loss of the photos. "It's gone," he comforted her, kissing the top of her head. "But I will find it for you.

I promise," he added.

She gave him one of her curious little gazes, a mix of suspicion and melancholy flashing through her eyes. When they were children, the boys used to steal the cherries from the tree outside her window. She was unable to get a confession out of either of them, but what she did get was the faint tremble in the dimple of his cheek and the red stains on his fingers. His dimple was wavering now as Iris looked at him. What did he want with her purse? she wondered.

She kissed his smoothly shaven cheek one last time and disappeared behind the tinted glass of the customs counter. As the plane lifted off, she knew two things with certainty: that he had stolen her purse and that the next time they would see each other again, it would be too late to put an end to whatever was happening to him. It was the last time she would ever see him as she knew him.

It turned out she didn't even have to think of a reason to start talking to the girl sitting on the steps in front of Sintra town hall. With her head on her knees, the tall brunette was sobbing her heart out, clenching her purse the way a child grips a stuffed toy.

"Are you all right?" started Iris, sitting down next to the girl, who shook her head vigorously. "Well, you know," she went on, "my father always says it takes both rain and sunshine to make rainbows."

The girl's chest shook with every word. "What does . . . aaaarrrrgggghhhh . . . your father do? Aaaarrrrgggghhh . . . is he . . . aaaarrrggghhh . . . the weatherman?"

"No, he's not the weatherman. He's an ambassador," Iris said almost apologetically. The girl began to sob twice as hard, and Iris thought she heard her say, "Not another one!"

"Not that it matters," continued Iris quickly. "I just mean to say that tomorrow will surely be better than today. Believe me, things will get better. Whatever your problem is, there must be a solution for it." She put her arm around the girl, almost forgetting why she came to speak with her. Like a child, the girl let herself be held.

"I don't know if you remember, but we have met once before," continued Iris. The girl put her head up examining Iris through the tears and shook her head. "It was on the subway. I complimented you on this very purse, and you told me it was a gift from your boyfriend. Do you remember now?"

Whether the girl did or didn't, the mention of the word *boyfriend* caused her to start sobbing again.

"What's the matter? Did I say something wrong?"

"Aaaaarrrrgggghhhh, my boyfriend . . . "

"Is that why you're crying? Because of a boy?" Iris asked and received a definite nod for an answer. "What has he done to upset you so? You know, no man is worth your tears, dear girl. And the ones who are won't make you cry. Believe me, I've learned that the hard way." Iris continued to stroke the girl's hair, and after a pause, she added, "Why don't you tell me what happened, and maybe I can help you. It is a known fact that 90 percent of all human conflict is the result of misunderstandings. Perhaps you misunderstood him, or he you. Maybe we can think of a way to fix this."

"No one can fix this," cried the girl. "He doesn't love me anymore."

These last words came out so loudly that they echoed throughout the piazza, causing the motley crowd of tourists and locals to turn and stare at the two girls.

\* \* \*

Oh, not that nosy reporter again, thought Perla, who was just crossing the nearby roundabout, sparkling like a supernova from the neck up under the glitters of the freshly shined Sophie necklace, which was framed by a rather low neckline. During the commotion of arrival, she had managed to escape the movie set and was now running loose in the piazza. What was the reporter doing there? She seemed to be talking to a vaguely familiar girl who was making a spectacle of herself hollering in broad daylight.

Perla picked up a Spanish *signorita* fan from a souvenir booth and covered her face with it. She scanned the plaza one last time and then quickly cut a diagonal around the corner of the pastry shop. The things we do for beauty, she thought adjusting her necklace not without a small measure of pride. And not any kind of beauty—but the *exquisite* kind.

"Oooops," she cried out as she collided with the chest of a very large man and ricocheted back into the drywall. The man grabbed her by the shoulders in an effort to stabilize her, and then bent down and picked up her fan. She looked up at the giant dressed in safari pants, and feeling lighter all of a sudden, she nodded in gratitude. The man gave her a smile and walked away, concealing his large fist in his front trouser pocket.

What a kind and unusually large man, she thought. And here she'd judged Mediterranean people to be short.

"He doesn't love me . . . aaaarrrrggghhhh." Perla could still hear the echo of the crying girl as she skipped to find the Spanish guru.

* * *

"How do you know this? How can you be sure?" Iris had reservations about going into this line of questioning given the girl's state, but it was too late to turn back.

"Because he loves another," sobbed Snejana.

"Then you must fight for him. You must show him you are the better woman."

"But I'm not the better woman. I'm merely a silly girl, while she is the most beautiful woman in the world."

It was the second time that day Iris had heard someone speak of the most beautiful woman in the world. What was it with people nowadays? How could any one woman be the most beautiful, and why did it matter if she was? Beauty was such a subjective quality. It seemed unfair to choose a single woman over all the others. As opposed to Athena, the girl was not using the term sarcastically. She went on telling Iris about the movie star they had chased on the way up to Sintra, about how her beloved had humiliated her in front of the other four men, and how she came all the way to Portugal to prevent him from falling prey to a secret admirer whom they hadn't even found yet.

"Extraordinary story," said Iris, suddenly feeling nauseated. She strongly disliked coincidences, and there were just too many of them to ignore. First, there was the limousine chasing their trailer on the road to Sintra while a flustered Perla watched from window and sighed. Then there was this girl, clasping a butterfly-shaped purse Iris had been missing for a number of years. These seemingly unrelated events were now brought together by the girl's story. It seemed her boyfriend had been desperately chasing a famous actress all the way up to Sintra. Although no names were mentioned, the probability of another gorgeous movie star filming in Sintra at the exact same time as Athena Jeudi seemed rather slim.

"Sure, it sounds like a fine adventure when it's not happening to you." The girl sniffled and tried to compose herself. "Being dumped is hard enough. Imagine being dumped for a famous actress in a foreign country. All I want is to go home where I can cry in the privacy of my room instead of in the middle of a town square, on a Portuguese mountain."

"How are you getting home? Do you have any money?" Iris reached for her handbag.

"Oh, I'll be fine," the girl bit her bottom lip as if trying to add mentally two impossibly long numbers. Slowly rocking back and forth, she continued to clasp her purse. Suddenly, she stopped biting her lip and poured out the contents of her purse in the dirt at her feet: a shiny phone, a makeup case, a flowery spray bottle, a couple of loose lip glosses and tampons, and a bottle of fire engine red nail polish.

"My life," she said, picking it up and stuffing it into a spare plastic bag she pulled out of one of the side pockets.

Mine also, thought Iris, suddenly overcome by feelings of sisterly affection. Well, except perhaps for the fire engine red nail polish. It wasn't a colour she could see herself wearing.

"I want you to have this," the girl said, giving Iris her handbag.

The older woman stared in disbelief and then began mumbling an incoherent yet polite refusal.

"I couldn't possibly . . . not under the circumstances . . . I can't possibly . . . take your purse," she said. My purse really, she thought. No matter. She could not take back her purse from this poor, betrayed, lip-gloss applying, tampon-using girl.

"No, you must. I insist. It's the least I can do. You mentioned you liked it, didn't you?"

Damn right! I bought it, Iris refrained from saying. She nodded ever so slightly.

"Then you go ahead and take it. I'm going to toss it to the dogs anyhow, being a present from him and all." She took Iris' hand in hers, generously overlooking the redhead's plain and rather short fingernails. She might not have been a lady, but she sure was a fine woman. "Thank you for your kindness. Perhaps someday we'll meet again under happier circumstances."

"Perhaps," nodded Iris. "Next time we meet I hope to see you happy, on the arm of some worthy young man."

"Maybe," she said in a small voice just before she stood up.

\* \* \*

Meanwhile, a discreetly touched-up yet visually stunning Virgin was scheduled to appear first to a tormented Lord Byron, the British collective prophet of Mediterranean Europe, and then to three little Portuguese children whose roles had just gotten smaller to accommodate Armin's cameo.

Decked out in the white ruffles worthy of a romantic poet, Armin Pector looked almost like a character out of a Thomas Mann novel. It was regrettable that this was not a vampire movie, thought Athena, watching Armin from the director's chair. He would have made a most memorable vampire. Not a Lestat, of course. But a rather handsomely confused Louis.

"Where's your mother?" Armin asked

"Why is it you're interested in every other woman except me?"

"I'm not interested in your mother, not in that way. It's just that I need to watch her for the documentary."

"Oh, Armin, cut the crap," she threw her head back. "I know why you're here, remember? I'm the one who provided the cover for your investigation with all that nonsense about the biography you're doing on me."

Armin's eyes widened proportionally to his mouth, which now hung open, making him look rather like the fountainhead from *Roman Holiday*. With a gracefully Hepburnesque lift of the hand, Athena closed it for him, and looked around to make sure no one had seen them.

"You knew about the investigation?" blurted out Armin. "How is that possible? How can we investigate you if you already know you're being investigated?"

"I'm being investigated! Who told you such a stupid thing? Why would I be investigated? I haven't done anything that needs investigating in years. You can find everything you need to know about me in the tabloids: whom I sleep with, what I eat and drink, my prescription pills, where I vacation, and when I choose to go tanning topless. What else is there to investigate? My life is out in the open. It is my mother who is being watched."

"Mrs. Galanis?" His mouth flicked back to the fountainhead position. "Is that why Iris wanted me to watch her? Why would anyone want to know about her?"

Athena rolled her eyes. "Because she's here to meet her secret lover. Well, she's here to see me, really, but we think she's brought her lover with her, and she's probably going to try and see him soon."

"Who is *we*? And how do you know all this?"

"My brother and I, of course," explained Athena, who was starting to get irritated with the boy's ignorance on the matter. "He's the one who planned the whole thing. He's the one who put me up to it and hired you and your lady friend to investigate Mummy." She waved her hands in a gesture of awareness. "Although I'm beginning to think it was not one of his cleverest ideas. I thought you were in charge of the operation. I mean, if that's not why you're here, then why are you here?"

"Good question." Armin shrugged his shoulders discombobulated. "I was told it was on a need-to-know basis," he muttered, sinking into the same seat Athena had just gotten up from before pacing around the corner of the set. For a moment he seemed to be sulking in confusion.

Then, suddenly he sprang to his feet. "Perla! Where is she?"

Athena said she hadn't seen her mother since before she went to get her makeup done. Right, blinked Armin, a tad conscious about his own charcoaled water lines. At least he wasn't wearing mascara. Trying to look as inconspicuous as humanly possible at this maddening juncture in his day, Armin, followed closely by the subdued yet striking Virgin, ran frantically from person to person, asking if they had seen Perla. The bald director raised his curiously hairy eyebrows at him and carried on explaining his vision to the costume designer. The driver seemed to know something, but a whole lot of good that did; the man spoke nothing but Portuguese. At last, he found Charlotte dozing off in the shade of a cypress tree, holding her agenda wide open on her knees.

"There you are," he said, startling the publicist into dropping her planner in the dirt. "Have you seen Athena's mother anywhere?"

Charlotte shook her head vigorously while she bent to pick up the fallen papers. "Why did I have to be the one to babysit her? Why couldn't the driver do it? Or the cameraman?" she muttered.

"It is paramount that I find Mummy, Charlotte. If you know where she went, tell me at once," intervened Athena.

"This must be a misunderstanding." Charlotte closed the agenda firmly and shoved it in her handbag. "No one told me I was to watch Mrs. Galanis."

"Yes, yes," Armin cut her off. "No one is holding you responsible. I was supposed to watch her. And if you can't tell me where she went, I'll get in a lot of trouble."

Charlotte hesitated and then said, "I saw her earlier. But I can't tell you where she was headed. She just sort of wandered off that way," she said, pointing toward the town square, just before the sight of a certain hairless feline sent her into a serious cough attack.

"Come," said Athena pulling at Armin's ruffles. "We'll follow the cat. Mummy can't be too far. She'd never leave that blasted cat alone for too long."

* * *

Athena couldn't have known those were the exact thoughts Regina had as she set off to find her mistress. It was the first time the cat had ever woken up from an afternoon nap to find itself abandoned, and the confusion of it left poor Regina in a state of sheer panic and caused her already outstanding eyeballs to bulge to the point of resembling the offspring of extraterrestrial life. At first, she tried to find refuge on the lap of the makeup artist. Who knew the rather plump human liked applying makeup without discrimination? The woman shouted—which in Regina's experience was never a good thing—a few words which did not match any of the commands that were already part of the cat's vocabulary and proceeded to chase the animal away with a very thick brush full of sparkling bronzing powder. No, thank you, was Regina's utmost thought as she bolted for the next available spot. She could never understand human fascination with darker pigmentation. Take her mistress for example. So much time in the sun couldn't have possibly been good for Perla's digestion now that she was past her prime mating season. Not to mention it made her head fur look dry and raggedy.

Of course, if Regina could speak, she would have long ago recommended trimming off the head fur altogether, so that human males would think that Perla too had a fine pedigree like her cat. As an added bonus, the lack of fur would have left the other house pet, the idiot with the scissors, out of work. Yes, hissed the feline, in her most evil hissing voice. Since the beginning of time, cats had worked hard at eliminating competition: dogs, mice, canaries, and as of late, hairdressers.

A set of sturdy legs moving by pulled her out of her kitty daydream and into the torrid Portuguese afternoon. In the interest of survival, the hairless cat decided to lower her standards a tad in her search for temporary asylum from the knees of the makeup artist to the ankles that had just walked by. She employed the oldest trick in the cat book and began to rub herself against the sturdy legs while purring like a chronic bronchitis patient fresh out of inhalers. Unfortunately, the legs belonged to the driver, who had not yet forgotten being pushed behind schedule that very morning because of the blasted cat. He discreetly checked to see if anyone was watching and then hooked his large foot under the cat's behind, setting it into flight. The cat recovered balance, but her ego emerged rather bruised.

One look at the three Portuguese children, who were quietly dangling their feet off a large bench, waiting for their scene to be filmed, told Regina she was indeed misunderstood. The children, who had never before seen a hairless cat, were crossing themselves the way grandparents taught them to cross when faced with some manifestation of the antichrist. A cat like me ought not to be mixing with the likes of them, she meowed, taking one last look at the movie set and the humans in it. Whipping her tail into a proud and straight vertical line, Regina set off to find her mistress, unaware she was being followed by Athena and Armin.

"Where do you suppose it's going?" whispered young Lord Byron to the Virgin hiding behind him.

"Following Mummy's scent, no doubt."

Her sense of smell had never been her strength. It had been altered from the age of kittenhood by countless beauty products: perfumes, hair balms, body creams, and as of late, the tanning enhancer kit. As they say, the absence of one sense leads to the enhancement of another. In this instance, it was Regina's sense of hearing that compensated for the cat's olfactory shortcomings. She could hear a pin drop across town, or as the case may be, she had the ability to pick out the clinking sound of a uniquely designed diamond necklace from all other background noises such as inquisitive groups of tourists, mothers concerned with preventing sunstroke, gossipy old ladies of the Sintra retirement home, baking trays banged against the oven wall, and head gaskets blowing off from the heat.

This necklace was known to the Galanis family as the Sophie necklace and to the Galanis family cat as the over-the-top human collar. It seemed to be somehow linked to Perla's mating season, although it had to be said that no tomcat, no matter how virile, would have been worth the trouble of lugging such a great big thing around one's neck. Then again, humans had a thing for big, sparkly rocks, while, curiously, they remained indifferent to rodents. Oh well. Regina had lived long enough to know that humans were better left to their own devices. As long as they provided food, shelter, and the occasional petting, one did not need to understand their species at all.

The clinking sound of the fancy human collar taunted the poor creature into exhaustion. She wasn't a hunter, not by nature or genetics. Her pedigree said she was, but that was a little like a human resume; it was designed to enhance one's skills and not necessarily to reflect reality. For at least three generations, no one in her family has had to chase a mouse or even so much as lift a finger to get a meal. The meal consisted of crunchy chicken or fish-flavoured kitty grains, chocolate bonbons, and sometimes, a garnished helping of *fois gras*. Given these circumstances, chasing the sound of a sparkly necklace was no fun at all. The only incentive was the hope to find Perla and a spot in the shade—unfortunately, in that precise order.

The greatest leap of faith for the generally cautious cat was the decision to cross the town square heading north toward the pastry shop. Parked in the middle of the roundabout was a white bus waiting for a group of Japanese tourists. Trying to find her bearings, Regina lingered for a moment in the shadow of the tour bus, unaware she was being watched by a middle-aged Asian woman who was quietly enjoying half a dozen cream puffs. The woman was wearing an oversized pink visor hat that could very well remind one of a welding helmet. The hat completely covered her face, but left the top of her head to bake in the sun.

Under the pink plastic shield, the woman had a very pleasant round face. She smiled at the lost animal, and came a little closer. Then, with the precision and economy of motion worthy of a ninja, the woman flicked the visor up, bent down, and lifted the cat to eye level.

The cat, who had never come face to face with a Japanese person before, shrieked in sheer panic, not knowing what to make of it. This met an opposing reaction of equal strength from the Japanese woman. The animal put up a valiant attempt at freeing herself from the loving arms of the visor-wearing tourist and had it not been for

Perla having had her recently declawed, she might have even stood a chance. Instead, her feeble efforts at biting the human were smothered with a honey-glazed cream puff. The woman put the cat up, looked around as superficially as any decent soul who found a $20 bill, which she is obligated to return, unless there isn't anyone to claim it. The visor moved 180 degrees from left to right. "Cat? Cat?" she repeated the only English word she knew. Going once. Going twice. Gone!

A few paces behind her, Athena, who had processed the meaning of these events much quicker than her ruffle-sleeved sidekick, blew her cover just after she whispered, "Carry on without me!"

"Wait! Where do you think you're going?" she yelled at the round faced Japanese woman, snatching the frightened feline out of her arms. "This is my cat! My cat!"

"Cat. Cat." The woman bowed, looking a little humiliated and very much saddened.

Regina meowed and purred when Athena took her in her arms. She had never been happier to see Athena, and almost forgot for a moment that the actress had done cruel and unusual things to her as a kitten. On the other hand, Athena wasted no time disposing of the cat with a swift kick in the bum as soon as they got in front of the pastry shop.

"Get lost you stupid rat," she said. "Go find Mummy!" Then, she waved discreetly to Armin, who was still pursuing the chase from behind a cypress tree. "My work here is done," she said loudly enough for him to hear. "I must return to the set before Harold starts filming my next scene."

The cat watched her walk back to the other side of the town square, presumably to the movie set. The subtle clinking of jewellery had grown louder, which could only mean one thing: she was getting closer to her mistress. Her tiny ears turned as she made her way up the street, passed an ice-cream stand, and went around the corner. The side street narrowed into a rather dark alley where a black limousine hid away from the sun. As Regina proceeded cautiously toward the limousine, one of the beige buildings to the near right made a rumbling sound and closed in from behind her.

"Wow, what a big rat!" spoke the moving building.

Frightened out of her wits, Regina hid behind the left rear wheel of the limousine. The familiar click-clank of the jewels came nearer and nearer, as the moving building approached with intermittent thumps. Confused, the cat peaked from her hiding place, searching for her mistress. But she was nowhere in sight. Inches close to trembling Regina, the car door opened, and two perfectly shined shoes made their way out.

"Hiya there, boss," spoke the beige building, greeting the shiny shoes. "I just saw a giant rat run under the car. Do you want me to smack it?"

"No, no smacking is necessary, Kim. We've got more important things to do."

It took the cat a good few minutes to stop its tiny heart from racing. Perhaps she had overestimated her hearing. After all, she was getting on in age. Deciding it had been a false alarm, Regina waited to come out from underneath the black limo until she could no longer hear the clinking sound. Luckily, on her way back, the lost, hairless cat bumped into the equally lost Armin, who was resting on the sidewalk next to the ice-cream stand, enjoying a Popsicle.

"There you are, kitty-kitty-kitty. I thought I'd lost you," he shook his ruffled sleeves at her. Regina stretched her long and wrinkly neck until her nose could almost touch his hand. "Where's your mommy? Is she nearby?" The cat's ears moved. Armin tilted his head to one side, imitating the animal. "I sincerely hope so, because to be perfectly honest, I can't take this heat much longer. By the looks of it, you can't either. So how about we find Perla and go back to a cool spot? Huh? I'll be in a heap of trouble if I don't find her. You're my last hope. What do you say?" He waved the colourful treat under the cat's nose. "Want a bit of my Popsicle? Here, I'll break a little piece for you if you promise to be a good kitty and take me to your mommy." Her whiskers touched the Popsicle and she shivered. Then, slowly, a tiny pink tongue cautiously probed the frozen treat. "You like it, don't you? That's a good kitty!"

Delicately licking the melting piece, Regina shuddered from her very first brain freeze. Armin had finished eating and flicked the wooden stick to the curb. He stood up and looked down at the hairless animal. Acting on an impulse of solidarity, the cat also stood up and waited for direction. Armin took a few exaggerated steps around the ice-cream stand, as if to teach the cat the science of walking. "Come on, kitty! Show me where the old cougar is."

The cat observed this with moderate interest and following Armin's lead, made a few steps of her own. Opting for a change in rhythm, Armin increased the pace of his walking tutorial. The cat overtook Armin and quickly circled the stand once, under the vigilant gaze of the ice-cream seller. The vendor looked up at Armin, without bothering to hide a sneer.

Taking this as a sign of provocation, Armin took one step forward and two steps back. He repeated this a few times over, completely confusing the animal whose sense of coordination gave best results only when used forward.

It was at this point that the ice-cream seller opened a can of Fanta orange soda and reached under the tabletop to press play on the boom box.

It was the cat's turn. To the sounds of the newest summer hit, Regina executed a swift somersault followed by a dissing meow somewhere along the lines of "Beat that!"

A middle-aged man wearing a white apron and a rolled-up

cigarette behind his ear emerged from the back door to the bakery behind them. He greeted the ice-cream seller, who started to explain something, gesticulating at the cat. The two men reached into their apron pockets and pulled a few colourful bills. They shook hands at once, and turned to watch Armin and the cat with interest.

Armin frowned for a moment. He stood there staring down at his red shoes, while the cat and the vendors observed quietly. Then, suddenly, the corner of his mouth widened into a triumphant smile. Armin straightened up and looked the cat in the eye. He had one last trick up his sleeve: the moonwalk.

* * *

On her way back to the set, Iris Bendal turned the corner and caught a glimpse of something that made her stop in her tracks, livid with anxiety. The three men made a very unlikely group. Had her brain been able to process anything beyond the point where her eyes encountered a pair of uniquely familiar arms, she would have surely noticed the gargantuan size of the taller man or that he dragged what seemed to resemble Perla's hairdresser, otherwise known as the good doctor from Hotel Almeida. However, when faced with an object of strong discomfort, the human brain seems to zoom in on said object and lose focus of details and decorum. For all she cared the giant could've been a dwarf. It was his companion's arms she had zoomed in on.

Over the years, she had become accustomed to seeing bits of him everywhere she went: his eyes on an Islamic woman, framed by a dark hijab; his nose on the actor who played Zorro; even his Frida Kahlo monobrow. But never his arms. Those were two of a kind. Of all the places their paths could have crossed, Sintra seemed to be the least likely. Still, there she was, not nearly as prepared as she thought herself to be. Not the best dress, not the perfect hair she would have liked, and not the most courageous heart she could've worn that morning. Yet there was one thing she owned that made up for all imperfections: her butterfly-shaped purse. Holding on to it, both hands around the handle, she slithered along the wall and peeked to see where they were headed. And this is why I'm highly suspicious of coincidences, she thought, following the three men on the set of the movie formerly known as *Fatima: Three Secrets*, now entitled *Fatima: Three Secrets and a Vision.*

# CHAPTER 21

# THE AFFAIR OF THE NECKLACE

Anxiety sounds like a bogus sort of condition until one experiences it firsthand, thought Perla, dabbing her forehead with her Hermes scarf. Compared to all the other respectable mental ailments, anxiety seems rather like an amateur amongst professionals. Depression gets one sad just by merely mentioning the word; multiple personality disorder gains legitimacy through numbers—the more personalities to deal with, the more serious the condition; schizophrenia brings to mind a very young Anthony Perkins or a very thin Christian Bale portraying Norman Bates. All other mental ailments appeared legitimate next to anxiety. Put an x and a y into any given word, and it will automatically increase its scientific value. "Anxiety!" It was just a fancy word for plain old worrying. Who would ever take that seriously?

The tabloids by the Lido poolside were always full of celebrities suffering from panic attacks. As if there was any reason to panic while vacationing on a pristine beach, having drinks with other celebrities, or signing autographs at the latest award show. Yet, every hot celebrity did it. Like rehab, panic attacks were the rite of passage in the world of who's who, reflected Perla. Come to think of it, did Atty ever suffer from anxiety? Maybe. For publicity purposes, of course. If they'd only known that this condition was in fact very real and that it left one feeling rather like a victim of disembowelment.

From the moment Perla had come to the realization that her precious necklace had disappeared, her stomach churned as if trying to contain a great big tornado, and her heart pounded with the speed and the volume of an African drum. Lost in a labyrinth of narrow streets, Perla had instinctively touched her neckline only to find her chest bone proudly sticking out. Overcome by a fit of panic, she shook her blouse vigorously and immediately checked inside her brassiere and trousers. She pulled out the Hermes scarf tucked to her breast and sticking from sweat. Holding the scarf by an edge, she shook it like a tablecloth. It revealed no more than a few rays of Portuguese sun, peaking out through the fine weaving. Dizzy with dread, Perla grabbed her hair with both hands and began to pull. She bellowed a series of undetermined sounds without paying any mind to the small balconies overlooking the street. Luckily, there was no one to witness her gasps for air as her face turned the colour of wine.

She sat in the dirt for a while, unable to move. Then, still trembling from every limb, she got up and made her way through the streets, occasionally holding on to the walls of a building. Visions of a family inquisition led by George and Denis pushed her over the edge of desperation. She could see herself sinking in a small wooden chair, being questioned by her son, slowly, precisely, and without mercy, until she'd break down and cry at the top of her lungs that YES, she had taken the Sophie necklace out of the family safe, and YES she had brought it to Portugal, because YES she was hoping to impress her younger lover, who she had also paid to bring here with George's money. Her son's small pupils would narrow into sharp dark dots, while George himself would stand up from his oak throne, look down at her with Arthurian dignity, and turn his back to his cheating, lying wife.

"I can bear that you have lied to me, because I know you have done it before," he would have started, pacing about the dining room. "I can even live with you making yourself into a harlot for the sake of some young stud. You wouldn't be the first immoral woman. But to be as stupid as to take Maman's priceless diamond necklace, which had been in my family for generations, bring it with you in a suitcase, and wear it in broad daylight as an accessory to a Marciano V-neck blouse in order to impress a yoga instructor, only to have it stolen, *that* is beyond my power to forgive. Do you have any idea how important that necklace was to my mother? To me? Not to mention that its value amounted to more than your lover makes in a decade. How could you be so reckless? How could you be so . . . dumb?" he would have settled on a less technical term, just before handing out the sentence to her crime. "You are beyond redemption, I'm afraid. I have worked too hard for my political career to let you end it with your folly. From this day forth, you are no longer to set foot out of the house—not to the Lido, not for shopping, not for any reason under the sun. You are to stay confined to our home, our pool, and our hired help. Which, by the way, I'd appreciate if you refrained from screwing. When you want to shop, you will do so over the Internet. The only time you will be allowed out will be to accompany me to various functions. Of course, you are welcome to fight my decision, but I assure you that a divorce based on adultery will only leave you as I found you: penniless in the gutter. Only this time you will no longer be the belle of the ball, but the old hag in the street. Do we understand each other?"

Perla shook her head, trying to clear it. She had betrayed her husband, a good—if boring—man, for the smouldering guru she hadn't even managed to find yet. Back on the movie set, Perla sat in the shade of what could have been a villa in a Mayan Riviera resort or a plaster scale model of the Fatima basilica.

She was confused about who she should look for first, the unknown thief or the misplaced lover. Think, she urged herself, aware it was not her strongest skill. Any moment, the damn reporters would return and chances of escaping them twice in one day were slim to none.

The dramatization was only a figment of her imagination. For now. But there was incontestable truth to that vision. She had to find the stolen necklace at once! Before the thief could leave town, and vanish forever. She also had to do so without bringing the police into it, without her daughter suspecting anything was amiss.

* * *

Perla Galanis was not the only woman in that particular neighbourhood of Sintra searching for something. The investigator waited behind one of the cars parked next to the narrow sidewalk, watching the three men cross the street toward a large beige building. Suddenly, he stopped a few feet short of the front entrance of the building and signalled to the other two to follow him behind the corner. Iris was sure she saw him point at the school, and for a moment wondered what business he had in it. Unless he was there for the movie. On a second thought, of course he was. She involuntarily slapped herself across the forehead, remembering her unusual meeting with the crying girl and the story about chasing a movie star. She clasped her butterfly-shaped purse tightly and leaped like a frog, crouching behind the next car over.

It was because of Armin that Iris failed to catch up to the three men she was following. Just as she was about to move one car closer to the corner, he came running, calling out her name. She stood still under the rusty sign above the entrance, afraid of being discovered. It read "*Escola Secundária de Santo Domingo.*"

With Armin came the lengthy and nonsensical explanation about an acrobatic cat; moonwalking as the upside of being a Michael Jackson fan; and a violent, angry, and most dangerous ice-cream vendor who lost a bet to the baker because Armin tripped off the curb while completing the said moonwalk. And here he stopped to catch his breath. Seeing she looked through him unimpressed, he waved his arms. "Hello? What's the matter with you? You look like you've just seen a ghost."

"Maybe I have," she said. "Who won the bet?"

"What bet?"

"You said there was a bet."

"The baker, of course. He bet on the cat. Not a fair bet, if you ask me. Bloody thing has nine lives. I've only got one. Anyway, the point is they're after me now. The ice-cream vendor tried to hit me with a bag of frozen Popsicles, but I managed to get away a few streets ago. I think he's still looking for me," he said, looking back to be sure. "Any luck finding the limo?"

"What limo?" she asked, staring at the same spot where the school turned a corner. She took a few steps past him, standing on her toes to see over the cars.

"The one you set out to search for. What have you been doing all this time?"

"Forget the limo," she waved her hand dismissively. "It's not important."

Armin exhaled sharply but said nothing. He adjusted the ruffles on his white shirt and gently rubbed the makeup running across the skin under his eyes. With her back at him, Iris made a few more steps toward that corner she had been watching.

His shoulders slumped again. "Can we get out of here?" he said in a resentful tone.

"Yes, let's get back to the others," she agreed, and they both flashed their press passes at the doorman dozing off under a large cowboy hat by the arched entrance to the movie set.

"Have you seen three men walking by just now?" she asked him.

"No m'am," replied the doorman in a heavy Southern accent, flicking his hat an inch higher with the top of his thumb. "Ain't no one gone by for at least an hour."

"Thanks then," smiled Iris, looking around at the external walls surrounding the square shaped building. Off on the left side, an open window on the second story caught her attention. Shaped as all Sintra windows, it too resembled a giant key hole. It had been left slightly ajar, but not enough to ventilate the room. "One more thing. Where does that window lead to?" she turned to the cowboy.

"Don't know m'am. These darn Portuguese houses ain't like the homes in Tennessee. The second floor looks to be locked up. So y'all ain't gonna be able to get up there."

"I see," she said. "Say for the sake of argument that the second floor wasn't locked. How would one get there? Is there a staircase that leads to it?"

"There is one by the main entrance." The man pushed his cowboy hat back with his index finger and pointed at another door. "But that's all covered by the set construction. It's right behind the scale model of the church in Fatima," he added, placing the accent of the second syllable of Fatima. "An' I reckon you shouldn't go wondering about the movie set. Y'all might cause some kinna trouble and upset the crew."

"Now you wait a minute," started Armin in his most outraged romantic poet tone, "do you know who I am? I'm a star in the movie!" He tousled his not-so-impeccably white sleeves at the cowboy.

"Us, trouble? Never!" winked Iris, pulling Armin by the hand before he could share his identity with the doorman. The boy pouted in silence, timing his steps to match hers.

"Where are we going?" he asked bitterly. "I thought we're getting back to the others."

"In a moment. I just need to check something," she said as Armin followed her sulking.

\* \* \*

The commotion brought Perla out of her reverie. Not fully recovered from the visions of her grim future as an adulterous wife, she peeked from the other side of the coloured clay facade. Maybe if she didn't move, they wouldn't hear her, and she could still get away from them. The only thing missing from her already terrible day was the media, she sighed. Trying to recollect her thoughts, Perla retraced her steps from the moment she took the Sophie necklace out of the safe.

Before she left the hotel room that morning, she had placed it at the bottom of the carryon bag, neatly wrapped up in one of her Hermes scarves. Then, she waited until they arrived in Sintra, and once the crew was busy setting up on the movie set, she reached into her carryon luggage and took out the Hermes scarf, stuffing it in her brassiere. She walked up to a public bathroom nearby, locked herself in a dubiously smelling stall and pulled out the scarf. She took the necklace out, and stuffing the scarf back in her brassiere, she used both hands to carefully place the Sophie necklace around her neck, fastening the clasp at the back with a small, metallic click.

Moments later, she headed for city hall to meet Leborio. Once she got there, she lingered briefly by a souvenir booth and bought a Spanish fan to cover her face. Suddenly, she caught a glimpse of the female reporter sitting on the steps, and holding the necklace tight to her bosom, as to prevent it from falling, Perla fled before the reporter could spot her. That was the last time she remembered touching it.

She wanted to sob and stomp her feet on the ground. But the sound of the reporters' voices reminded her that she was not alone. Instead, sitting behind the clay facade of the movie set, Perla Galanis repeatedly hit the back of her head against the wall, covering her mouth with both hands.

\* \* \*

They entered the quad in silence. Unaware the object of his mission was within physical reach, Armin wandered if now was a good time to bring up the small detail of having been lied to and brought to a foreign country under false pretences. After having heard everything Athena had to say, he was sure Iris had something to hide. He took this quite personally, as would most infatuated young people. Then again, there was the matter of the hairless cat and its disappearance, which ultimately resulted in Armin having failed his mission. Relieved she had forgotten all about his assignment to watch Perla, he opted for polite conversation and against confronting her right then and there.

"Is that a new purse?" he inquired, running the tips of his fingers over the leather. "Interesting design. One of those arts and crafts local items I suppose. I had no idea the Portuguese were so handy with handbags. The Italians seem to be known for that sort of thing. Florence in particular. Goes to show how little we know about other people."

Iris nodded, scrutinizing the four sides of the quad. She didn't seem to be paying attention to what he was saying. Seeing she didn't answer, he went on, "Well, I'm glad you had a good time in town, and you found something you liked. Although I must say it looks a little worn out for a new purse," he added, fishing for the faintest reaction.

"Oh, this?" she clasped the butterfly-shaped handbag. "It's not new. I bought it a long time ago. Then it got stolen. The strangest thing, this was the second time I ran into the girl who had it. I once spoke with her back home, if you can believe it! And now she was here in Sintra, crying in the middle of town square."

They were standing outside of the scale model now. There was a narrow opening separating the real building from the movie prop, and Iris quickly slipped through it. Armin followed her behind the scale model.

"Why was she crying?" he asked.

She shrugged, scanning the area cautiously. "Something to do with her boyfriend," she said, brushing her fingers against the wall. "Anyway, whoever stole it, I'm glad to have it back. Life is full of surprises, don't you think? A few more minutes and I might never have seen my old purse again."

* * *

Luckily for Perla, who hadn't had much luck thus far, she saw them coming and was able to circumvent toward the other side of the kitschy construction. Still struggling with fuzzy memories of her afternoon, Perla remembered fleeing town square to hide from the reporter and the girl who was crying. She also remembered the girl looked vaguely familiar. Moments later, she had bumped into that unusually large man. There was something there, in those flashes of memory, she said to herself, leaning against the plaster wall.

Perla might have never been able to recall what it was she had seen, if not for the brief exchange between Armin and Iris. On the other side of the plastered basilica, Perla Galanis caught the ending of Iris' story the way a child catches the string to a wondering kite. The girl in town square! She thought she'd seen her before. Suddenly, she remembered where.

It was at the Lido spa. She was the young ostrich from the massage parlour, the one who booked Leborio's appointments. What was she doing here at the same time with Perla and Leborio? Did the entire staff of the Lido spa decide to vacation in Sintra? What sort of coincidence was this? The female reporter mentioned she'd found her *stolen* purse with the girl. Stolen! Just like her necklace. Something told Perla opportunity would not strike twice. Careful not to make a sound, she slipped away and ran back toward town square, as she had never ran before, causing her tightly wound curls to bob up and down like suspension springs.

* * *

"Why are we hiding?" whispered Armin. He tugged at her wrist, following her lead and ducking behind the wooden boards holding up the plaster facade of the miniature Fatima basilica. "I said why are we hiding? We have clearance to be on the set. I'm in the movie, remember?"

Iris shook his hand off her wrist. "How could I forget?" she smirked. "But we're not hiding from the movie crew."

"Then from whom?"

She did not reply. Emerging from behind the wooden boards, Iris found herself in front of a large wrought iron door held together by a rusty chain. She picked up the lock hanging loosely by a broken handle at the lower end of the chain. The broken lock hung on a hoop like a lose earring on a pierced lobe.

"Damn! They broke the lock," she muttered. She turned, grasping the purse with one hand and the chain with the other.

"Who broke the lock?"

"Never mind," Iris shook her head, staring right past him. "Why don't you get back to the others?"

"You know what, I'm sick and tired of you treating me like a babbling child," Armin raised his voice, taking a few stompy steps back. She did not reply.

"I'm a grown man, in case you haven't noticed."

Still, she said nothing, and continued to stare past him.

"Did you think I would never find out why we're really here?" he sneered. "Did you think I would fall for that on a need-to-know basis nonsense? Well, I know all about the affair, and I know who you're really investigating." Armin paused for additional effect.

"Good," she replied neutrally. "That saves me having to fill you in on recent developments. Come now, we have to catch up before anyone else sees them."

"Them who?"

Before Iris could answer, a deafening sound broke the quaint silence of siesta hour. It was ironically reminiscent of the prison sirens that go off when an inmate makes a run for freedom.

Sitting in the director's chair with a bottle of water, Athena, who could hardly believe her eyes, caught a glimpse of her mother's hair bouncing on its way out the movie set. As Perla almost made a seamless escape through the gate of the *Escola Secundária de Santo Domingo*, her daughter sprung to her feet and picked up the director's megaphone. Proving that almost is never as good as absolutely, Athena spontaneously threw herself into what some might argue was to be the most convincing role of her career: that of a jailhouse siren. She screamed long enough to resurrect a small cemetery from its everlasting sleep. But alas, genius is invariably weighed down by the limitations of human condition, and Athena's voice gave out in the end, making way for coherent speech. "Help!" she shouted, throwing the megaphone down. "Somebody help me! *Somebody*! Now!"

Behind the plaster church facade, Armin covered his ears. Next to him, Iris peeked out at the source of the insufferable ruckus and pulled Armin's hands away from his head.

"Make her stop! She's ruining my investigation," she whispered and nudged him. But Armin could barely hear her over Athena's screams.

"Somebody! Follow her!" screeched the actress.

Iris scanned the inner court and the windows overlooking it. Without a moment to waste, she pushed Lord Byron into the filming quad with a surprising amount of strength. "Here's your chance at being *somebody*," added Iris, as Armin stumbled from behind the plaster facade of the basilica and landed face-to-face with Athena Jeudi.

"Stop yelling." He put his arms out bracing himself for an impact with the director's chair. Luckily, the chair was quite sturdy and he was able to find his balance again. "It's not very ladylike, you know," he straightened up and gave her a look. "You're supposed to be this unattainable movie star, not a bloody fire drill."

Her face was flustered and her hair had come undone. Athena pushed the loose strands behind her perfectly proportioned ears, and tidied her costume with the tips of her fingers.

"I just saw Mummy getting away is all," she whimpered, lowering her gaze. "We don't want to lose her for the second time today."

His eyes opened widely for an instant, and he quickly glanced at the metal gate. "Who said anything about losing her? I had her all along," he boasted. "What do you think I was doing just now? She was about to take me to the rendezvous point just before you blew my cover with the sound effects. Though I must say you've got fierce lung capacity for a girl your size," added Armin, turning to face her.

Athena shook the confusion by flicking her hair over her shoulder. She straightened her posture, pushing her chest outward, and lifted her heels off the ground a little. Her fleshy lips opened up ever so slightly, as if ready to reciprocate an imaginary kiss. Hesitant, she leaned on his arm as the costume mistress and the security cowboy had come running to see what the screaming was all about.

* * *

"Bloody hell," whispered Leborio, observing the object of his plan of seduction from the second-story window where he and Kim had taken cover. Through the dirty glass, he could see Athena hanging on the arm of a pale young man dressed in white ruffles.

"Don't worry boss, they can't see us up here." The giant took a step back.

"Oh, I don't care about that," said the guru. "I think I just figured out why the actress doesn't want me."

"Why is that, boss?"

"It appears someone's already working her," he replied, nodding his head in Armin's direction. This was not something he had expected. Leborio had gone through a lot of trouble to bypass security and get close enough to watch her, certain that once he did so, he'd figure out how to charm Athena. "Can anyone explain to me what on earth that little maggot is doing here?"

Kim peeked through the window, careful not to eclipse the view in the chain of command. Dressed a little like those men his mother warned him of, Armin Pector waved his ruffled sleeves to the incoming personnel alerted by Athena's siren performance.

"That's the boss' son," he noted, and almost immediately corrected himself, "The other boss. Do you think the other boss sent him, boss? Do you think he knows where we are?"

"I don't know," Leborio's neck tightened. "If he did, I doubt he'd send that imbecile to round us up. No, he must be here on his own. But why?" He rested his forehead against the cool surface of the window.

"Why don't you read his mind?" inquired Gino from the back of the room, staring smugly at the guru. "Or are we too far from him? I'm sorry; I don't know how this metaphysical stuff works. Perhaps you can levitate closer to him and then read his mind."

Leborio straightened up and turned to face the hair stylist. "You're starting to irritate me," he said. "Kim, find a chair to tie him to."

"No, no," Gino put his hands up. "I was only making a joke. I apologize. If you just take me back to Lisbon, you won't hear another peep out of me. Honest!"

"I'm not in a particularly humorous mood," said Leborio coldly. "Go ahead, Kim."

Over the muffled sounds of the hairdresser's cries for help, the giant stuck a dried and dusty blackboard sponge into Gino's mouth. He punched the man in the stomach, rendering him semiconscious, and then, as steadfastly as a surgeon, he shredded a fallen curtain into neat strips that he then used to tie the man up.

"Let's go back, Kim," muttered Leborio lingering behind the window. "No sense in hanging around here for now."

"What about the actress, boss?"

Leborio looked up. This time he was smiling confidently. "Give her a few days in the company of Armin Pector and she'll be good and ready for me. In the meanwhile, we'll swing by town hall and see if the old hag is still there." Taking one last look at the tied-up hairdresser, he added, "A bird in hand is worth two in the bush. Maybe this trip won't be a total waste if I can get my hands on the old gal's bling."

Kim dusted the chalk off his massive hands and then pushed them in his trousers pockets.

"I think this place is a school, boss," he decided, looking about him.

"Remind me to teach you how to read," said the guru as they walked out of one of the upper story classrooms of the *Escola Secundária de Santo Domingo*.

* * *

It was just as well that his saliva had turned into chalk. At least it prevented him from swallowing the pasty mixture of dust, wiped-out lessons, and fear secretion. If only he had married the dentist's daughter, Maryam. He could have opened up a carpet shop in a posh area of Teheran, could have owned a big house with a large living room painted silver or gold, and a back yard where Maryam and he could smoke apple-flavoured hookah, drink tea, and suck on dates. He would have taken the kids to Dubai once a year, for their family vacation, and splash in what was probably the only water park built in the middle of a desert. He could have been a proper Persian man, doing the things that proper Persian men do, visiting relatives with his proper Persian wife, and raising his kids to mentally multiply three-digit numbers. Instead, he chose to run off, cut hair badly, and do the bidding of a mad, old woman.

"Goodness, Doctor Gino, is that you?"

The pretty redhead from the hotel stared at him from the doorway before taking the sponge out of his mouth. It made a sound similar to splitting Velcro. The outer layer of his tongue, calcified by now, came off with it. He blabbered and drooled in her hand, while she reached for a box of tissues from the teacher's desk. She wiped his face and held a half-full bottle of water up to his mouth.

"I drank from it already, but in your condition I'd say that would hardly be a concern," she said. He rinsed his mouth, spat, and then swallowed a second gulp.

"Thank you, that's awfully kind of you," he said to her. "I don't know what would have happened to me if you hadn't come."

"Who did this to you?"

"I was mugged," he lied. "That sort of stuff happens to tourists all the time."

"Who mugged you?"

"Two Portuguese men," he replied. "Aren't you going to untie me?"

"In a moment," she said coldly. "Two men, you say. How do you know they were Portuguese?"

"Huh?"

"If you're sure they were locals, all we have to do to catch them is call the police. They usually keep files about all their felons, and you should be able to identify the men who did this to you in no time," she explained. "That's if you're positive they were Portuguese."

"I don't know," began Gino, confused about the implications of involving the police. It could be days until they let him go, and they were bound to stumble onto discrepancies in his story. What a glorious end to his tragic story, to be thrown in jail for withholding information from the police, half a world away from his home. "I guess I assumed they must have been. Maybe they were not."

"How can you not be sure? They must have spoken to each other.

Did they speak Portuguese?"

"I don't remember. Everything happened so fast. Will you please untie me now?"

She took a step back. "Fast, you say. Then they must have attacked you here, in this room. And here I was, thinking they dragged you in here from outside."

He nodded his head quickly and willingly, holding out his curtain-tied wrists.

Iris folded her hands in her lap, interlocking her fingers. "Of course, you trespassing on a movie set or school property—whichever you prefer—begs the question of what your business was in this room. The entrance to the second story was locked. And if you arrived here before the thieves, then you must have been the one who broke in. That would place you in a position of delinquency and would force me to consider leaving you tied up to wait for the police."

His eyes bulged out. "No! Please don't call the police. I'll tell you the truth. The muggers forced me to lie. They dragged me here from the street and said that if I told anyone they would kill me."

"Poor Doctor Gino," she empathized. "You've been through so much today. I understand that. And it will soon be over. In fact, it will be over just as soon as you tell me why the muggers chose to spare you the gold necklace, ring, and watch you're wearing. It is my understanding muggers generally thrive on those particular items."

"Sentimental value," he tried. "I told them they were gifts from my late mother."

Iris paced slowly and stopped to face him. Gently touching his shoulder, she leaned forward until their eyes met. "Such kind souls, these muggers. Makes one wonder how they had it in them to tie you up in the first place. I haven't heard of such compassion from a thief since Robin Hood. But you know what? I bet you if I check your pocket for a wallet, there will be money in it." Her hand dropped away from his shoulder and she straightened up. "Please spare me the thrill of going through your front trouser pocket and tell me why that is. Did the thieves only take the amount they needed? Kind of like withdrawing from an ATM machine? Or perhaps you agreed to pay them in instalments."

Gino kicked the chair with his heels in a futile effort to set himself free. To be consistent with the other fifty-seven times it had been kicked by the man over the past hour, the chair refused to break.

"Could I have a bit more water, please?" he tried, grimacing.

"Why? Having trouble bullshitting me with your mouth dry? I'll give you water just as soon as you tell me the truth," she said, twisting the cap off the water bottle.

From under the dishevelled fringe hanging about his forehead, the hairdresser gave her a look. "Are you some kind of detective?" Seeing there was no reply, Gino burst out, "Listen lady, mind telling me what your problem is? If you're going for the Spanish Inquisition, I think you've got the wrong country. Try a little to the east."

Iris slowly shook her head, a look of discontent etched across her face. She twisted the cap back on the water bottle. Just as she opened her mouth to say something, behind them, someone cleared their throat as means of announcing their presence. Gino would have followed the redhead's lead in turning to face the intruder if only he could move. But as it happened, he was still quite tied up.

"Who's this guy?" asked the newcomer.

"You scared me," she said. "This here is Doctor Gino."

"Why is he tied to a chair? Did you do it?"

"Of course not. He was already tied when I got here."

"Then why don't you untie him?"

"What an outstandingly pertinent question!" exclaimed the good doctor.

"Quiet." She hit him gently across the head with the almost emptied out water bottle. "I'm in the process of getting to the bottom of things," she explained to the newcomer. "You may stay and watch, or you may go. It's entirely up to you."

The young man, dressed a tad too flamboyantly for Gino's taste, walked into his visual field craning his neck over him as if he were the centrepiece at an art exhibit. He gazed at Gino from multiple angles and propped himself on the teacher's desk, where he sat quietly for the next few moments.

"Is this your friend?" asked Gino with an ingratiating smile.

"This is my associate," she answered, making an introductory flourish with her empty water bottle, "Lord Byron."

That explained the milky white skin, inferred the self-proclaimed psychiatrist or psychologist— whichever applied. Everyone knew British aristocrats shagged their cousins into some pretty dubious genetic side-effects, one of which being alarmingly unhealthy coloration.

"Your Excellence!" he bowed his head, uncertain of how he should address the inbred noble. "It's an honour to meet a veritable British Lord. I would shake your hand, but I'm afraid I'm a little tied up at the moment. Unless Your Excellence—or is it Your Grace?—would care to untie me."

"He insists on lying to me about whoever tied him up," explained Iris, removing a piece of lint from her dress.

"Have you tried torture?" suggested the younger man without the slightest British accent. "I saw this incredibly large bodyguard do it to a hooker once, and it seemed to work well. If you want, I think I can reproduce it. It's still fresh in my memory," he said, tapping a knuckle to his head. "The smell of cheap perfume mixed with warm blood and turpentine, the sound of screams and pleas for mercy."

Gino's eyes gawked out in sheer horror. He had always been suspicious of the British, he reflected. There was something creepy in their calm demeanour.

"Glad to hear it," replied the redhead in a sarcastic tone. "I think we'll just sit it out a while longer. Doctor Gino was just about to tell me the truth about how he came to be tied up to this chair. Weren't you, Doctor?"

"What was the turpentine for?" asked the fraudulent hairdresser.

"No idea," said the young man. "I got there after she confessed to having opened up her own business after working hours. By that point the bodyguard was pretty much wrapping it up with a couple of farewell smacks."

"Smacks?" repeated Gino, as the spark plugs to his dehydrated brain made a small but significant connection.

"Well, listen," said Lord Byron, "I can see you've got a handle on things here, so I'll get out of your hair." He hesitated for a moment. "I just came up to tell you I bumped into an old buddy of mine a few minutes ago. He's here on holiday, and would you believe it, he's staying at the same hotel as us." There was no reply, and the young man continued. "He and his girlfriend got lost from their group, and they need a ride back to Lisbon. It would be the decent thing to do to invite them to ride in our trailer. But I told them I'd check with you before giving them a definite answer. Wouldn't want anything to interfere with our investigation."

Iris considered it for a moment and nodded her head. "Fine, tell them to come. As long as they're able to behave properly," she added, raising an inquisitive eyebrow at Armin.

"Oh, yes, no need to worry. My buddy is a super Christian," he bragged. "All he ever does is pray. He's probably better behaved than you," he said, getting off the desk. "Well, then, carry on up here! I've got to get back to work now." His voice resounded with pride. "They're shooting my scene, and I must say, I didn't think I would be quite as excited, but I am. I mean, it's not a spoken part or anything, but Athena says my part is vital to the entire film."

At the mention of her name, Gino's eyes bugged out just a little, as he let out an involuntary cough. It was attributed to thirst and ignored. As discretion was the mark of a good hairdresser, Gino stopped coughing and continued to draw mental connections.

"I bet she does," answered the redhead somewhat distantly.

"Well, Iris, I regret to inform you not everyone is of the opinion that my role is irrelevant to the movie. In fact, many would argue it is a central role, even without the words."

She waited quietly for a few moments, lending an ear to the siesta silence outside. Not a bird chirping, not a camera squeaking, not an actress screeching. Only the complete silence of a torrid summer day.

"You'd better run back to the set," she grinned. "Sounds like they're filming your part."

The boy forgot himself for a moment. His eyes welled up and he almost burst out crying. "Nice meeting you, Doctor Gino," he said storming out of the dusty classroom.

"Ta-ta, Your Excellence! Lovely to meet you. What sort of part is he playing in the movie?" he asked his inquisitor.

"The part of Lord Byron."

"Most interesting! So he'll be playing himself? He must be pretty well known then."

"Now where were we?" Iris turned to the man in the chair. "Ah, you were just about to tell me the truth, and in return, I was about to offer to untie you. If it's a really good story, I'll throw in a ride back to Lisbon. What do you say?"

# CHAPTER 22

# LISBON AWAITS

Collapsed on the sofa couch aboard the white Mercedes trailer, Perla Galanis sobbed into her Hermes scarf. For the past few hours, she had run all around Sintra without really being sure of what she searched for. While running like a headless chicken, however, a few things occurred to her. First, it came to mind that despite her very best efforts, she never actually managed to meet Leborio. Not even for a moment. How was it possible that after almost a week in Portugal, travelling through the same places and lodging in the same hotel, she never once saw her intended? Second, Perla saw no reason why the ostrich girl from hotel Lido should have been in Sintra unless she came along with Leborio. And if that was the case, the third thing that occurred to Perla was that there was a very big chance she had been had. In hindsight, she recalled the compliments Leborio gave her were mostly directed at her jewellery. She also recalled the manner in which Leborio's hands seemed to always find their way around her necklace. What an old fool I have been, she thought to herself, blowing her nose in the scarf. Not only had she lost the Sophie necklace, but she had also lost her cat.

As a last resort, she called her son and reported the theft of the jewels and the loss of the pet. Dennis seemed significantly more interested in the first. Obviously, he had never given feline companionship a fair chance. Still, he was on his way to Portugal to recover the stolen necklace. Her heart as black as ink, the sexagenarian fell asleep, sobbing.

* * *

The sun descended slowly behind the soft peak of the mountain until all that was left of it was a fascicle of rays pointing at the clouds above like a flashlight through the fog. The driver held his perfectly convex belly with both hands, summoning the crew one last time. The vibration of his baritone voice carried over the neighbourhood of the *Escola Secundária de Santo Domingo*, and even though the American crew remained oblivious to the exact translation of his call, they gathered the gist of its meaning and rushed back to the trailer. The first ones to arrive were Charlotte McMahon and the makeup artist, followed by Harold and Athena, who seemed to be very much engaged in a religious debate.

"I think the word *virgin* can be interpreted metaphorically," gesticulated Athena, lifting the robe to her costume above the knees while she crossed the street. "To say she had a pure heart is not to say she didn't care about looking good," she insisted. "I'm not telling you to turn her into Lady Gaga, but I have a feeling a little makeup would have helped with public relations." Walking ahead of her, Harold climbed aboard the trailer shaking his head vehemently.

"Wait up!" yelled Armin as he ran uphill. He was followed by a tall, well-built blond man holding a plastic water bottle. An equally tall girl, with long and wobbly legs, followed him. Halfway up the folding stepladder, Athena waited for them to get close. Holding on to the trailer door, she looked down to the two strangers, inspecting the girl for a moment.

"Who are they?" She turned to Armin.

Armin wiped his forehead with one of his ruffled cuffs, revealing red blotches across his milky complexion. Panting and wheezing, he pushed the blond man forward and spoke, "This is my friend, Umberto Bore. He is the house deejay in my father's nightclub." Then turning to Umberto he started, "Umberto, this is my . . . colleague?" he looked at her for confirmation.

"I know who you are," the blond man gushed, shaking her hand. "I'm probably your biggest fan."

Athena rolled her eyes. "Doubtful," she said, turning her attention to Armin. Still panting from the run, he gave her a look. "What?" She shrugged. "They all say they are."

"Listen," said Armin, pulling himself up the steps until they were at eye level. "I was hoping they could catch a ride with us back to Lisbon. They're staying at the same hotel as us, so it would be no trouble."

Athena peeled her eyes away from Armin's, staring down at the two newcomers. Her distrustful gaze lingered on the girl. Her shoulders were weary, slouching negligently away from her thin and unusually long neck. The girl had circles around her bloodshot eyes, and her hair appeared unwashed and stringy. She looked tired and worn out, like a rag doll discarded by a fickle child. For a moment, she leaned against Umberto, taking his arm to hold herself up. Umberto took the cap off the plastic bottle and gently passed her the water.

"All right," Athena nodded, her eyes sparkling from the excitement of a new idea. "On one condition. Lose the other one."

Armin scratched his head, "The other what?"

"You know what I mean," she winked. "Lose the one you came with."

"Who did you come with?" asked Umberto, screwing the lid back on his bottle.

Armin did not reply. He gave Athena a sharp gaze and descended from the steps. Then, as if to excuse her behaviour, he explained, "I came here as part of a team of investigators on an assignment. She wants me to drop my partner," he nodded in Athena's direction, "because she's jealous of her."

"Hey," yelled the actress from the trailer door. "I'm still within earshot."

"Investigator?" muttered Umberto.

"Good," Armin yelled back. "I was hoping you could hear me, you shrew!"

"Shrew!" shrieked Athena, stomping her foot against the metal step. Her well-defined cheeks were flushed. "If it wasn't for this shrew, you'd still be chasing after your own tail, hoping to get the redhead to take you seriously."

"Redhead?" repeated Umberto, letting go of Snejana's arm. He looked as if he was in a trance.

"If it wasn't for me, you wouldn't even be in the movie," she sizzled with anger, as she descended to street level. Making a fist with both hands, Athena started toward Armin. "You'd still be her gopher, clueless to your own investigation. Is that what you want for yourself?" She pushed him back, red with frustration, huffing curses at him. In an effort to defend himself, Armin grabbed her by the wrists, pressing them together against his feeble, pale chest. He used the other arm to hold her steady, and hastened to lift her off the ground, backing her into the metal side of the trailer. Kicking her stilettos off, she wrapped her legs around his waist, trying to hit him with her bare heels. Their noses almost touching, Athena squirmed for a moment before she looked up at him and exhaled, parting her lips to exhale.

"What the hell is going on out here?"

Both Athena and Armin turned their heads to see Harold standing at the top of the steps. Panting, they released one another.

"Nothing," she answered first, dusting her costume off. "Just rehearsing."

Harold glanced at the two newcomers and asked, "Rehearsing for a scene I'm not aware of?" He shook his shiny head like a parent who had just caught his children fighting.

"You'd better cool it, Byron," he put up his index finger. "I've let a few of them remarks go by today. But you'd better cool it while you can, or there might not be enough redheads in the world to save your scrawny ass."

Armin's brow furrowed as he opened him mouth to reply. But before he could do so, the director pointed to the school entrance. "Speaking of redheads, there she is. Are we ready to go now?"

All eyes turned in Iris' direction. Closing the school gate behind a man dressed in a white smock, Iris pushed him along and crossed over toward the trailer. Suddenly, as she looked up, her eyes met Umberto's. She stopped in her tracks, a wide smile lighting up her face. He dropped his plastic bottle to the ground, walked up to her, and rushed her off her feet, spinning her around in the air.

"What is *he* doing here?" asked the man in the white smock, staring at Umberto in disbelief.

"Is this another scene I'm not aware of?" grimaced the director from the top of the steps.

Picking up his hanging jaw, Armin stepped away from Athena and muttered, "I don't think any of us were aware of *this* scene."

Umberto put Iris down, and they stood still for a moment, just looking at each other.

"I had a feeling it would be you," he broke the silence, smiling from ear to ear.

She smiled back, taking his hands in hers. "Look at you," she said. "You're a grown man, Bert."

"Bert?" Armin gagged. "Did I miss something?"

"You two know each other?" The man in the white smock asked the question on everyone's minds.

Iris nodded without taking her eyes off Umberto. "Yes," she said plainly. "We grew up together."

Then, as if remembering something, she gasped. "Oh, I'm sorry. I forgot to introduce my guest," she turned to the man in the white smock. "This here is Doctor Gino," she said, flashing her eyes at the hairdresser.

With her back leaning against the Mercedes trailer, Athena let out an involuntary snort.

"He'll be travelling back to Lisbon with us," continued Iris, ignoring Athena. "Isn't that right, Doctor?" she turned to Gino.

Shifting on his legs, the hairdresser sank his hands in the wide pockets of his smock. "I'm not really," he mumbled, shrivelling in embarrassment.

Iris placed a comforting hand on his shoulder. "Not really what? Travelling back to Lisbon?"

"Not really a doctor," interjected Athena, walking up to the man to get a closer look. "Not unless he's got a PhD in backcombing. This is my mother's hairdresser," she snivelled.

Gino's chest narrowed, and his eyes fell to the ground, avoiding contact with the others. He opened his mouth but not a sound came out. Clearing his voice, he looked up at Iris and said with a quivering lip, "I should have . . . I should have told you."

"Yes, you should have," she shrugged. "But that doesn't mean I didn't know you were lying."

"I understand if you don't want to take me back to Lisbon," he said in a small voice.

"Oh, let him come," Athena waved her hand magnanimously. "Mummy will need someone to cheer her up after what she's been through." For the first time that evening, Iris and Armin exchanged glances. "Oh yeah, that's right!" carried on Athena. "You guys weren't around for her return. Do you want the good news or the bad news first?" And without allowing for an answer, she made a long face, "The bad news is that Mummy got a very expensive family heirloom stolen. A diamond necklace that would have been mine after she .. . well, you know," she slumped. "But the good news," added Athena with a cheerful smile, "is that the cat was also lost."

Everyone stared at her quietly for a moment. Gino gasped and took a small step back. He stood up on his toes, trying to peak through the tinted glass inside the trailer. Instinctively, he reached into his pocket and pulled out the fine-toothed comb he used to set Perla's hair. A few feet away, Armin pressed his shoe against the asphalt, overcome by a sudden urge to moonwalk. He shook his head to clear his thoughts and made for the trailer door, forcing Harold to go back inside.

"Let's get out of here," he said, scanning the thickening darkness around him with an ominous look. "Does anyone else hear bells?"

Athena shook her head and followed him into the trailer. Behind her, Umberto and Iris climbed aboard with their arms entwined. Snejana, who had been leaning against one of the headlights ever since Umberto ran off to meet Iris, was staring quietly at the hairdresser.

"What did you do?" she said, pointing to his face. "Eat chalk?"

Gino wiped his mouth with the back of his hand. "In a matter of speaking," he said, helping her up the folding stepladder.

* * *

Sometime later, the white Mercedes trailer made its way down the dark, winding road back to Lisbon, oblivious to the small but vicious tricycle struggling to catch up to it. Still carrying a grudge against Armin for having lost him a significant bet to the baker, the ice-cream vendor peddled his little heart out, cursing at the dimming sight of the white trailer.

Inside the trailer, a number of passengers slightly greater than before dozed off in silence. Athena, with her lovely head resting on Armin's shoulder, made a soft snoring sound, like an intermittent gurgle, competing against the steadier stream coming from the director's throat. Charlotte, the publicist, had passed out with her face buried in the leather-bound agenda, while Doctor Gino, who had been reunited with his patient, stroked Perla's dishevelled hair with the tail of his comb as her breath fluttered. She had spent the past few hours crying and had not finished doing so even after having fallen asleep.

Yes, all was silent aboard the white Mercedes trailer—all but Umberto and Iris, wedged between a seat and the carpeted floor, gesticulating to a whispered story that Armin, struggling to listen in from a distance, could not make out.

# CHAPTER 23

# THE PHILOSOPHER GURU

Just because the crew had returned to Lisbon did not mean filming ended. Filming ended because the new leading man in the movie *Fatima: Three Secrets and a Vision* was unable to get any sleep the night before, causing him to look more like Uncle Fester and less like a romantic English poet. And although his part was silent, it was not blind.

Armin tossed and turned, alone in the large oak bed, unable to shake the image from the trailer. He carried the luggage to room 112 with the cheerfulness of an old mule. There wasn't much to carry—just the equipment they rented to film the documentary. But the idea of her going off in the middle of the night made him want to chew his fingers off.

They had taken the stairs to avoid jamming the elevators against the sleepy contingent of the white Mercedes trailer, and somewhere between the first and second floor, he'd lost her. Iris held the door to the staircase open, and then she asked if he was going to be okay. The next thing he knew, she was gone.

His first impulse was to go back and look for her. Then he remembered Athena's advice and decided he wasn't going to get very far with Iris by chasing her. No! This time, he was going to stick to the plan, act distant and aloof, and make her come to him. He was going to be charming and deliberate, one of those guys who light up the room just by stepping into it. He was going to dress sharply and speak cleverly, smile at no one in particular, and welcome the hungry eyes of all women. Then she would want him, wouldn't she? Would she ever? What if she didn't?

If only there was a way to be sure. If only there were formulas for these sorts of things. One would think that men of science could spare some of the time spent on finding the answer to cold fusion to solve the mystery of unrequited love. Was love not important enough? It felt painfully important to him. Kind of like a root canal without the freezing. His heart throbbed and squirmed like the infected pulp of a tooth, making him want to bang his head against a wall until jealousy, misery, or consciousness—whichever happened to be first—would cease to exist. He feared he lost her before he even had her. He feared asking, being rejected, and looking like a fool. And now that he had been infected with this pain, this craving, this insanity, he mostly feared a lifetime of fighting the torment off, like some sort of chronic disease.

Visions of Iris having cocktails by the bar with Umberto—his hand brushing against hers—jolted Armin in and out of momentary naps. He tossed and turned, covering his head with a pillow. Should have let the bigot SOB walk back to Lisbon. After all, he could have guessed what effect she had on unassuming men. All she had to do was squint her eyes ever so slightly, and the poor bastards would forget themselves. Armin, Harold the director, Doctor Gino—all victims of the same weapon: the eye squint.

Bastard, he spat over the polished edge of the veranda, staring at the distant semicircle of the moon. He paced around the infinity pool, stopping to check the street below every few minutes. An incontrollable need to know itched him like a bad rash. In the case of severe itches, mind triumphs over matter only if there is enough of it. And because it was no secret that Armin's mind was not his most striking feature, the tormented lover gave in and scratched.

He put on a black shirt and a pair of cargo pants, pumping himself into field operations mode. And proving that Athena was on to something in regards to his talent for imitation, he thought of the last season of *24* he'd watched. He took cover by the wall, blending in against the ivory revival wallpaper where topaz pheasants rested on pink cherry blossoms, showing no concern for the immutable laws of gravity. He held up his Swiss Army knife with both hands, ready to shoot imaginary bullets out of its corkscrew opener, and made short, geometrical steps all the way down to the Hotel Almeida bar.

* * *

Later that morning, well after the sun had risen, a very elegant woman came out of a taxicab, and entered the lobby area of Hotel Almeida. Seemingly unimpressed with the exquisite decorum of the famous hotel, the woman walked up to the front desk and asked the Valentino for a room, but not before scrutinizing the lobby for unwanted attention.

"Certainly, madam. Do you have a reservation?"

She gave him the name under which a reservation had been made and anxiously looked around her from under the wide brim of her black sun hat. No one could know she was here. After all, appearances must be maintained, she thought, fixing the high-wasted cinch belt that balanced the dark pencil-shaped dress she wore.

"Madam, perhaps I misunderstood," said the Valentino after a few moments. "You already have a room with us. Did you want the key to your room?"

She nodded her hat at him, put her hand out to receive the key card, and marched straight to the elevator. The woman got off on the second floor, looked for the room, and swiftly swiped the card, closing the door behind her. Inside, besides the large oak bed, a few ottomans, and a loveseat, the room was dark and empty.

She slipped out of her heels and cautiously walked to the veranda, looking to see if anyone was there. Damn, she thought, they must have been out. Focus! Focus! There must be something lying around here. She opened the drawers to the night table and checked for clues. Not much except for a pack of gum, a hairbrush, and a hotel Bible. Behind her, a hollow telephone ring made her shudder. She took a piece of gum to calm her nerves. What she really would have liked was a cigarette. But she'd given that up years ago.

The hair between the bristles of the brush was long and warm-coloured. In all likelihood, the woman was a redhead.

Dring-dring! Dring-dring! The phone ring kept echoing about the room as she checked the closet and the bathroom. She found nothing more than half a dozen chiffon dresses and a familiar pair of men's red runners left to dry in the bathroom. Where were they? Damn it! She wasn't about to sit and wait for them to return. She picked up the phone and waited for someone at the other end to speak.

"Hello? Ms. Bendal?"

"Uhm," she agreed.

"I've been trying to get a hold of you all morning," said the nasal female voice at the other end. "We're phoning about the printouts you're expecting."

"Uhm."

"We have them."

"Hmm," improvised the impostor, sounding puzzlingly disinterested.

"The paternity test, Ms. Bendal. The test is positive. Perfect match between the father and the son," said the nasal voice. "You wanted the printouts," she concluded, sounding rather deflated.

"Uhm," let out the woman in the wide brimmed hat, mostly out of habit, before hanging up and bursting into a frenzy of incongruent motions. "I knew it! I knew it all along. The son of a bitch!"

And without further ado, she fell back on the bed, causing her elegant hat to wheel across the room and onto the veranda. At about the same time, the alarming thump of a very large body repeatedly crashing against the front door caused her to follow her hat outside the living quarters of the suite. Wishing she'd locked the door behind her, she hid behind the white curtains, holding on to the black hat.

"He's not here, boss." She heard the all-too-familiar voice without being able to make out the other man's reply. "If you don't mind me asking boss, what's the plan now? Do we go after the boy? Or do we wait up here until he returns?"

Moved by instincts older than herself, the woman came out from behind the curtains. "Until who returns?" she asked, causing the jaws of both men to hang open with surprise. "You expecting someone?"

"Amalia," Leborio said, smiling and opening his exquisitely shaped arms to embrace her.

"Don't you dare touch me, you pathetic excuse for a human being!" Holding her head up high, she scrutinized the confused-looking giant next to him. "And you, you big ape, after everything my husband has done for you, after everything you've gained from working for my family, you run off with Satan's minister here?"

"I . . . I . . ." tried the giant. "I didn't run off. We're on holiday."

"On holiday?" repeated Amalia.

"Yes ma'am. Holiday without pay. What's the name I'm looking for, boss?" he turned to Leborio. "I mean, younger boss."

"Leave of absence."

"That's it! I'm on a leave of absence."

"And does your leave of absence include investigating my son?"

The giant shuffled his feet and looked at Leborio for answers. He was, however, out of luck. The guru appeared to be as baffled as his sidekick. His spiritual training alerted him that keeping the silence would not work to his advantage.

"Come now, Amalia. I'm not sure what you mean. Your son is doing very well. In fact, I just saw him the other day on the movie set."

"What movie set?"

"Of the movie he plays in," explained Kim slowly, the way his mother did when he had difficulty understanding something. "I think he's hooked up with Athena Jeudi. You know, the actress," he winked, just before Leborio froze the rest of the explanation with a subglacial glance. "Sorry, boss, but I think that's the truth."

She raised an incredulous eyebrow. But a mother remains a mother even when her son is rumoured to be an item with the single most famous celebrity of her time. More concerned than starstruck, Amalia cut to the chase, "What is my son doing in a movie?"

"He's playing in it," explained the giant, batting his crossed eyes at the woman. "Isn't that why he's here?"

"I know exactly why he's here," she shouted, turning her attention to the spiritual master, her fiery brown eyes transfixing him. "I know all about your devious plan to convince Placido that Armin is not his son. And I know all about the detective you hired to do your dirty work." She paused for a reaction, and then hissed, "Your plan has failed!"

"Amalia, please!" Leborio took a step back. "You're giving me a headache. Calm yourself down."

"What's going on?" asked a new voice behind them, putting an end to their argument. All eyes turned to the door to face a distraught young man with dark circles around his equally dark eyes, holding up a Swiss Army knife. "Mom, what are you doing here? With them?"

He pointed the corkscrew at the other two men. "I don't understand. What are you all doing in my room?"

"Your room? Isn't this the room of the detective?"

Armin stood in the doorway. "Yes, Mom." He nodded wretchedly. "The room was reserved under her name. We're staying here together. And wait a minute, how did you know about her?"

"Her?" whispered Leborio, as the proverbial penny dropped. It was all beginning to make sense.

"Oh, don't play innocent, you sleek bastard!" Amalia turned to the guru, raising her voice. "Placido told me all about your detective friend," she said, getting a few steps closer to look him in the eyes. "He was reluctant at first, but I got it out of him. He confessed everything. He told me it was your idea to get a paternity test."

Armin's eyes sank in a little deeper, giving out the air of two suction cups stuck to the inside of a white balloon. "You know Iris?" he turned to Leborio.

"Of course I know Iris," replied the guru, offended by the absurdity of the question. He rubbed his scruffy chin, pacing about the room wondering quietly where Umberto might be found at that fine, dawn-cracking hour. The answer, plain as it was, hovered in the air at the speed of an imminent threat. "Where is she?" asked the guru, and seeing there was no reply, he added, "And you really shouldn't call her a detective. She hates that. She prefers the term investigator."

Armin's suction cups sank in a little more. Iris did hate being referred to as a detective. One had to know her well enough to be aware of this. He took a few steps back, watching the guru with a gloomy expression.

Frowning with worry, Amalia grabbed her son's hand, pulling him away, "Come, Armin, you need to come back with me right away."

"Why?" he pulled his hands out of his mother's clasp. "Why do I need to come back with you right away?"

Amalia stared her son at a loss for words. She hadn't thought of that. It only made sense to her that once she found her Armin and rescued him, he would want to return home with her, where she could protect him. "Well, because we have to go home," she stumbled. "You have to get back to your life."

"What life? I am an eighteen-year-old freshman, which would be exactly right if I were a freshman in college. But, as it happens, I am a freshman in junior high, as I have been for the past five years." He put up his fingers for added effect. "Clearly, you must know by now I am not made of the stuff of academics. I am also not made of the stuff Dad is made of," he said, wistfully. "I could never rule the streets any more than the streets could rule me. I've got nothing in common with the streets, except for the fact they meet with the wheels on my Ferrari about six or seven times a day. To be honest, I'm surprised anyone noticed I was gone at all. Dad most of all. Unless I drop by Neon Lounge, I don't cross paths with him. And I hardly ever drop by. I mean, what's the point? He's busy with this one here," he pointed at the guru. "And between the two of them, there aren't any women left to talk to in the club. So there really are no perks in being there. Not that I would want to touch any woman they've touched. And I'm sorry if this sprinkles salt on the wound," he turned to his mother, "but I suspect it doesn't come as a shock to you that Dad has other women."

Amalia sat on the bed, placing her wide-brimmed hat beside her. "So, you see, I have nothing to come back to," he concluded. "I just got a role in a Hollywood production and the chance to make something of myself. Some even say I'm good at it," he said, standing a little taller. "Acting, I mean. Who would have thought? Well, Athena did. And she's far from perfect— although men seem to think she is a goddess—but if you can't have the one you love, they say you must love the one you're with. With a little effort and emotional maturity, I might come to care for her one day. After all, she is the only person who ever believed in me," he added affectionately. "That's gotta be worth something, right?"

"You are aware you're speaking of Athena Jeudi," inquired the guru. "The most beautiful woman in the world?"

"That's a matter of taste," said Armin. The mixture of sadness, disappointment, and exhaustion made him look almost wise. "To me, she is not the most beautiful woman."

"You poor boy," smiled Leborio. "You've fallen in love with her, haven't you? She has that effect on most people."

"Are you deaf? He said he hasn't."

"No, Amalia. He said he hasn't fallen in love with Athena Jeudi. That's not who I'm referring to."

Armin put his head down, looking rather like a schoolboy whose bladder has refused to grow as fast as the rest of his body, spilling its contents in the middle of a test.

"Pity," continued Leborio, "to have the alpha mare and go for a bloodweed." He walked to the loveseat, paced around it like a great big cat, and decided on a spot to sink into. He crossed his legs into a lotus-like pretzel, paying no mind to the subtle cracking of bones breaking the pensive silence of the room. From his dark corner, the Spanish guru spoke, his low-timbered voice projecting against the ceiling. "It is because of men like you that unremarkable women end up having remarkable lives. A sin that should be punished, in my opinion. And I will tell you why," he said, cracking his fingers.

"Every woman is told by someone at some point in her life that she is beautiful. This banal word has the unsuspected power of setting an entire chain of events in motion. Just like the secret chants of ritualistic initiations open up spiritual doors one might never otherwise have walked through, telling a woman she is beautiful causes said woman to lose her common sense," he paused, shaking his head in disproval. "Cynical women would pose as nonbelievers and brush off the compliment as clumsily as any man. But deep down," he added, bringing his hand to his heart, "inside the carcase where femininity conceals, a little mechanism opens up like the astronomical clock in Prague, filling the woman with a warm feeling of being sure of herself, if even for a mere moment. Gratification is the result of many centuries where a woman's only power was her beauty. It's as logical as any evolutionary leap. And evolution could not be undermined by women's liberation."

His eyes fell on Amalia, fixing her from under his monobrow. "Next to motherhood," he said, gesturing toward her, "gratification is the only moment where a woman feels at peace with herself entirely. As if she has fulfilled some mission she was born and trained for. It only takes one heartfelt compliment in a woman's lifetime to trigger the secret craving to be seen as beautiful. And who would like to live life knowing they are not beautiful nor will they ever be?"

As he paused, all eyes, including his own, descended on the half-concealed shape of his magnificent arms. Feeling the pang of imperfection, Armin became acutely aware of his pallor and awkwardness. He wondered how much work one had to put into looking like Leborio. Probably more than three times a week at the local gym, doing twenty minutes of cardio and lifting weights for fifteen. Maybe he could step it up a notch and get a personal trainer. But what if that didn't work? He feared genetics played a dominant role in looking this good. Some people were just naturally gorgeous. Unfortunately, he was not one of those people. Looking over at his mother, Armin could tell she had been a great beauty. So that left his father entirely responsible for the genetic calamity he felt he was. On the upside, the paternity test left no room for uncertainty. Placido could be blamed with a clear sense of being in the right. Turning his attention back to the Spanish guru, who was still going on about the importance of beauty in the female universe, he wondered if Leborio had always been this perfect. Armin would have given anything to know his secret.

"But I digress," he heard Leborio say. "My purpose was to explain to you how irresponsible it is of you to show an unremarkable woman that you love her. In that reckless act you create and empower a tricky little monster," he lifted up a finger, in a gesture of warning. "At first, women doubt that they truly are beautiful—as they should," carried on the guru. "I'm not being cruel, only rational. Now, you may imagine, there can only be so many truly gorgeous women at a time, just as there can only be so many truly gorgeous horses in one herd. But as time goes by, the memory of that one compliment starts to work on the psyche of the woman, gains the mythical proportions of a sacred memory, and becomes part of her convictions. Why shouldn't it? It makes life bearable for her to think she is one of the beautiful horses in the herd. Secretly, all women doubt themselves," he whispered, turning to the males in the room. He seemed to take no notice of Amalia's incessant eye rolls and went on speaking and gesturing like a professor behind his lecturing podium.

"The paradox is that while they doubt themselves, they also think themselves beautiful. Even the ugly ones. Perhaps not on the whole, but some part of them: they have exquisite eyes, lips, hair, legs—you name it. No matter how unremarkable, deep down inside, women think they're beautiful. And Iris Bendal is no exception," he said, turning his attention entirely to Armin. "She's not the gorgeous horse of the heard. She's no Athena Jeudi. But she's one of the pretty, robust mares. She has probably received more than one compliment in her life, and so she has genuinely come to believe she is beautiful. What she doesn't understand, is why the alpha male, the head stallion," he stretched out his arms, bursting his buttons with pride, "has not made a play for her. Can you imagine the mixed messages she must have received? 'You've got eyes like the ocean after a storm, Iris!'; 'You've got lips I could die kissing!' —all setting her up for failure. Because at the end of the day, she is not the type of mare the head stallion will go after. But she believes herself to be. Rather sad, don't you think?" he wrinkled his nose for a moment, before reaching his conclusion.

"So you see, it is our duty, as the superior sex, to remind women they are commonplace and ordinary. It is our duty to keep them from the irrational high of confidence. We have to keep them from thinking they have the power to chose, the power to deny us, the power to judge our actions."

There was no immediate reply from the other three. Amalia exchanged glances with her son, while Kim waited with his mouth slightly open, nodding his head ever so slightly.

"I suppose you're the head stallion in this story," huffed Armin.

Counting on silence to be an answer in itself, the Spanish guru closed his eyes and threw his head back on the seat rest, as if awaiting a round of applause. But Armin would not give up that easily.

"How is it that you know Iris? Does she take your yoga class?"

Leborio took his time before shaking his head, "She's not the group fitness type."

"So how do you know her? Did you need a detective and found her in the phonebook?"

"She's not listed," grinned the guru, refusing to give a clear answer. "Anyway, time's a wasting. Lots of things on my agenda this morning. I wish the two of you good luck sorting things out, and should you decide to return home, have a lovely trip," he stood up. "Kim and I must bid you farewell."

With the unexpected agility of a Great Dane, Kim jumped to his feet and was by the door before Amalia and Armin could blink.

"Not so fast!" said the woman, barring the hallway with her arm. Her expensive watch sparkled in the light of the Baroque wall lamp. "You haven't told us what you were doing here. How did you get into my son's room and for what purpose?"

The guru turned to Armin but found an equally avid interest to hear the answer to Amalia's question. "We heard he was in the hotel and wanted to say hi," he tried.

"You're gonna have to do better than that."

This time Leborio decided to tell the truth. "All right. I came to make sure Armin would not interfere with my plans. I intend to take Athena out tonight. But I suppose you don't care, do you?" He stared at the forlorn boy.

"Oh, come on!" Amalia raised her voice. "Do you expect us to believe you broke in to, what, tie my son to a chair while you're taking some actress out?"

"Yes?" blinked the guru, overwhelmed by an unusual wave of sincerity.

"Pfew," she burst out. "Why don't you confess you came here hoping to find the results to the paternity test? You were hoping to prove Armin is not his father's son and then take his place by Placido's side."

Leborio scratched the top of his head, checked his watch, and conceded with a nod.

"Yes, you got me," he said. "My bad."

Amalia's arm descended like a subway turnstile, allowing Leborio to make his way out of the suite.

"He confessed," she sighed, picking up the phone receiver to dial a number. "You heard him. Wait until your father finds out!"

Armin ran his fingers through his hair nervously, paying no mind to his mother's voice on the telephone. He could not have cared less about Leborio's confession, sincere or otherwise. The guru's despicable character was hardly newsworthy. Thus far, Leborio had taken everything from him: the respect of his father, the delusion young people indulge in that they just might be special and unique, and the healthy conceit all young men use to kick-start their destinies. Because of Leborio, Armin was painfully aware he would never amount to very much. Not with his ordinary mind, pasty white skin, and tubercular good looks. Yet he could live with this knowledge, as long as there was a chance that Iris might not pick up on it, as long as she did not come across a Leborio, out there, to capture her interest in a way Armin never could. He paced around the room, flaring his nostrils in a complete state of panic.

"Okay, let's get out of here." Amalia turned to her son after she hung up the phone. "I could use a cup of coffee. How about you?"

He nodded, grabbed his key card, and closed the door to suite 112 behind his mother.

"Remind me not to do yoga again," she said, talking the stairs down.

"Why not?" he followed absentmindedly.

"It seems to be founded on a profound disregard for women. Did you hear what he said about women being the inferior sex?"

"Perhaps that's just Spanish yoga."

"You think? Makes sense, what with the machismo culture and all."

"I could have sworn I heard it somewhere that yoga was exclusively an Asian tradition," said the son. "Goes to show you all things worth mentioning originated in Europe: intelligent humans, money, chocolate, and pop music. And now, even yoga."

"I thought Homo sapiens came from Africa," disputed the mother.

"They might have," he agreed with a superior nod. "And now they all live in the San Francisco area."

# CHAPTER 24

# AT LAST WE MEET

In times of personal turmoil, the human mind shuts off all external stimuli and turns its undivided attention upon itself. This is why Amalia and Armin Pector closed the door to suite 112 behind them without spotting the latch had been jammed with a business card, which, when unfolded, would have read:

The Lido Hotel Pool and Spa Presents

**Leborio Borzelini**

*Spanish Guru*

(Master in the Art of Meditation)

The card had not been sanctioned by the Lido hotel, although in Leborio's view it ought to have been, especially after the numerous requests he had filed. Somehow, the idea of printing business cards for a member of the entertainment team met with resistance from management. But in the end, fate could not be tipped over by the narrow view of a few hotel managers. The card emerged as the brainchild of the guru himself, designed and produced with the aid of a certain art student who looked like an ostrich, and in return was allowed the great privilege of drawing the master as he was deep in post-coital meditation. Leborio had always known having a business card would one day come in handy. Radiating with self-gratification, he waited in the staircase until the mother and son disappeared from view.

"Watch and learn, my large friend," he addressed the giant, while holding out his left wrist to the swipe lock.

"It knows the secret handshake?"

"Something like that," laughed the resourceful guru, pressing his magnetic bracelet collection against the unit until the little light went green and the door clicked open.

"If you don't mind me asking, boss, what is it that we're looking for?"

"A notebook, I imagine."

The giant's right hand disappeared in the front pocket of his linen khakis, as he dragged his feet behind the spiritual master.

"I make it a point to lift only items worth doing time for," he muttered. "A notebook is not one of these items."

The giant's crossed eyes bounced around the room and intersected on the nearest exit. He checked his pocket once again, brushing his thick fingers against the abrasive surface of a small bundle. A little trip bonus, he thought, playing with the pear-shaped gems. Using the oldest trick in the book, he'd created a diversion bumping into the woman who wore it, and snatched it from right around her neck. He had a feeling it was worth a pretty penny, and as soon as he could manage to get away from Leborio, he would check with a jeweller and see how much he could get for it.

While Leborio ransacked the room, the giant listened intently for footsteps. It was high time they split. Getting caught for petty thievery in a hotel room was not part of his plan. He suddenly missed Umberto and his perpetual crusade against sin. But alas, the poor bugger must have been halfway across the continent by now, sharing Bible stories with the Russian girl, and if Kim had gotten it right, she was depleting the air travel industry of tissue supplies. That girl could surely cry! Though she couldn't cook worth a damn.

The giant wondered how long it would take him to slip out unnoticed and decided it was entirely a matter of chance. It all depended on Leborio's attention deficit, something the giant had noticed to be an issue whenever the guru pounced on a new target. For the moment, searching for a notebook took up most of his concentration. Kim's dilemma was quickly brought to an end once the grand guru slid the closet door open, revealing a cornucopia of chiffon dresses.

"Eureka!" he cried out. "I knew it."

His hand reached behind the dresses, on the back shelf of the closet, from whence he pulled out a navy blue shoebox. He removed the lid and pulled out a medium–sized purple notebook.

"Have a seat, Kim. This could be a while."

* * *

Meanwhile, at the Lisbon international airport, Alfonso the driver was holding up a cardboard sign once again, playing the guessing game with a little less confidence. How would a Mr. Galanis look? Medium height, moustache, and a horseshoe hairline. Of course, one couldn't say for sure. Not after having met the gigolo with an accountant name. The driver would not have been very far off in his assumption, had the vision pertained to Mr. Galanis, the elder. In fact, it would have described George rather well.

Mr. Galanis the younger, however, was an entirely different matter. A tall and slender man, with curious, weasely eyes, hair combed neatly and parted to the side in a lovely shade of mouse-brown that matched his suit impeccably. Alfonso held the limo door open for him before setting off for what was becoming point B of his daily routine: the resplendent Hotel Almeida.

Mr. Galanis the younger ordered the partition to be raised, and whipping his gold-rimmed spectacles out of his briefcase, buried his nose in a small stack of proposals. Technically, he was on vacation, so he decided to begin with marketing proposals and save budgeting and mergers for a later time. He couldn't shake the feeling that he'd forgotten something of great importance. And soon enough, his suspicion was confirmed. Even with the tinted windows, Denis found the sun to be quite bothersome. He cracked the partition open and asked the driver to find him a decent place to buy sunglasses.

"Not the hotel kind," he added. "I'll need them to be prescription."

Moments later, Alfonso pulled by the curb in front of an optical store, letting his distinguished client out. The man gave him the slight nod of a person accustomed to having servants and walked out of the sun like a vampire at the sight of dawn. Alfonso sighed in his seat, turning the air conditioning down. Why did people like this man come to his country? The sun, the air, the atmosphere—all lost on a man like him. He'd much preferred the loud and boisterous tourist families, who from the moment they got off the plane, persisted in lugging their half a dozen suitcases on their own, asked if there was a bus to Lisbon, and settled on negotiating with a cab driver. He liked to watch their expressions as he passed the taxi on the freeway. Eyes wide open, staring at the perfect blue sky. They had smiles that lit up their faces, and the children pulled at their mothers' sleeves, bewildered. Now, they knew how to appreciate a slice of heaven. But those were not the clients Alfonso would get. He got the starchy businessmen wearing mouse-brown suits, carrying a briefcase for luggage, and making a permanent attachment of their phone's earpiece. And, of course, the occasional Leborio Borzelini, he thought, raising an eyebrow.

Inside the store, the earpiece lit up neon blue for a split second, while the clerk behind the impeccably polished counter greeted Denis with a warm retail smile.

"I've been trying to get a hold of you all morning," Denis said.

"Sorry?" froze the salesclerk, looking confused.

Denis pointed at the earpiece, causing the clerk a great deal of relief. "Yes, yes," he went on, "please spare me the details of your personal life. I'm calling about our situation. Any recent developments?" He took out a folded piece of paper from his wallet and showed the store clerk the appropriate abbreviation for his order. The clerk nodded and followed him as he paced about the store looking at the different shapes of sunglasses. Denis appeared partial to the oval rimless style. "I understand. We'll have to meet right away," he decided, pointing to a brown polarized pair of shades. The clerk unlocked the display counter and carefully pulled it out, handing it to the customer.

Denis tried them on in front of a small mirror and nodded his head. "No, not at the hotel. Hang on!" and turning to the clerk, "Thanks, don't bother wrapping those up. I'll wear them out. Could you tell me the name of a decent cafe around here? Some place where there's air conditioning?"

Happy to have sold a very expensive and unpopular style, the clerk recommended a small bistro around the corner. "Listen, meet me in twenty minutes inside Ferreira Cafe on the Rua Augusta," Denis said, ending his phone conversation.

* * *

"I gotta go," Iris said to Umberto, fixing her hair into a tangled bun. Although she didn't look tired after a night spent between the rustic comforts of the trailer floor on her way down from Sintra and the rigid edges of a hotel barstool, she didn't strike one as the freshest of flowers.

"What, now?" He seemed deflated.

"I know. I'm sorry," she let go of his hand. "It's work. I have to meet a client. You and the girl can stay in my room. It's probably not safe to go back to yours. Here's my key card—just don't leave the room until I get back, or I'll be locked out."

He took the key card somewhat reluctantly, and for the first time in twelve hours, checked his watch.

"Wait a minute," he said, running after her. "How come we didn't spend the night in your room?"

"Oh, because of Armin," she replied casually. "He would have had a hard time sleeping."

"You're staying with him?"

"Or he with me; it's not entirely clear. But yes, we're sharing a suite."

"Are you two . . . ?" Umberto couldn't bring himself to finish the sentence.

"Of course not, don't be ridiculous! But you should probably know he's got a thing for me. So take it easy on him."

"Of course he does," he muttered. "And what if he's still in the room?"

If she considered the possibility, she made a very good job of concealing it. Moments later, she swiped the card through, and the two tiptoed into the suite. Showering was no longer an option, she sighed, catching a whiff of her own smoke-imbibed hair. Armin would need a good ten minutes of reasoning before he would give up wanting to bash Umberto's face in. And that was without incidentals.

"Good morning, sunshine," she heard the low-timbered voice before freezing in her tracks.

When Iris took into account incidentals, she failed to consider the possibility of finding Leborio Borzelini comfortably sunken in her loveseat. As her eyes adjusted to the darkness, the sight of her purple notebook split open on his lap had the effect of a battering club to the head. Her legs suddenly grew weak and were it not for her companion's chest to break the fall, she would have hit the ground face up.

"What are *you* doing here?" asked Umberto in a tone that suggested were it not for the half-fainted girl in his arms, he would have charged ahead for a less-than-friendly body check with the guru.

"I could ask you the very same question, brother," he answered, flipping to the next page. Without so much as raising his eyes form the purple notebook, he added, "I'm here to see my girl and do a bit of light reading. Now you go!"

Umberto gently lowered Iris on the unmade bed, piling the pillows as a backrest. "I'm here to make sure nothing happens to her," he said, holding her head up with one hand, in the way of a ventriloquist puppeteer trying to convince the audience that Pinocchio really is a boy. "It seems there's a dangerous criminal in town, who has yet to be apprehended by the police."

"Really? What sort of criminal?"

"A thief," said Umberto, pausing for a reaction that never came.

The guru looked up bemused, "What did he steal, her heart?"

Without a second thought, Umberto threw himself at Leborio like a bull onto the red cape of the matador. Inches away from the guru, the bull hit the impenetrable surface of a large body emerging from behind the curtains. His head took the hardest hit, knocking the poor bastard out of the realm of consciousness and into a state of painful concussion.

"All right, Kim. Take him up to our room and tie him to something. When he recovers, you have my permission to smack the living daylights out of him. He should have a good reason for hating me so much."

The giant greeted the semiconscious woman on the bed in passing and shuffled away, dragging Leborio's cousin across the floor by his collar.

\* \* \*

"What do you think you're doing?"

"Ah, Kitten, feeling better?" he asked, without lifting his eyes off the paper.

"Is that a rhetorical question?"

"Of course not," he said, looking up at her for the first time. She could see the whites of his eyes through the curtain-covered darkness. "You have my undivided attention."

"Why are you in my room?"

"I was actually in Armin Pector's room, but it appears these days the two aren't mutually exclusive." Lowering his voice, he added, "Are the two of you . . . ?"

"That's none of your business," she lashed out. "In fact, nothing in this room is your business. Now, I have somewhere to be, so if you'll excuse me, I'm gonna have to ask you to leave."

"You'd better reschedule," he replied as calm as ever. The grand spiritual master unpretzelled himself and got up from the loveseat only long enough to pick up the phone and ring room service. With the thorough tone of a housewife going through her grocery list, he ordered two goat stakes and a tomato salad.

"Don't look at me like that, Kitten. We've got to eat sooner or later. Who's to say we can't enjoy a meal while we chat?"

"Chat? Is that what we're doing? Because, to me, this looks an awful lot like a hostage situation."

He raised an eyebrow. "Hostage? That's too strong of a word," he shook his head, crossing his legs back into a lotus and exuding pious serenity. "You're free to go any time you please. It's just that I, personally, am not going anywhere until you answer my questions."

"Well then, if you're not going, I'll have to go." She got up from the bed, making an effort to conceal the weakness in her knees.

For someone who had been sitting like a pretzel for some time, Leborio found his balance in record interval. He lashed out with the agility of a panther, cutting off the investigator's escape route. Without giving her time to escape, he lifted her off ground by the shoulders and pushed her back into the wall tapestry.

"I thought I was free to go," cried Iris.

"I lied," he hissed. "Surprised? Now you listen to me, Kitten," he whispered into her neck as she turned her head the other way. "Neither one of us is leaving until I understand what it is that you're doing in Portugal. I've read enough of your notes to put the general picture together, but I still need you to fill in the blanks." He paused for a moment. "It's your choice, Kitten. What will it be? Answer a few questions and get out of here or continue fighting me? You know I would never cause you any harm," he said, lowering her to the ground. "But I could make our time together extremely unpleasant."

"Please stop calling me Kitten, Tom. It adds insult to injury."

"Tell you what. I'll stop calling you Kitten," he whispered, "if you promise to stop referring to me as Tom. No one has called me that since high school. I've changed my first name. I go by Leborio nowadays. Leborio Borzelini."

"So I hear. May I ask why?"

"It's my stage name," he explained. "A man like me was bound to outgrow his given name. In any case, Tom was such a plain one. I find my new name adds character, don't you think?"

Her eyebrows rose beyond what was considered polite, "You must be very famous, no doubt. With the name and all," the corners of her mouth fluttered while she spoke. "I suppose you got what you've always wanted. Besides money, I mean."

"What can I say? Fortune is the root of all bliss," he met her sarcastic stare. "You know what they say. Money talks."

"And when it does, you listen, oh so carefully."

Leborio shrugged, still holding her against the wall. "Nothing wrong with a man wanting to live up to his potential."

"So what do you do nowadays, Leborio?"

He let go of her shoulders, sighing at the complexity of the answer, "Spiritual matters take up most of my time, I'm afraid. I am not who

*C.R. Preston*

you knew me to be. Much has changed since last we saw each other, Iris."

"Is that so? What in particular?"

"Well, I have made some changes. I have become . . . a guru," his voice trailed off.

Iris laughed. "You have become a what?"

Leborio cleared his throat and repeated with a certain measure of pride, "A guru."

\* \* \*

"Did Athena like him back?" Perla asked, holding her breath, as her head fell back into the sink.

"Not to my knowledge," said Gino, rinsing her hair with warm water. "But does that really matter?"

"I suppose not," she pressed her lips together until they turned pale. He wrapped a white towel around her head and helped her to the mirror.

Perla peeled a cotton pad away from the others and squeezed a blob of makeup remover in the middle of it. She was very close to the mirror, so close that her breath fogged up the glass. She drew big circles around her eyes, removing the build-up of mascara, eye shadow, and blush.

"I thought you ought to know," Gino spoke again. "I'm sorry."

"Do you think I look old?" she asked, her voice as small as a child's.

Her hairdresser looked away without saying anything. It was strange that she would ask this now, when her face was naked from colours and shine. Perhaps it was the sound of her voice, hurt and unsure, or the colour of her skin, pale and almost gray, that made her look older than ever. Gino watched her from the corner of the hotel room, as she stared at her own tears in the magnifying mirror.

"No fool like an old fool," she sighed. "I've always wondered about that expression, about what they really meant by it. I mean a fool is a fool at any age. But there is something to be said about feeling like a fool past a certain stage in one's life. Something to do with decency, I suppose."

With a pair of silver clamps, he picked a few ice cubes out of a bucket and poured her a tall glass of Bourbon. She sank into the sofa, staring at the coffee table, where a colourful romance novel was spread out like a cheap magazine.

"Drink this," said Gino. "You'll feel better when the glass is empty."

She closed her eyes and obeyed quietly. Instinctually, her hand reached out on the sofa and brushed against the embroidery. "Regina," she cried out and burst into tears.

Gino poured himself a drink and sat next to her. He placed his arm awkwardly around Perla's shoulders, and she turned sobbing to his chest. "There, there," he shushed her, and not knowing what to do, repeated something he heard his mother say, "Such is the end of youth."

"I've lost the necklace," she whimpered. "George will be devastated."

"He will," nodded the hairdresser. "But you will miss the cat more. And you have a better chance at recovering it."

She emptied the glass and pushed it on the coffee table with the tips of her fingers, causing the brightly coloured romance novel to fall on the carpet. Then, for a brief moment, her hand rested on his, as she spoke. "Let's go home, Gino."

* * *

Leborio's fork scraped his plate. "Have you put on a bit of weight?" he inquired between mouthfuls of medium rare goat stake.

"Perhaps," she said. "Have you lost a bit of hair?"

He grinned and nodded, passing her a napkin. Iris was indeed a brilliant sport. She might not have had that androgynous quality defining modern beauty, but she certainly had a masculine sense of humour that more than made up for the womanly presence she exuded. Leborio pushed a fork into her hand and nodded in the direction of the tomato salad. She pretended not to notice the single bowl between them and pressed on with her questions.

"So," she said, "you're a guru now. What does that mean exactly?"

"It means I am a spiritual guide for others."

"I know what it means. But what do you actually do?"

Leborio thought of the best way of phrasing his job description at the Lido and decided to omit the backdrop of his present career.

"I teach a select few how to transcend the illusions of this world. It would be hard to explain to the uninitiated mind what this entails. One day I will show you."

She smiled graciously and placed the fork he had shoved in her hand beside the empty plate. Leborio picked up his own fork and began harpooning tomato slices as if they were miniature whales in the ocean of their single bowl of salad. Iris watched him eat more than a half of the bowl before he looked up, his big eyes filled with wonder. "Why aren't you eating? Don't you like tomatoes anymore?"

"I'd much rather prefer having my own bowl."

"But we always share it," he objected.

She imagined the taste of it and looked away. It was still her favourite food.

"How's His Excellence?" he asked.

"Father? He's in Greece at the moment. Busy, as always."

"Does he still hate me?"

"He doesn't take you seriously enough to hate you. He just dislikes you."

"I remember. He thinks I'm not good enough for you. I bet he would eat his words now," he said proudly.

"Because you're a guru? I'm afraid father would not think very much of that at all. He's got a more pragmatic approach to life. As he says, a man is not a man unless he leads a successful life by moral means."

"Old-fashioned," he sighed. "No matter. Soon enough he'll know that he was wrong about me." Then, in a casual tone, he added, "You know, I haven't had tomatoes since—well, since you, I suppose. Funny how time goes by and yet we never bump into each other. I had to come all the way to Portugal to see my oldest friend. What brought you here anyway?" he asked, gazing at her with the most deliberate and undivided interest.

Her lips puckered imperceptibly as she picked up her fork and smeared a few tomato slices through the feta crumbs. They shared what was left of the salad before she replied, "Placido Pector, of course. He contacted me after you gave him my number." She fixed him with a stare. "Why did you, anyway?"

"I thought it would be nice for us to work for the same…company."

"He's not the sort of man I'd want to know."

"Then why did you accept the job?" he smiled, not without maliciousness.

Iris bit her lip. She meticulously folded the napkin into a small square and placed it on the plate in front of her. They both remained silent for a moment, she gazing out the window behind him. He watched her with a smirk. At last, Leborio leaned over the table, and gliding his arm over the plates, he placed a hand over hers.

"Are Armin and the actress an item?"

She pulled her hand away and flashed her eyes at him without saying a word. But Leborio, seemingly immune to her look, leaned back in his seat and repeated his question.

"No," she said, careful not to reveal more than she had to.

This time he was the one to glare at her as if trying to see right through her skin. She shifted uncomfortably against the backrest, avoiding his eyes. Next he'll want to know if Armin is in love with me, she thought.

"Of course he is," he uttered and paused, studying her reaction. "It showed all over his face when I mentioned your name."

Iris looked away, without saying a word. But his eyes followed the outline of her neck, down the delicate patterns of her chiffon dress, narrowing in on her navel point. Folded over in her lap, her hands trembled unnoticeably.

"What? Are you surprised it's still working?" he lowered his voice. "Your ability to read the face of an infatuated teenager?"

"No, our telepathy."

She dismissed the thought with a flick of the wrist. "Spend enough time with anyone, and you'll communicate just the same. There's nothing special about two people who grew up together being able to guess each other's thoughts. It happens every day to millions of people."

He sighed and rolled his eyes, "If only you knew how unattractive this is. A woman ought to be softer, more inclined to forgiveness, less . . . what's the word I'm looking for?"

"Intelligent?"

"Precisely!" he gesticulated with his fork. "Intelligent women are often inconvenient, I find. They ask too many questions and don't even bother to pretend believing the answers. It's as if they're not afraid to lose a man to the truth."

"Why should they be?"

"Because, my dear—can I call you my dear?—the man, you will find in time, is more important than the truth."

"That depends on the truth," she said, wiping her downturned mouth with a napkin. "Listen, I don't have the time to argue with you on issues of moral philosophy. I really do have somewhere to be."

"This thing we've got," he said, raising his voice to drown out hers, "does it happen to you with Umberto? Because it sure as hell doesn't happen to me. I mean, we all grew up together," he added, getting up from the table and falling back on the sofa again. He tapped the coffee table with his toe and then propped both of his feet over the tabletop. "It may happen collectively to millions of people. But only *once* to each one of them."

Still sitting upright like a schoolgirl, Iris waited until he stopped talking and muttered, "Yeah, well, it's too bad our *once* had to be with someone irremediably incompatible."

Leborio shook his head slowly. "See, that's what I mean," he said, stretching his arms across the backrest. "That's so unattractive! Why do you always have to do that? Beat me to the punch like a man. Your tongue is sharper than a blade. Sharper than you intend it to be. A man would not be as harsh as you, you know that?"

She wiped away a few breadcrumbs from her side of the tablecloth. Their eyes met for a moment, and Iris found herself inexplicably drawn to his gaze, unable to look away. Concealed in the flickering shade of the curtains, he looked like a crucifix, arms spread out, legs entwined, the weight of the world on his shoulders. His eyes were heavy with darkness, and there were deep creases around his mouth.

"A man *is* just that harsh," she said after a while. "Only your harshness is a credit to your mind, while my mind is no more than the root of my sharp tongue. If I stopped to think about being attractive, I'd be left in the gutter along with the others."

"It would be different you know," he looked down at the bare coffee table in front of him. "I would be different with you." And, then, added almost imperceptibly, "This time."

"But I wouldn't," she said ruefully, reaching for her handbag under the table. The handle was worn out, made soft by clasps and sweat. She pressed it between her fingers, feeling the rigid core underneath the leather binding. "I can't—not anymore."

Struggling against a strange and unusual knot-like restraint at the base of his throat, Leborio felt sorry and almost articulated it. But when his mouth opened, what he did say was, "Why was my cousin accusing me of stealing earlier?"

Iris almost let go of the handbag. "You can't be serious!" she shook her head. "To think you'd expect me to be that stupid! You're a lousy liar and a rotten thief."

Leborio put his feet down from the tabletop and leaned forward with an outraged expression. "Thief! What are you talking about? This is the second time I've been called that today. I swear to you I have not stolen a thing," he crossed his heart before adding, "Yet."

"You swear?" she sneered, lifting her butterfly-shaped handbag up into the light and dropping it on the table in front of her.

Leborio swallowed hard. "That one was different . . . " His voice trailed off into an incomprehensible explanation. "The pictures were— well, I have my image to think of . . . and none of it is gone. I have everything . . . within reach, that is. But I don't expect you to under-stand," he sighed, reclining against the backrest and into the obscurity of curtain shadows. "I found the thief after you left. Did you want me to beat him senseless? I mean what, was I supposed to send it to you?" he waited for an answer that never came. The clean lines of her profile stood out against the wallpaper, and for a moment, he closed his eyes as if to memorize it.

"In the end it evens out, you know," he slurred. "She really liked the purse. It made her happy . . . and your stuff, the stuff you had in it, it's all in good hands, making people happy. You can look at it as a good deed."

"Stop it," she held up her hand. Her voice was soft but firm. "Stop embarrassing yourself. I am done with you, and that is what I stayed to tell you. Now that I have said it, I am on my way to meeting with Perla's son to confirm that you are the one who stole the Sophie necklace." Fixing him with a glacial expression, she added, "So you'd better get out of here while you still can."

Leborio looked up disoriented. "Sophie necklace?" he asked dubiously. "It has a name? I presume you're referring to that blinding god-awful choker she keeps wearing at all hours of the day. I admit I thought of unburdening her of it, just for the sake of good taste. The sodding thing makes her look absolutely ridiculous. But I haven't gotten around to it yet. Something else came up, you see."

"You mean another scam."

"Why do I bother explaining things to you?" he shook his head.

"Because you don't want me to pull the plug on you," she replied dismissively. "Perla's son is a powerful enemy to make. In fact, I'd get as far from here as possible, as soon as possible."

"Why would you do that?" said Leborio without really expecting an answer. "I'm telling you the truth. I didn't steal anything. I haven't even seen Perla—only her hairdresser. You can confirm it with him," he put up a hopeful hand, only to drop it right back. "Actually, you can't. I left him tied up to a chair in Sintra the other day."

Iris turned her face away from Leborio and closed her eyes. He was not lying. There was no dimple in his cheek. That, and of course, she had interrogated Gino herself.

He got up from the sofa and slowly walked up to her. "Please, Iris," he whispered. Here was a word entirely new to his vocabulary, she thought. Iris had never known him to ask nicely. He enlisted people to complete tasks with a shameless sense of entitlement. Sensing her hesitation, Leborio bent forward and placing both hands around her small shoulders, inhaled deeply. "You don't have to do this. We can still be what we are to each other."

She weighed the implications, but in the end couldn't help asking, "And what would that be?"

Leborio magnanimously waved his magnificent arms in the air, in an all-encompassing gesture meant to suggest the absence of boundaries.

"What about the actress?" she persisted.

Sincere in his intention of eating his cake while having it, the spiritual master shrugged.

"I'll tire of her."

Iris wiped her beautiful downturned mouth with a linen napkin and stood up from the table. Leborio was telling the truth. Someone else had stolen the necklace and that was his misfortune. Given the opportunity, she knew he would have stolen it, as he had done before. Justice had a hard time catching up with Leborio Borzelini, she thought, smiling faintly at this new name he had taken.

Outside, a passing fleet of speeding scooters zoomed by, leaving a trail of adolescent verve behind. She leaned by the opened doors of the veranda, aware he was watching her still. Young people never think anything bad can happen to them, she reflected. Until the day something does. Suddenly, what she had to do was very clear to her. It would be like getting Al Capone on tax evasion.

* * *

No cars ever bothered pedestrians taking their lazy midday strolls along Rua Augusta. Alfonso the driver pulled under the shade of a Moorish balcony on an adjacent street, waving to let Denis know he would wait there. The man in the mouse-brown suit pushed his earpiece in with the tip of his pinkie nail, for better sound quality, and placed his newly purchased shades on the narrow bridge of his nose.

Around him, the buzzing of the street circled like an indistinct echo. Motley sounds, smells, and colours blended into a dizzying feast for senses. A rich scent of roasted pistachios, pastries, and salted fish rose up past the hanging street lamps into the cobalt coloured sky. Covered by a patio umbrella, an old woman selling used books hummed a fado tune in a hauntingly lonely pitch, while African and South American craftsmen seated on hand woven carpets chipped at wood figurines of exotic gods. Without taking notice of street performers, artists, or peddlers, Mr. Galanis the younger checked his wristwatch impatiently and disappeared inside the Ferreira Cafe, the only air-conditioned establishment within a fifty-meter radius, which was the longest distance he was willing to travel by foot in this heat.

By the time Iris Bendal made it to the cafe, Denis was adding the tip to his bill. He looked up at the investigator, dishevelled from sleeplessness, heat, and running, and ripped out a copy of the charges, handing it to the waiter.

"You're late," he said. "I dislike waiting for people who are late, especially when they're on my payroll."

"I'm sorry. I was delayed on my way here. But I do have a full report for you. And a rather successful one, if I might add."

She handed him an envelope and watched him tear it open. Her heart suddenly felt the size of a raisin. She stood up from the table with the wretched expression of a tourist who strayed away from his group in Monaco, found himself in the Casino, and gambled too much on roulette. Denis looked up at her over his sunglasses.

"Are you certain this is our man?"

"Without a shadow of doubt. I've seen the necklace with my own eyes," she lied.

He seemed visibly pleased and took out his checkbook to write her a very handsome fee.

"I trust this will cover revamping Legoland into a proper office," he smirked.

Iris folded the check over and tucked it away inside the butterfly-shaped handbag. Her mouth wilted into a desolate pout, and for a moment, she felt a little like Judas pocketing the thirty pieces of silver. She too sold a friend out for money, conveniently disguised under the generic term of business. Only Leborio was not the saviour, and the office really could use some grown-up furniture.

"When you do catch him, do me a favour," she asked Denis on her way out. "Tell him a man should never go through a woman's purse."

* * *

Back at the Hotel Almeida, in suite 425, a very large man was dozing off on the bottom part of what used to be a bunk bed, his right fist clenched into the front pocket of his trouser. Crouched on the floor and tied up to the coffee table, Umberto watched the giant's extremities jerk about every so often, as he fell deeper and deeper into sleep.

Imbecile, he thought. He lifted the table up and slid his restraints down the wooden legs of the neatly sculpted table. He stretched as he stood up and looked around the room for something to eat. He settled on one of Leborio's power bars and used Snejana's cuticle scissors to open it up quietly. The girl had found her way back to their room immediately after arriving in Lisbon, and as far as Umberto could tell, she was passed out on the love seat, clueless to past and present commotions. He decided not to wake her yet. Rescuing Iris from Leborio was challenging enough without a perpetually weeping sidekick.

Silently, he made his way to the door. Just as his hand grabbed a hold of the knob, a white envelope slipped through, right between his two feet. Startled, Umberto jumped back against the wall and waited. But not a sound could be heard from the other side. The light on the latch remained red, the giant continued to snore, and the girl did not move an inch. Slowly, he bent down and picked up the envelope on his way out, deciding to open it out of earshot.

He took the stairs down to the first floor, stretching for time to develop a rescue strategy. With the giant out of the way, there was no telling who would win in a fight. For all his perfect muscle groupings, the guru had never been seen in combat, much less winning a fight. No one could deny he had what it took to win—the strength, cleverness, and arrogance. Leborio was never one to shy from making gratuitous threats. But did he have the spirit? Did he have the drive, the proper motivation? Armed only with the strength of his grudge, which he skilfully disguised under the righteous cloak of conviction, Umberto launched his guerrilla attack by knocking at the door of suite 112. Back against the wall, fists ready to spring into action, the guru's cousin awaited for the door to open.

He waited.

And he waited.

Then he waited some more.

Not a sound came from within the suite.

Stuck on the threshold, the cardboard corner of a folded business card peeked out from under the door. He picked it up, turned it over, and crumpled it up with one hand. It belonged to his cousin, the grand spiritual master. Umberto huffed and threw it away spitefully. He had to give it to Leborio. The man knew how to put on a great show. If he hadn't known any better, Umberto might have believed his cousin could actually speak Spanish and meditate the living daylights out of a nonexistent yoga creed. Yes, these props certainly helped the Spanish guru believe in his own spiritual powers. A guru having his own business card was like an actor getting into costume before a performance. In a bright moment of clarity, Umberto realized he perhaps had rushed into renouncing religious fervour a little too soon. Above all, belief was tool of empowerment, a tool that his cousin had wielded for himself and in his own image. Granted, Umberto was pretty pissed off about being handed off to a bodyguard like a common punk. The question that begged to be answered was whether he was pissed off enough to stand a chance against Leborio and his magnificent arms.

But, alas, faint heart never won fair lady. The thought of Iris lying there defenceless, as he had left her, made the risk worthwhile. Taking one decisive breath, the chivalrous ex-believer threw his body weight into the door and with a muffled thump, fell right through, belly up. Of course, the door had been left ajar, he panted in frustration. Feeling as keen as mustard, Umberto stared up at the ceiling, cursing the gods he no longer believed in, which was just about as useful as cursing Santa right after finding out he doesn't actually exist. Then he remembered about the envelope and tore it open with feverish hands.

It contained an urgent telegram addressed to Leborio Borzelini. *Care of: Hotel Almeida, Suite 425, Lisbon*

Mr. LEBORIO BORZELINI

AS SOLE LIVING RELATIVE OF MR. GIGI BORZELINI (DECEASED), YOU ARE THE BENEFICIARY OF HIS ESTATE, AS PER STATE LAND RETRIBUTION ACT 143B. STOP.

ESTATE MUST BE CLAIMED BY BENEFICIARY IMMEDI-ATELY, IN PERSON OR BY PROXI. STOP.

PS: LOCATION OF ESTATE IS BONGOVILLE, GABON, AFRICA. STOP.

V. L. BEGA, ESQ.

Umberto scratched his head with ape-like clarity. Gigi Borzelini had seldom come up in family reunion conversation as anything other than the deceased epileptic brother Leborio's father and Umberto's mother shared. He'd been dead for longer than the boys had been alive. Why would anyone dig up a long-lost inheritance now, almost thirty years from his death? And how was it they did not know Umberto was also a relative of his? More importantly, why would they bother to insist the estate was under some sort of deadline?

Of course, back home, Land Retribution Act 143 B had something of a mythical quality about it. Everyone had heard of someone who benefitted from it, but no one had actually seen the benefits. For thirty years, this land had been unclaimed, and now Leborio, hardly the sole living relative of uncle Gigi, was expected to claim it or lose it. Umberto frowned, wondering why uncle Gigi would own land in a place that sounded like a cross between a chance game and a post-revolutionary American settlement, defiantly placed on the wrong continent.

Bongoville, he cackled. What sort of place was that? No, the whole thing had the makings of an infantile prank. Umberto was too practical to fall for it. But maybe his cousin would, he smiled devilishly. He could just picture the guru's monobrow come up in surprise, his eyes lighting up with the first flickers of hope for that blindingly grandiose future he'd always imagined for himself, the corners of his mouth raise in contempt of all mere mortals who'd ever failed to see his value. He'd show them all, the illustrious master of the Bongoville land, the great proprietor flaunting his inheritance papers like a certificate of personal worth. He'd organize a great big coming-out party, where he could dress like a debutante and parade his ticket to fame and fortune to all those who'd ever known him. Then, thought Umberto, Leborio would anonymously alert the media from a payphone and run back home to book his own interview appointments for tell-all stories of his grand success.

Lastly, he'd write himself a praise-filled page on Wikipedia, just in case anyone should ever Google his name. Yes, Leborio will surely go nuts over this telegram! Umberto laughed out loud, wishing he could be a fly on the wall to watch it all happen. He folded the paper neatly and placed it back into the envelope, which he then licked methodically, hoping to revive the last traces of adhesive and seal it.

* * *

The triumphal archway on the Rua Augusta is the converging point of the lively pedestrian street itself and the Plaza Comercio. It was befitting that at this very crossroads, under the arch's filigreed clock, a tall man dressed in a brown business suit, too busy talking into his earpiece, engaged into a head-on collision with a not-so-tall woman wearing a vision-impairing wide-brimmed hat.

"I'm sorry. Excuse me," they both scrambled. The woman's black hat hit the ground and circled itself like the drain cover of a sewer.

"Here you go," said the man, picking it up with a chivalrous bow.

"Denis!" she gasped, as they both dropped the hat. "Is that really you?"

The man in the brown suit stood as upright as a flagpole, struggling to decide between a limited number of reactions deemed to be appropriate. To say hello and smile graciously was beyond his power. He had pretended she was dead for so many years that he had actually come to believe it a little. And one cannot smile and greet a dead person the same way they do a living one. To simulate he was late for a very important meeting in order to escape her seemed like a waste of an opportunity that may never return. He might never again see this woman. For lack of a better idea, he put out his hand the way he did upon finalizing a business merger. Disconcerted, the woman stared at his hand in passing, as she came up on her toes and put her arms around his rigid neck. His arms wavered for a moment before softly locking around her waist.

"Yes, Amalia. It really is me."

"I can't believe it," she said letting go of him. She took a few steps back for perspective. "You look good. Like a businessman on vacation."

The man laughed self-consciously, "Thanks, I guess. So do you. Look good, I mean," he added. "You haven't aged a day. What are you doing here? In Lisbon . . ."

The radiant smile lighting up her face disappeared behind a momentary cloud, revealing the delicate net of lines framing her eyes. "As a matter of fact, I came to meet my son, Armin."

"Yes, well, congratulations. I heard you had a son. How old is he now?"

"He's almost nineteen," she said, not without pride. "Can you believe it? And it seems he is to be an actor. He was recently discovered by a Hollywood director, and he's starring in a movie as we speak. I must say I was quite surprised. We never saw that coming. My son the movie actor."

"Yes, well, having actors in one's family can be a mixed blessing. My little sister is an actress, and god knows she very seldom comes out of character. But," he stopped himself, "oh, wow, you have a nineteen-year-old son! Almost the same age we were the last time I saw you. That is truly amazing, Amalia. Good for you! How long has it been since we've seen each other? My god, how time flies!"

"Twenty years," the woman whispered. "Yes, it really does fly."

They were both silent for a moment, thinking of all the days that make up twenty years. This was what a human life amounted to: meetings, mergers, helping Armin with his math homework, taking Armin to the zoo, investments, dating a model, waiting for Placido to come home, pretending not to see the lipstick stains on his shirt, breaking up with a model and dating her friend, hiding outside Neon Lounge to see the other woman, Sunday dinner at the Galanis residence, bringing down Armin's fever, carrying a brown briefcase, waiting alone, dating an executive lawyer with long legs and blond highlights, watching soap operas where the men are faithful and romantic, breaking up, getting Armin back in school, not dating, waiting, waiting, waiting alone. And every once in a while, when the world stopped spinning, they silently wondered what if . . .

"What about you? Did you ever . . . ?"

"No, I'm not married," said the man. "Marriage is not for everyone, I guess."

"Oh, don't worry." She smiled modestly. "Marriage is not all that it's cracked up to be. Sometimes it's better not to be married at all."

"I suppose it depends on whom you marry," he added, picking her hat off the ground and dusting it gently.

Amalia took the hat and thanked him to buy herself thinking time. She wanted to say, "Or don't marry," but instead smiled graciously and hid her trembling hands under the hat. "So what brings you to Lisbon, Denis?"

"Listen," he blurted, taking his new sunglasses off, "why don't we do this the right way, over a cup of coffee?"

Sensing her hesitation, he went on, "It's not every day we bump into each other, you know. And it's already midafternoon. From here on, it'll only get hotter. We'd better find a nice little patio to hide in."

"I've already had a coffee with my son," she started, without a clear sense of how she would end.

"Well, I just finished my coffee when I bumped into you. What does that have to do with anything?" he smiled, gently nudging her. "One can never have enough coffee. Besides, if you really want to stay away from caffeine, I'll get you an ice cream."

She ran her fingers around the inside rim, making an impression of a circle. Ice cream had always been her kryptonite. All these years, being married to Placido, she thought herself above temptation. Yet different people succumb to different lures. Amalia's weakness turned out to be less obvious than her husband's, and she wondered if ice cream could be also considered a pleasure of the flesh. If it was, then all the better. It was high time she caught up with Placido. Only for her, temptation felt sinful even when the sin was overdue.

"Pistachio gelato?" suggested Denis, slurping an imaginary cone. "Mmm, you know you can't resist it. I'll even throw in a scoop of nocciola."

Doubting her husband had ever known her favourite ice-cream flavour, Amalia gave in.

"But only if the earpiece comes off."

In a gesture highly uncharacteristic of his person, the man in the brown suit pulled the bud out of his ear and threw it over his shoulder, "Done!"

# CHAPTER 25

# NEW BEGINNINGS

On a hot July evening, in a little house made of mud bricks not too far from the Lisbon harbour, a round-faced, middle-aged Japanese woman finished chopping green onions on a plastic cutting board to the cheerful sounds of *Feliz Navidad* coming from a yellow CD player, that hung from the window by a wire that also served as a radio antenna. She threw the chopped vegetables into a steaming pot, which she then covered with a lid. The sweet smell of cooked vegetables spread throughout the small kitchen and into the living area. The woman cracked the window open, letting in the sea air.

She set the table and sat across from her husband's empty chair. "*Feliz Navidad, Feliz Navidad,*" she chanted. Her lips parted a little as she mimicked the sounds of the song. Her husband, the fisherman, had told the woman she would learn the language quicker by listening to local music and watching local television. The television set was currently being used as a potting jar for vegetables, which left the CD player as the only viable option. The fisherman owned only four CDs, two rap compilations he pulled into his net one afternoon—together with twenty-three cod and a squid— one salsa mix he got as a gift from a Korean friend, and one international Christmas carol collection he found in a cereal box. Before he left home that morning, the fisherman forgot to tell his new wife that none of these CDs were actually in Portuguese. But that was the thing about newlyweds. They often forgot to tell each other seemingly unimportant things. Older newlywed couples were no exception.

In turn, that evening, after they ate dinner, his wife forgot to tell the fisherman that she had revamped his bait box into a pet house for the cat she had brought back from her excursion to Sintra. At first, the man had been opposed to bringing in another mouth to feed. But in the end, he gave his blessing. She was, after all, by herself for most of the day, and it could get quite lonely in a strange country. After she washed the dinner plates, the wife emptied out the bait box, leaving only a few of the most colourful tackles to cheer up the glum cat and placed the animal inside for the night.

The cat, who had never seen such desolate decorum as the little mud brick house, was too wretched to find the motivation to get out. She went to sleep dreaming of napping in the back seat of a brand-new Maybach and woke up several times that night to see a scary-looking creature zoom across the kitchen floor.

It too was hairless. From what the cat could tell, the creature was gray. It had a long thin tail and it was faster than anything she'd ever seen. Before the night was over, the creature brought his friends along and together they raided the rice box. One of them looked up with small, red eyes and hissed at the frightened cat, causing her to duck back into the bait box and cover her eyes with padded paws. She could hear their little feet tap frantically across the linoleum floor, sending chills down her bendable spine. If only she could find something to shield herself with, she thought, stretching to grab onto the closest object that promised to shelter against the army of gray, long tailed intruders.

Before the crack of dawn, the half-asleep fisherman, who had dozed off right after dinner, grabbed the bait box, threw in a couple of cans of beer, and placed the box behind the cabin of his wooden fishing boat. The cat, hoping to escape its current predicament, didn't make a sound till about high noon, when the growls in her tiny stomach became too difficult to ignore. Tucked in the bottom shelf of the bait box, she tenderly sniffed the two cans of beer. To a cat whose sense of smell was less than keen, they smelt just like the cans of Whiskas her mistress used to feed her.

* * *

The trouble with cobblestone roads built by German masons a couple hundred years ago was that no one really knew how to fix them. Not the laid-back city workers who set up orange pylons to map out their perimeter, not the guy backing the cement truck into the pot holes, and not the new mayor, who had German engineers brought on board to supervise the entire process. One of the engineers claimed to be the descendant of a long line of cobblemasters that had somehow gone extinct after the Great War. His great grandfather once told him the stones were taken from the bottom of the Rhine River, where they had lain still for hundreds of years, allowing the running water to shape them and round the rougher edges off. Then, they were brought up to the surface by divers and carried far away by oxen caravans. They were then sold to the road masons who were employed by the kings and queens of Europe to pave their cities with the smooth but resilient stones. One by one, the stones were placed over the dirt like the pieces of a giant puzzle. At the end, a dozen of the most beautiful maidens of the city would come to brush egg whites across the cobbles and give the road its sheen. Whether the story was myth of reality, clearly the process could not be replicated. Even if the bedrock of the Rhine River could be brought to the surface by stone divers, and even

C.R. Preston

if the city could manage to stop all traffic for however long it took to complete the cobble puzzle, where would they find a dozen maidens in this day and age?

So, the door of the yellow building with purple shutters wedged between Aviation Boulevard and Renaissance Street was to remain wobbly indefinitely, or at least as long as it could manage to pass under the radar before the new directives following European Union standards would come in and whip the city into a comprehensible—if prosaic—shape. From the cosiness of her newly renovated office, Iris Bendal read the reviews for an upcoming blockbuster about the miracle of Fatima. *Fatima: Three Secrets and a Vision* would not come out until the next spring, but the cast and the plotline were already up. By the looks of it, Lord Byron was to play second-fiddle to the Virgin herself.

"Ding," called the oven bell by the front door, announcing a guest.

"Note to self," muttered Iris, "buy a proper motion sensor."

"Good afternoon, Miss," spoke the thin girl standing in the doorway, her tiny voice trembling with anxiety. "I hope I'm not too late. You see, I couldn't find the building. It was right here, but I didn't see it. My glasses, they fog when I change temperature, and I took a cab here, and there was air-conditioning, and when I came out I couldn't see a thing, and . . ."

"Don't worry about it," said Iris, offering the girl a glass of water. "Have a seat and calm down."

The girl obeyed, sinking into a brand-new IKEA pong chair. She wiped her dark–rimmed, square glasses with the edge of her plaid skirt and waited with a wretched look.

"So," began Iris, pacing about the desk, "I had a chance to look at your resume. It seems you have limited experience working as an office secretary. Do you mind me asking why that is?"

The girl turned a beaming shade of red before answering, "It is because of school, Miss. You see, I am still a student. But not for much longer. I'm almost finished my undergraduate degree. And I can work as much as thirty hours per week. Even more in the summer," she ranted. "I would just need two days off where I can schedule all my courses, and you wouldn't even know I'm in school. I am a very hard worker."

"Hmm," was all Iris said for a moment, unwillingly sending the girl into severe palpitations. "I see. And what is your take on working with investigators?"

"I am very discreet," the girl blurted a line she had rehearsed on the way to the interview. "And I pay particular attention to detail."

"Very well," said Iris. "We are in a business where unpleasant things happen when you least expect them. How would you handle a difficult situation?"

The girl frowned and shut her eyes for a moment. Then opened them. Then closed them again, this time with more determination. But nothing came out of it. Her mind was drawing a complete and utter blank.

"I am a discreet person. And I pay great attention to detail," she repeated.

"Excellent qualities." Iris smiled. "I always say that a discreet, detail-oriented person is the best sort of person one can have for an employee."

The girl looked up at Iris gratefully. She smiled back with a small, mousy tweak of the nose.

"That being said," Iris went on, rephrasing the only highlighted question on a short list she had jotted down on a notepad in anticipation of her one and only applicant, how do you think such a person would deal with, say, a difficult customer? A rude customer who would try to intimidate the employee into taking on a morally questionable case."

"Why, this person would tell the customer that this is not that sort of agency," the girl sat up as straight as a board. "And then direct them to the phonebook." She had finished wiping the dark-rimmed glasses just in time to see Iris pick her daily planner off the desk and drop it in her butterfly-shaped handbag.

"Well," said the investigator, "I would need you here for a minimum of twenty hours a week. More, of course, during the summer. That's when our business picks up. I don't work weekends, so you'll need to come in at least on Saturdays. Actually, I know it's short notice, but it would be of great help if you could start right away." She raised an inquisitive eyebrow. "A friend of mine is buying a house as we speak, and he'd like to get my opinion before he closes the deal. So can you stay?"

The girl nodded eagerly, and Iris took a moment showing her how to use the phone.

"You pick it up here, and you switch lines from here," she explained.

"Heloooooooooooooo."

The girl with the dark-rimmed glasses was about to place the receiver back down when the faint metallic sound of a screaming voice pierced through.

"Good afternoon. You've reached the offices of Private Affairs Investigators. Gretchen speaking. How may I help you?"

She made a beckoning gesture toward her new boss, who was watching her from the doorway, with her jaw hanging. The girl was a natural. "One moment please. I'm going to have to put you on hold," and then to Iris, "It's for you, Miss . . . Iris, I'm guessing."

"Yes, I'm sorry. That'll be me. Hello?" she spoke into the phone.

"Who answered your phone?"

"My new secretary," said Iris proudly, twisting a spiralled strand of auburn hair around her index finger. Smiling from ear to ear, the girl made herself busy tidying up the desk.

"The reason I'm calling is to see if you'd like to have dinner after you see the house." The voice wavered on the other end of the line. "To celebrate, I mean. It's not every day one buys a house." Seeing the answer wasn't as forthcoming as he'd hoped, the man on the line carried on, "We can go to any restaurant you'd like, of course. Or not, if you don't want to. We don't have to eat. Maybe coffee? Unless you'd rather not. In which case we can go for a walk, if you have time. If you're not busy, that is. But if you are, that's cool. Totally! We can hook up some other time."

Iris raised an eyebrow and slowly shook her head. One of the great advantages of telephone conversations, she thought, is that people don't get to see each other's reactions. "How about we hook up now?"

"For a walk? Or for coffee? Or are you on board with the dinner idea?"

"All of the above."

The man grinned and before he could stop himself, he blurted out, "Thank you!"

"You're welcome?" she raised another eyebrow. Decidedly, Umberto had never been the smoothest of operators. Fortunately, what he lacked in technique, he positively made up for in . . . in . . . now that she thought of it, it seemed hard to determine what he excelled at. Those who knew him well would have described him as constant, loyal, and generally well intended. But in light of his recent conversion from being a devout Christian to being a devout atheist, perhaps his only certified character trait was devotion. Not a bad start. Not by a long shot. Iris allowed herself to imagine, as she applied a coat of lip balm over the plump softness of her downturned mouth. It seemed that everything was falling into place, now that she was at last free of her past. She exhaled, relieved fate would never again throw her face-to-face with Leborio Borzelini. That chapter of her life was now over.

"Oh, Gretchen, I meant to ask you. What are you studying in

school?" she asked on her way out.

The girl pushed her glasses on top of her nose. "Criminology," she said. Iris nodded graciously, and smiling from ear to ear, closed the door behind her.

Moments after Iris had set off to meet the prospective homebuyer, the newest employee of Private Affairs Investigators picked up the phone after fashionably letting it ring twice.

"Private Affairs Investigators. Gretchen speaking. How may I help you?"

"Good day, Gretchen," said the woman at the other end of the line. "I am phoning about a missing person. Is there a detective I could talk to?"

"The investigator is out for the day, but if you're looking for a missing person, shouldn't you go to the police first?"

"I already have," replied the woman in an accent Gretchen could not really place. It was heavy and slow, with vowels that rounded the words into a kind of song. "They tell me to wait, but, you see, I can't wait. I am a mother. My daughter disappeared, and I am worried sick."

"When was the last time you saw her?" Gretchen grabbed a pen and began taking notes.

"Eight days ago. But she called me the next morning from her boyfriend's house. So, really, I haven't heard from her in seven days. Lord knows what he's done to her!"

"Why do you think he is responsible for her disappearance?" asked Gretchen, scribbling quickly on her notepad.

"Because he is a terrible man," said the woman, emphasising her vowels with extra oomph. Slavic! The accent was Slavic, thought Gretchen, listening to the story.

"He's the kind who uses women to get anything from money to favours. Why he'll use my poor child up and sell her off to the highest bidder. Please, you must help me find her!"

"Very well," reflected the newest secretary of Private Affairs Investigators, pushing the dark-rims of her rectangular glasses on the bridge of her thin nose. "On behalf of my employer, I feel confident in telling you that we may be able to help you. As a starting point, I'll need the name and address of your daughter's boyfriend."

"He lives in one of the old buildings on Fortune Street," she explained. "And his name is Leborio. Leborio Borzelini."

The secretary wrote the name down on a yellow notepad and booked an early appointment for the distraught mother to meet with Iris. She highlighted the name of the suspect and placed it on top of Iris' desk. Gretchen felt proud of the way she handled this first customer. Her new boss was bound to be pleased with the case. Yes, she thought, smiling, first thing in the morning Iris would be very pleased indeed.

# CHAPTER 1

# EPILOGUE

In the shade of a colourful umbrella, Mrs. Perla Galanis put away a copy of the latest Dr. Pill relationship rescue book to ponder on the importance of spousal communication. According to the good doctor, trust and love was the product of hard work and large amounts of time spent taking an interest in each other's passions.

"You really ought to get out of the sun, Georgie," she said, sipping on lemon water. "Recent studies indicate that sun exposure can damage your skin and cause it to age."

"You don't say?" George lifted off his sunglasses as she took another gulp from the loop-around straw. "Oh my,," he gasped, "isn't that Rita in the middle of the pool?"

Indeed it was. Like a large sea mammal following a catastrophic oil spill, Rita floated on a see-through air mattress, looking as cheerful as cancer. Perla confirmed with a grave nod and reached in her handbag for a compact mirror.

"She looks terrible. What happened to her?"

His wife shushed him, checking to see if anyone had overheard.

"Can't a woman look natural without you men criticizing her? Rita's going through a hard time," she explained. "She was very fond of the yoga instructor we had before, and I think she's taking his disappearance a little hard."

"Whatever happened to that Spanish guru you used to rave about?" asked George, making an effort to conceal his resentment. Now that his wife was back, there was no sense in digging up old graves. Perla had been through enough, according to Denis. As far as George was concerned, pretending not to know was the kind thing to do.

"Oh, it's actually the same guy," she replied, taking another sip from her drink. "The girls here at the Lido refer to him as a guru. They're all nuts about him, you see. All but me," she added bitterly. "I could see right through him from the very beginning, and I'd have to say he was a little too green to last in a discipline like yoga. To be perfectly honest, I think calling him a guru is a bit of an overstatement. He was more of an instructor, an entertainer if you will."

George raised his eyebrows to show he cared and flipped to the editorial of *Politics Today*. His wife picked at her hair with the tips of her fingers, looking into the small compact mirror.

"I must say, Gino outdid himself this morning," said George, glaring at her over his newspaper. "You look lovely, my dear."

Perla blushed for a moment and covered her eyes with a bejewelled hand. She sighed like a food critic after a satisfying meal, dozing off in the cool shade of the parasol. She dreamed of sleeping a very long sleep in a Taj-Mahal-shaped mausoleum, next to her balding husband.

\* \* \*

It is never pleasant to be sought after by the police. It is even less pleasant to be a wanted man in a foreign country, where the only language clues a man on the run may be able to pick-up on are those of body language. Being a guru should have given Leborio the edge over the Portuguese officers combing the streets of Lisbon in search for a diamond thief who matched his description. But unfortunately for the spiritual master, the edge quickly dissipated when confronted with the reality of being broke and owning an unusually distinctive pair of arms. The only long-sleeved shirt he'd brought was a resplendent shade of purple, adorned with white fleur-de-lis the size of a grown man's head. Where could a guy dressed to match the wallpaper at Versailles hide? How could he move through and away from the city of Lisbon without attracting the usual abundance of attention? After a whole night of running and hiding, without a shower and without a bed, even the resourceful guru had a rough time answering these questions.

Behind the smelly dumpster of a harbour-front seafood restaurant, the Spanish guru took a load off on top of a wooden apple crate. With his head in his hands, he closed his eyes and attempted to focus. He was the prime suspect in the theft of an invaluable diamond necklace, and though he had not committed the crime, the evidence pointed toward him. By now, the police would be alerted about the theft. There would be pictures of him at the airports checkpoints and the train stations. It was only a matter of time until the canine unit would be brought aboard to pick up his scent. His only way out of Portugal was by water. If only he could charter a small boat out of Lisbon, perhaps he could salvage what was left of his grand destiny.

"Thank you," he heard the girl say in a small voice. "Thank you for choosing me to be the one you're running away with."

Not much of a choice, he thought, keeping his eyes closed. He would have preferred Kim, of course, but the giant had vanished without a trace. It made sense that the rats would abandon a sinking ship, he reflected, grinding his teeth at the thought of it. He raised his chin a little higher, until he could feel the sun beaming across his face, reminding him of another glorious creation that was meant to shine. Leborio Borzelini was no sinking ship. In fact, he was no ship at all. He was much grander than that, even if some failed to recognize it. Their loss, he decided, feeling suddenly invigorated. Like the sun, he would rise again and again, fighting off the fleeting clouds and their insignificant shadows.

"What are you doing?" Snejana's high-pitched voice interrupted his thoughts.

He opened his eyes and looked down at the girl. Her hair looked stringy and her cheeks were sunken in from crying herself to sleep the night before—or perhaps from a steady diet of carrots, water, and oxygen. Sitting at his feet, in the white dust of the curb, she looked up at him with big, hopeful eyes, one tail wag away from licking his hand.

"I'm meditating."

"And is it working?"

"Yes, insofar as getting us out of here."

"You can do that?" she grabbed his ankle with both hands. "You can trans . . . trans . . . transportate us to a different place? Like in *Star Trek*! I always thought there must be some truth to that whole thing, but of course, I had no way of proving it. I mean, if my mom can heal people with her hands, I can only imagine what you can do with your mind. You're so much smarter than her."

"We're not trans-anything out of here," he cut her off, feeling her forehead for temperature with the back of his hand. "You really ought to eat something; I fear you're becoming delirious. Listen to yourself, going on about *Star Trek* and teleportation! I grant you that I am far more intelligent than your mother," he conceded, "but I wouldn't waste my paranormal energy on conjuring spaceships when there are plenty of other reasonable means of transportation we could employ. In fact, I've already found the perfect getaway plan." He paused for effect, but seeing Snejana stared at him devoid of expression, he muttered, "We're taking a boat ride, if you must know."

"A boat ride?" she clapped her hands, suddenly excited. "Where to? Oh, I know, we could go snorkelling! I've never seen tropical fish somewhere other than in a fish tank. Or we could go to Ibiza! They have the most amazing deejays spinning this time of the year. Why, just the other day, a girl from school lent me a really neat ambient mix, and I thought it would be great to go to this place someday. And I think they speak Spanish over there. How perfect is that? You speak Spanish, right?" Seeing she received no answer she added, "I mean, you're a Spanish guru, right?"

Leborio shrugged. "Hate to break it to you, Big Bird, my Spanish is about as fluent as your Portuguese. Besides, I hate dancing, and I hate clubs. We're not going to Ibiza."

"But you spend all your nights at Neon Lounge."

"That's different," he made a dismissive gesture with the back of his hand. "It was a career move. I thought Neon Lounge would be mine someday," said Leborio, with a tinge of bitterness. "No, I'm through with clubs, poolsides, and come to think of it, I could even do without beaches and other such places where dress code consists of swimming trunks. What we need is a new adventure. A new quest to bring us closer to my destiny." And then he added, "It's just as well that we don't go back home. It was a dead-end anyway."

Snejana listened quietly, blinking at regular intervals, and staring attentively over her droopy nose. "You're just saying that because we can't go back," she said, her voice still resonating with the nasal pitch of objection. "They're all looking for you. You made many enemies working for Placido, and now that you no longer enjoy his protection, they'll be coming after you. Not to mention Placido himself. They'll be lining up for you."

"Then we'll have to make sure they line up in the wrong place," he stood up. "Come on Big Bird, the old continent has nothing left to offer. Let's get out of this dying, aged world and its decaying spirit. Europe, with its old money, its moral promiscuity, its endless hierarchies—Europe will forever stifle true talent into despair. Europe, with its incestuous dead poets and their beautiful Hollywood whores," he muttered, less than audibly. "What is Europe to make of me? Of my destiny?" his eyes lifted to the skyline as he uttered this last word. "Too long, I have selflessly guided others on their journeys of discovery. Too long, I have dreamed up my future. It is high time I set forth into the big wide world. And you may come with, if you so desire," he added benevolently.

"And where might that be?" asked the girl, whose excitement had picked up again.

With a single pull of the arm, unexpected from a person who had not slept in a couple of days, Leborio hoisted himself on top of the promenade ledge, landing on his feet with the agility of a tomcat. Down below, Snejana dusted off her slightly torn jean shorts, and followed, unsure of what to do next. She waited silently as he looked out from the railing, hand angled over the eyes to block the sun, looking rather like a flamboyant Captain Grant in a Jules Verne sequel. The girl sank her hands into the back of her shorts, flicking a paper in her pocket with the back of her nails. Across the horizon line, as far as he could see, the sapphire waters of the Atlantic melted into the cloudless azure sky. He stretched his arms sideways and brought his lashes together until it all became an endless blue blur. Just like the planet, he thought, conjuring up the image of the globe in search of a proper spot to shove a pushpin into and call it home. The globe spun twice in Leborio's head, and on both occasions, the Americas seemed to wink from right about where the Great Lakes were situated.

"Oh, here," he heard the girl say. "I forgot to give you this," she reached up and handed him the sealed white envelope. "I found it on the floor in our hotel room. It's got your name on it."

With one eye open and another squinting at the sun, the Spanish guru tore the envelope and read its content in silence. From the cooling haven of his shadow, Snejana watched him read the telegram over, before whispering, "143 B."

"Huh?" she wrinkled her nose.

"Land Retribution Act 143 B," he said, kissing the envelope with a loud smack. Then, without any further ado, he picked up speed in the

*C.R. Preston*

general direction of the nearest boathouse. She ran after him, "What happened? Where are you going?"

But nothing could stop the guru from his pursuit for a boat to carry him out of Lisbon. Nothing, that is, except for a spiffy olive-skinned seaman sporting an impeccably white sailing hat. He looked down his nose at Leborio and after hearing out a very apt explanation which combined sign language and words that presumably would have made a fine springboard for the Esperando language, he shook his head from side to side in what could only be interpreted as a universal no.

"Sne, come here!" hissed Leborio.

The girl rushed over, glad to be involved in this mysterious yet exciting commotion. He grabbed her by the arm, and pushed her forth in a way that reminded Snejana of her mother presenting her to the son of a good friend—a nice boy—after Sunday mass. "*Signor*, stop!" called out the guru. "*Achtung! Arretez! Questa signorina e mucha . . . jolie.*" The man spent no more than a glance in Snejana's direction and went about his seafaring business. "*Krasivaya,*" tried Leborio, "*Ragazza de la Russia. Molto buena!*"

"What are you doing?" cried out the girl, pulling away from his grasp. "Are you trying to sell me?"

"Only provisionally," he shushed. "Once we're on the boat, you could just play shy. Men like a chase."

"What do you mean provisionally?" she shouted. "You must be out of your mind to think I'd go along with this. He's going to take me for a prostitute."

Leborio clasped her lanky arm and shook her by the shoulders. "He can think whatever he wants as long as he gets us to where we need to go," he hissed close to her ear. "Women have been doing that for thousands of years, and with every passing century, they've gotten better at it. It's the oldest profession on the planet. Besides, there's nothing wrong with using your body to get what you want."

Plump tears rolled out of her eyes, blotting a brand-new path down to her chin. She wiped them with the back of her hand, and with a dignified curl of the lip, she opened her mouth, "Maybe not, but there's plenty of wrong using *my* body to get what *you* want. I don't care what women have been doing. I wasn't raised that way," she sobbed. "If my poor mother could see me now! She would die—die I tell you!"

Irritated by the superfluous display of emotion taking place a few feet away from his perfectly white boat, the starchy seaman started the engine and pulled anchor. Leborio watched the white boat part the waves with the elegance of a swan, leaving a trail of foam behind it.

"Now look what you've done," he turned to scold Snejana. "That's just great! Maybe we ought to swim to our next destination."

"Which is?"

Clearly, she did not deserve to be brought up to speed. The stupid creature had ruined his escape plan with her irrational behaviour. He turned away, repulsed by the prospect of spending another minute in her company. The freshness than had once emanated from her eye-catching awkwardness had dimmed into an obscure, and, arguably, pointless sort of martyrdom she now depended upon to bear out a far-reaching grasp at conjugality. Conjugality, he thought, was an unlikely factor in the grand scheme of his destiny, a catch-22 whose odds of ever being sorted out were hardly worth the energy. If ever he were to feel love for a woman, she'd have to be the intelligent sort. And those, he found, were highly inconvenient. Not to mention risky. No, intelligent women were not an option he cared to explore. If love was not to be in the cards for him, it would be because he chose a greater destiny than that of being dumped.

The next boat he spotted while staggering down the harbour front was a wooden affair painted in the colours of the Portuguese flag. Painted was an overstatement. The small deck and the booth-like structure covered by a single linen sheet that used to be white, where presumably the helm resided, kept only vague traces of the peeling colour. If someone with limited knowledge of boat carpentry decided to turn a raft into a fishing boat, the product would have looked very much like this particular vessel. Leborio cleared his throat to announce his arrival, unsure of etiquette when calling in on a boat. Seeing no one took notice of his delicate symphony of rasps, he worked up the gall to knock on the wood.

An Asian man wearing a Vietnamese conical hat came up from the belly of the boat. He propped himself on a long bamboo stick and gaped his mouth into a toothless grin. The guru nodded his head and pressed his palms together in what he imagined to be an Asian greeting.

"Hello, friend," waved the fisherman, in a crisp English accent.

Relieved, the guru greeted him back and made an unrelated comment about the lovely weather.

"Weazer always nice," lisped the fisherman. "You need ride?"

Leborio shook his head, working up an angle on what he could offer the boatman in exchange. Because Snejana was at the top of his bartering list, he looked behind to be sure she came across as presentable. Then again, the fisherman smelled very much like what he did, which combined with the cavernous smile of a man who's only got a couple of gums to chew with, did not place him in a position to be fussy.

"Where do you want to go?"

"Not much farther than Tangier perhaps. Anywhere in Morocco would be good."

"Is going to cost," remarked the fisherman with Confucius-sais certainty. "You have money?"

"No," said the guru, deflated. He looked back to the girl. "We don't. But she's pretty good company," he raised his eyebrows suggestively.

"I have good wife," the man shook his head. "But I like shirt," he said, pointing at the fleur-de-lis extravaganza.

Leborio would have preferred to keep his shirt, but given the circumstances, he really had no choice. With a graceful slide of hand he extracted his gold-plated pen from one of the shirt pockets and making sure the fisherman did not notice, he stuffed it in the back-pocket of his pants. Then, he unbuttoned fastidiously and climbed aboard the wooden fishing boat, faithfully followed by his female companion.

The fisherman put on the silk shirt and marvelled at the softness of the fabric.

"Iz nice and smooz. My wife will like," he grinned, pointing at the faded picture of a round-faced Asian woman nailed to the stirring wheel. Leborio smiled politely in the general direction of the picture. The fisherman pulled anchor and changed direction at 180 degrees, causing his wife's face to turn upside down.

What a life, noted the guru. To toil day after day in order to please a round head in a picture frame. Now that he was a landowner, thanks to Uncle Gigi and Land Retribution Act 143B, nothing could make him willingly enter the institution of marriage. He would live free as a bird, enjoying the benefits of a life without commitments in the beautiful town of Bongoville. Yes, Leborio Borzelini would be the catch of the town, the eligible bachelor at the centre of every social event. They would throw balls for him and garden parties where he would sit in the shade of a tall tree and tell equally tall stories of his adventures to the wide-eyed beauties of Gabon. Perhaps he would even give autographs to a fortunate few, he smiled, sinking his hand in his trouser poket to touch his retractable gold-plated pen.

"I'm feeling a little queasy," Snejana disturbed his daydreaming with her high-pitched voice. "Where is he taking us?"

With that, she bent overboard, throwing up a water-like substance that was very likely to be just that, because she had not consumed any-thing else in over two days. Leborio turned away disgusted. Suddenly, he saw no reason for bringing her along and contemplated giving her a gentle shove over the railing upon which she hung vomiting and into the Mediterranean Sea. Nothing too harsh, just an ever-so-light push. After all, the shore was within swimming distance and a little bit of exercise was bound to improve her appetite. He took a few steps in her direction, checking to make sure the fisherman was busy stirring the boat. The girl, bottom up over the railing, hanged like an ostrich with its head in the sand. He almost uttered "Bon voyage," just before nudging her into the sea. But as luck would have it, at the exact moment Leborio jostled her, the same white boat he'd tried to charter less than an hour before passed them by at arm's length, with the same determined grace of an alpha swan passing a baby duck. Damn, thought Leborio, pulling the girl back up. He caught her by the waist, waving to the spiffy olive-skinned captain of the white boat, who, in turn, raised the tip of his nose a notch higher and looked the other way.

The intercom on the white boat let out a wheezing sound. "Yes, sir," the captain wearing the white hat lowered his nose.

"Did you increase speed?" asked the voice at the other end of the intercom.

"I did, sir. Just wanted to overtake the fishing boats."

"I told you to maintain a steady speed at all times, all the way to Morocco," said the voice sharply. "Don't make me come out and smack you!"

The man swallowed with difficulty, "Sorry, sir! It won't happen again." He took off his impeccable white hat and wiped his forehead of sweat. Whoever the gigantic man in the living quarters of the boat was, one did not want to risk getting on his bad side. Granted, there was something visibly shady about this client and his desire to get out of Lisbon at once, but he paid well. Besides, this man was from the same place as the captain. It wasn't every day a man who spoke no other language than his mother tongue bumped into a compatriot with whom he could exchange a few words.

Back on the fishing boat, the toothless fisherman showed little concern for his cargo's well-being. After all, if they happened to fall over, he could call it a day and get back to his wife. He jerked the wheel around a few times testing their balancing skills, and somewhat disappointed with the outcome, decided to resort to trickery.

"You want cold beer?" he asked the spiritual master, who under normal circumstances would have most definitely declined the offer. But seeing how he had inherited a large estate in an influential African town, Leborio resolved to make an exception.

"Iz in metal box," said the fisherman, pointing behind the wooden hut from whence he stirred the helm. He buttoned up the purple silk shirt, whistling a jolly tune, while Leborio returned to the back of the boat where Snejana had stopped vomiting.

"That was close," said the girl, panting from fright. "Thanks for catching me," she smiled, her eyes welling up. She sat on the deck and twisted her arms around the wooden railing for hold and security and wiped a few tears of gratitude from her drawn cheeks. "Are you going to tell me where we're going, or is it a surprise?"

Looking for the bait box, Leborio took a moment to reconcile visions of a debonair lifestyle as a landowner with the difficult task of serving as a master to one overly emotional female slave. Difficult, but not entirely impossible, especially for one who planned to remain unattached. Instead of a wife, he'd have a personal worshiper, for lack of better terminology. So, there! His life would be spent next to a creature resembling an ostrich. And if she happened to pick up his socks and do his laundry, then so much the better. Of course, she'd have to improve her culinary skills, but overall, having a female *Passepartout* along for the voyage could come in handy despite the excessive sobbing. Lifting up the metal bait box from under the wobbly bench where the fisherman sat when he fished, Leborio took her by the hand, and answered, "Bongoville. We're going to Bongoville. It's a city in Gabon."

The former guru, who was now a celebrating landowner, opened up the bait box and reached for a cold brewski. What he got instead was one of the two most precious items belonging to Perla Galanis.

Not the one he had set out to get.

It was a hairless cat wearing a pink welding visor.

"Hick," the cat hiccupped once, before winding its thin neck like a serpent and barfing out the contents of the empty beer can.

He leaned back against the wooden railing of the boat, and covered his eyes with one hand. Between a cat that looked like a rat and a girl who looked like an ostrich, Leborio fought off a fleeting feeling of doom.

Staring at him with hopeful eyes, Snejana took one last grasp at her dream of dancing on the beach. "Gabon," she repeated. "Sounds pretty cool. How far would you say that is from Ibiza?"

*Stay tuned for the sequel to this book, to be released in 2011.*

# THE OSTRICH FARMER

Follow Leborio Borzelini to Africa, as he sets on an adventure to claim his inheritance. For a chance to get an early peak at the first few chapters and an opportunity to pre-order your copy of the book, sign up to receive our newsletter at www.leborio.com.

## *Follow Leborio:*

Twitter:     http://www.twitter.com/Leborio
Facebook:  http://www.facebook.com/Leborio
Myspace:   http://www.myspace.com/Leborio

5116635R0

Made in the USA
Charleston, SC
02 May 2010